Awake in the Dark

STORIES

Shira Nayman

Scribner

NEW YORK   LONDON   TORONTO   SYDNEY

SCRIBNER
1230 Avenue of the Americas
New York, NY 10020

Copyright © 2006 by Shira Nayman

SCRIBNER and design are trademarks of Macmillan Library Reference USA, Inc., used under license by Simon & Schuster, the publisher of this work.

For information about special discounts for bulk purchases, please contact Simon & Schuster Special Sales at 1-800-456-6798 or business@simonandschuster.com.

Designed by Kyoko Watanabe
Set in Aldine 721

Manufactured in the United States of America

1   3   5   7   9   10   8   6   4   2

Library of Congress Control Number: 2006048444

ISBN-13: 978-0-7432-9268-9
ISBN-10: 0-7432-9268-5

The story "The House on Kronenstrasse" first appeared in *The Atlantic Monthly*.

Australian Government

Australia Council
for the Arts

*This project has been assisted by the Australian Government through the
Australia Council, its arts funding and advisory body.*

For Louis, Juliana, and Lucas

Contents

I

II

I do not know what haunts me
This sad and nameless pain
Perhaps an ancient brooding tale
Coursing through my veins

—From "Die Lorelei,"
by Heinrich Heine

PART I

The House
on Kronenstrasse

Christiane. New York City, 1985

In this memory, which has haunted me the whole of my life, I am perhaps two and a half years old, and dressed in a special dress made of maroon velvet and lace. I am playing in a fountain that is ornate—and dry. The dryness is a striking fact, for until this moment of recollection, I know it only as a fountain that furiously spurts; I am accustomed to leaping away from its spray.

I have virtually no memories of my early years aside from this one, which I attribute to the fact of a wartime childhood.

In the memory I am filled with a distinctive mood I've not known since, and which I can only describe as a feeling of luxury—not of a trivial, material kind but in the fullness of the word's meaning: safety and ease, the promise of endless comfort, the implicit guarantee that all is right with the world and always will be.

My mother is nearby; I can sense her, if I do not see her. Then the moment blurs, and time skips long minutes, perhaps even hours. The sun has moved; it is now overhead and hot on the crown of my head. I look down to see that my dress is crumpled, its hem soiled. I see my mother crouched over the steps leading up to our grand home. She seems busy with something, though I cannot make out what.

At that moment she turns. She smiles. I am momentarily puzzled. I do not know why I am puzzled. That puzzlement has marked my relations with my kind soul of a mother for as long as I can remember. It is something I learned early on to try to hide from her. Only when I became a woman myself did I realize that my efforts had been unsuccessful—that my mother was all too aware of the odd distance between us. This distance came from me, I feel certain, and has been a great sorrow for my mother, with all the losses she has suffered, and me her only child.

I glance over to where my mother now lies. Her body is so reduced by illness that she is almost invisible among the bedclothes. I recoil from the rattle of her breath. I grit my teeth against my own selfishness, and struggle to find something to say, though my mother no longer seems conscious. But they say the dying can hear, whether they appear to or not.

I approach the bed, lower myself beside her, and rest my head on the pillow next to hers.

Her eyes are closed. Her face looks unfamiliar; the deep lines I'm used to seeing are oddly smoothed away, as if she were undergoing a rapid undoing of years. I gaze into her softened features, imagining that this is how she gazed into my sleeping face when I was an infant. I struggle to imagine how she felt in just such a moment, but cannot catch on to it. I reach up to stroke her face.

Her eyes snap open, alert in a way I've not seen in months. "I failed you," she says, her voice almost robust. This comes as a shock, because my mother has not spoken in weeks.

"Hilde, whatever are you saying?" I reply. I have called my mother by her first name since I was a teenager, just one of the many little oddities in our relations. Her eyes are clouded with distress. She touches my face.

"Christiane, my Christiane," she says, her eyes leaking tears that settle in the creases of her cheeks, which seem to have reappeared with her alertness. "You've been a good daughter. I know how hard you've tried."

Something clutches in my chest. I know I've not been much of a daughter to her; I feel I've not been a daughter at all. I try to stifle the rising sob without much success.

"Sssh," my mother says, batting at the tears that are now slipping down my cheeks. "It's not your fault. You see, I took it all away."

A terrible confusion takes hold of me. I feel as if a gauzy black curtain were being pulled around me.

"Hilde, what are you talking about? What is it you're trying to say?"

Her arm drops; she closes her eyes. Again, that odd dissolving of the heavy creases in her face.

"The house on Kronenstrasse. You know the number? Number fifty-eight."

I want to grab her, to shake her, to shriek at my mother: *What? What did you take? What is not my fault?* But I say nothing. I just lie there, the tears now flooding my eyes, looking into the smooth face that is no longer the face of my mother, that is now only a mask.

*   *   *

My father was killed in the early weeks of the war. All I know is that he fell on Polish soil, though even this my mother did not tell me; it was revealed during one of my surreptitious raids on the small stash of items she had hidden—she mistakenly supposed—beneath her bed. She had kept the notification of his death, an official Nazi document stating that my father, Hermann Kueper, was killed on September 13, 1939, west of Warsaw, in the Battle of Bzura: a hero, in the name of the Third Reich.

The rest I've pieced together using intuition and the few bare facts at my disposal. We fled Heidelberg after my father's death, when my mother was no longer able to find work to support us. I don't know what happened to the house in my memory, or to the wealth that must have gone along with it. My mother never wanted to talk about the past. At some point I stopped asking. I do know that we ended up retreating to Bad Gandersheim, in the Harz Mountains, where we stayed with a distant cousin.

I don't know how my mother secured passage to America after the war ended—only that we arrived in New York Harbor with refugee status. We had no relatives in New York or anywhere else in the United States, at least none that I ever heard of or met.

I know that my mother was grateful to be on American soil, and that this gratitude did not waver. She never complained that she was reduced in our new land to working as a maid. She took on her work with commitment and dignity. A good livelihood was cause for thanks, she said. She was proud to be on staff at the Plaza, such an old and respected hotel.

I know why I cherish the memory of playing in the fountain. I also know why it pains me still. Within that moment is a fullness of feeling I don't otherwise have in my life.

*   *   *

I give my mother a simple funeral. She had few friends. Eight people attend: the priest and me, four retired fellow workers from the Plaza, and two of my mother's elderly neighbors.

A week later I pack a small suitcase, take two of the many vacation weeks I have accrued, and buy a ticket to Frankfurt, with a train link to Heidelberg.

I have never been back to the country of my birth.

I do not think of myself as German, though neither do I think of myself as American.

From the train station in Heidelberg I take a taxi directly to my hotel, a small pension around the corner from the grand old Hotel Zum Ritter. I deposit my suitcase and walk for two hours or more, surprised by the magnificence of the city. I don't know what I expected, but I know it was other than what I have found. I walk along the river, past the Old Bridge, with its impressive stone arches and stern guard tower, and beyond the last of the bridges, where the river curves and the city opens out into the expansive greenery of its parks. On the way back I pause by Karl's Gate and stand for a moment, looking up at the huge arch, a visual echo of Germany's historical military passion. I take Hauptstrasse past the castle and then wend my way back toward the town hall.

My mother and I spoke German to each other until I was a teenager, when, like many children of immigrants, I started refusing to speak anything but English. Now, though, in the first little transactions I make—talking to a taxi driver, and to a waiter in a café—my German comes back in fits and starts. It's like trying to get an irascible old workhorse back into action—brutish and reluctant, but in the end obliging and strong.

I consult the map I bought at the airport and locate the government building where housing records are kept. On my way there I stop at a small café and drink an espresso at the bar.

Tracking down the owner of the house is remarkably easy: one Herr Eduard Stürmer. The city registry is orderly and efficient, true to German stereotype.

I call from a public telephone on the street outside the housing office. The phone is answered by a man who sounds about my age and who informs me that Herr Stürmer, his father, died a little more than a week ago.

"I'm terribly sorry," I say, aware of my American accent and also of the uncanny coincidence. A little over two weeks ago my own mother breathed her last.

"I'm so sorry," I repeat.

"We had the funeral only yesterday. We wanted to wait for my sister to fly in from New York."

A sister in New York. I can hear the pounding of my heart in my ears.

Only now does the man on the line think to ask why I am calling. I know all too well the strange overturning of etiquette that comes with new grief. I recall how, after my mother was packed away in the slightly shabby and oddly inappropriate blue van en route to the funeral parlor, I went into the kitchen, washed the few dishes I'd left in the sink—which included a glass from which my mother had, earlier in the day, taken her last sips of water—and then turned off the lights, locked the apartment, and went back out into the world. I found myself entering the corner deli where my mother had bought liverwurst and ham for more than forty years. Around me the day was alive with people going about their Saturday-morning business. *How could they all be so calm?* I thought. I wanted to shout out to the deli owner, "Don't you realize what has happened? My mother has died! Nothing will ever be the same!"

A well-dressed young woman standing next to me, who was surveying the pastry case, turned and gave me a polite smile. I felt like slapping her face. Instead I ordered a quarter pound of liverwurst and the same of ham, my mother's regular order in the years since I'd stopped living with her.

Outside the store I deposited my purchase in a trash can.

"The house," I say to the man on the other end of the telephone line, who is waiting for my reply.

"We haven't decided yet what we're going to do with it. My father's death was very sudden, you understand."

"Perhaps in the meantime you'd be willing to rent it?" Without any forethought this absurd and impractical suggestion slips from my mouth.

"That might be a good idea. Let me talk it over with my sister."

I hang up the phone and look out onto the street, aware of how everything seems uncannily familiar and yet completely unknown.

My mind is racing with practical details that ten minutes ago would have made no sense whatsoever. Quitting my job, subletting my apartment in New York, dealing with my mother's landlord to put her belongings in storage. Canceling subscriptions, transferring utilities, sending for some of my things. I will enlist my best friend to help put the pieces in place. I'll call my bank to transfer funds from my savings.

Several hours of phone calls, I figure, looking out onto a square where sooty little sparrows hop cheerfully up and

down the arm of a statue of a German poet from a lost age—
that's all I'll need to undo my life.

This undoing is disconcertingly easy. When I call my boss
at Columbia University, where for ten years I have served as
assistant dean of the School of General Studies, he takes the
news of my request for leave just a little too much in stride.
We will have no trouble filling the position in your absence,
he assures me; don't give the matter another thought. My best
friend also seems just a bit too nonchalant. Yes, certainly she
can tie up the loose ends—she's happy to do so. *I'll miss you,
Christiane.* Both seem to have been waiting for just this
unlikely scenario, and to wish to wrap things up as quickly as
possible.

In any case, here I am, three days later, with all the arrangements made, my life in New York put neatly in storage.

We meet at the son's residence, in a leafy suburb. I come
to a quick and ready agreement with Herr Stürmer's son and
daughter for what seems a ridiculously low rent, given the
grandeur of the house as it stands in my memory. No doubt
my childhood perception enlarged and embellished the
place. Besides, Herr Stürmer's children are probably people
of means, and are perhaps simply grateful to have a final dis-
position of the house pushed off into the future.

The son types up an agreement, which all three of us sign:
I will take the house for six months.

Two days is all they need, they say, to clear the house of
their father's personal belongings. "My father lived a simple
life," the son tells me. "Besides, the house is small; the move
shouldn't take long." As for the furniture and household
goods, they'll leave them for me.

"You can bring your suitcase and just move in," the
daughter says, mustering more cheer in her state of mourn-

ing than I am able to achieve in mine. "It will feel like home in no time."

I am a little taken aback. How can anyone refer to the house as small, even taking into account the distortion of childhood memory?

They do not seem to think it odd that I don't ask to see the house first. When I stand to leave, we shake hands. I fancy I detect in the daughter's eyes a peculiar, knowing expression.

"How long did your father live in the house?" I blurt out. I hope this is not becoming a habit—my mouth bypassing my conscious faculties, issuing statements and questions of its own accord.

"Why, it's the house we grew up in," the daughter replies, the peculiar look deepening. "During the war . . . so many houses were abandoned. We took it over toward the end . . ." Her voice trails off. I think I see a glint of distrust in her eyes.

"You must be mistaken," I say to the taxi driver as he pulls up in front of an attached house on a dingy, treeless street. The driver repeats the address and then points decisively at the brick façade, which is slightly crumbling in places. It is a two-story house with comfortably high ceilings, but with none of the grandeur I had expected.

The driver turns off the engine and exits the car to retrieve my suitcase from the trunk.

Stepping out into the gray late afternoon, I find myself trying to stifle a childish sob of disappointment. Where is the fountain? The imposing wide steps? And where is my mother, crouched over something she's doing? Where has it all gone? I should have known, from the modesty of the rent they settled on. How could my mother have made such a mistake? Could she have directed me to the wrong house?

I catch myself. What does it matter? This address is a mistake—the taxi driver's mistake, most likely. Kronenstrasse is, after all, a common street name, like Maple or Pine in leafy suburbs all over America. A tonier neighborhood across town, no doubt, harbors a far grander Kronenstrasse, with the large brick house and fountain and grounds of my memory.

I am cold, standing there on the street. I have packed inadequately, assuming that early fall would be much warmer in Germany than in New York, which I always think of, irrationally, as the coldest place on earth from October to late March. Now, in my jeans and thin sweater, I shiver. I need to go in.

I climb the three brick steps to the front door. The key turns easily.

So the taxi driver was not mistaken. Perhaps my mother's mind failed her in the moments before her death. Reaching for one thing, she happened upon another, a neurological short circuit. Thinking she was handing me the key to my lost past, she instead shunted me to a meaningless dead end. Who knows whose address this once was, or why the street name and house number long ago lodged themselves in her brain? Perhaps she took piano lessons here, or visited cousins of lesser means.

In any case, I have landed here. In my purse is the neatly folded contract for a six-month stay. Besides, as I open the door and peer into the dark, narrow hallway, a murky intuition tells me that this house, wrong as it is, will offer up some kind of knowledge.

I slide my hand along the wall and flick on a switch. A dim bulb fills the hallway with insubstantial light, by which

I see a worn floral carpet in fading pinks and browns, and an attractive staircase with polished mahogany balustrades and banister.

I recognize the close, musty smell of a house uninhabited by youth, of an old person's habits and lack of interest in freshness, brightness, and the new. I glance into the parlor to my left; I make out the shapes of several pieces of heavy old furniture, too large for the small dimensions of the room. I take the stairs and find another switch on the landing, which turns on a slightly brighter but still inadequate light. Herr Stürmer had either an aversion to bright light or a frugal concern for his electric bills. Here the walls are papered in vertical stripes of faded green. I tiptoe from room to room, finding three bedrooms, one converted to a sitting room, and the same weak lighting in each.

I brought with me a small bag of groceries—dark bread, a can of soup, apples, coffee, milk. I leave my suitcase in the largest of the bedrooms and make my way downstairs to the kitchen, where I rummage around for a pot, a can opener, a plate, a bowl, a knife, and a spoon. I settle at the small wooden table in the kitchen, rather than in the formal dining room, to eat my first meal in this wrong and musty and dark little house on Kronenstrasse that has drawn me to itself, though clearly under some cosmically mistaken premise.

After my meal I wash the dishes and climb the stairs. In a hallway closet I find blankets and sheets. I make up the bed in the room I have chosen, undress, and get into the bed. The sheets are worn and soft. Immediately I drift into a deep sleep. I am awakened by a draft that seems maliciously directed at my ears, which have always been sensitive. I rise, locate my light sweater, and wrap it around my head, not having thought to bring a scarf. In the morning I awake with aching ears and the uncomfortable fullness in my head that heralds a bad cold.

I spend the day wandering around the city and sitting in cafés, reading newspapers and magazines, which I find I can understand almost completely. Every now and then I consult the small dictionary I bought at a stationery store. When I have the need to talk to anyone, I am aware that my American accent is not quite so pronounced.

That night I drag my bed into the middle of the room and stuff a towel along the windowsill to fill the gap I have discovered beneath the pane. This helps a little, but not enough. My ears become so sensitive that every little sound is jarring.

The next day I buy a scarf and sleep with it wrapped tightly around my head.

My days take on a rhythm of walking, reading, walking some more. I drink a lot of very strong coffee, and sometimes forget to eat. When I walk, I enjoy a feeling of floating—after an hour or two all sense of effort evaporates, and I feel swept along by an external force, freed of agency. My mind, too, spins free, and I have the sense that I am hovering pleasantly some distance from my own body, like a small, friendly bird assigned to accompany my physical self on some important secret mission.

At night, the draft seems to be getting worse. On the fifth night I decide to change bedrooms. I strip the blankets and sheets from the bed and take them into the adjacent room, where I make up the bed and check the window, which seems to be newer than the one in the first room, and without gaps. I run my hand around the frame: no draft. I feel cheered and go to retrieve my things from the closet in the other room. I wonder why I didn't think to change rooms earlier.

I return with an armful of clothing and then stop short. I

survey the room. In one corner is a small side table holding a basket of silk flowers. The bed, a bedside table, and a dresser complete the furnishings. Three smooth walls, painted pinky-beige, the fourth wall broken only by the well-sealed window.

No closet.

I put the clothing on the bed and find myself walking the perimeter of the room, running my hand along the wall. These old houses often have few if any closets; clothing was hung in armoires. But something about the layout of the space is odd. A closet on the other side of this wall, in the bed-room I've slept in these past five nights, but no closet here, on the complementary side of the wall, as one would expect.

I return to the first room. Open and shut the closet door. Examine the wall, trying to imagine an explanation for what seems a kind of optical illusion related to the design of these rooms.

I sit down on the bed and glance around me, aware of a heightened feeling of eyes. I have often had the sense that other people are watching me, though I've learned to dismiss such feelings as a quirky neurosis. I date this odd sense to my seventh birthday, when my memory, having been almost wholly erased up to then, seems to have kicked back in. Ever since, it has existed only in fits and starts—vividly comprehensive regarding some periods or events, wholly amnesic regarding others.

I don't recall all of that birthday, just one pulsing moment.

I am sitting at a table, and before me is a cake, fashioned ingeniously by my mother from coarse ration flour, a lump of lard, a single egg, and a precious cupful of sugar. How proud she was that morning as she assembled those ingredients. She was particularly pleased with the sugar, which was very hard to come by and must have cost what was to us at that time a small fortune. Slowly she touched her finger to her tongue and then placed it in the cup of sugar. A few granules clung to her fingertip, which she put to my lips. "Isn't it delicious?" she said.

She also saved a candle stub, and here I am, sitting before the cake, looking at the wavering flame. "A wish," my mother is saying. "You have to make a wish." I look around the table: my mother's cousin, a woman who can't be over forty but looks old to me, and her husband, a clerk, both of them wearing expressions of irritation and distaste; their three children, much older than I, already in their teens. All of them are looking at me in that sideways manner they have when addressing me, as if they can't quite stomach looking at me full on.

We are only just tolerated, my mother and I; we are not a welcome presence. To pay for our keep my mother hands over much of the pittance she earns doing housework for her cousin's colleagues. I know that these relatives are sitting at the table only for the rare benefit, in that time of terrible scarcity, of a piece of cake, however skimpy in richness, texture, and taste it might prove to be.

Fervent wishes regularly passed through my child's imagination at that time, intense longings incubated by the suffering I'd witnessed and by our many deprivations. But one wish only burns in my mind as I look around at those faces, at all those sideways eyes fixed on my face with a distaste I do not understand, and which makes me feel hollow and achy inside. I close my eyes and give it full voice: *Stop looking at me.*

I open my eyes to find that my wish has come true. My mother, smiling a rare smile, is cutting the cake—and now all eyes are on her. She hands me the first slice. Then she leans down, her smile full and warm, though she has tears in her eyes.

"Happy birthday, Christiane," she says. "Seven years old! Imagine that!"

Now, in the house on Kronenstrasse, I feel overcome by tiredness. I lie down among the clothes I have put on the bed and doze.

When I awake, I am in darkness. The bulb of the lamp must have chosen this moment to blow. I stumble up, still half lost in a rapidly dispersing dream, and fumble for the switch on the wall. A scuttling on the floor to my right tells me I am not alone. A mouse, perhaps? I leap back onto the bed, but in the dark, and still unsteady on my feet, I miscalculate. One leg makes it up onto the bed, but the other misses, and I find myself falling awkwardly forward. I fling my arms out and tumble headlong into the wall. The lip of the baseboard catches my cheek sharply, while my forehead thuds the wall above. I lie there disoriented and frightened. I get to my feet and switch on the overhead light. I can feel a trickle of warmth down my cheek; I touch the spot, and my fingers come back red.

It is only when I am in the bathroom, dabbing at my cheek with a wet towel and staring into the mirror at the swelling lump on my forehead, that I realize something was odd about the sound my head made when it banged against the wall. This old house is solid—solid as a rock. But when my head made contact with the wall, it produced a hollow thud.

I flash on my mother's face, her dying words, the peculiar urgency in her eyes. No, her giving me this address was not a mistake, not the utterance of an addled mind in the moments before death. She intended this, intended that I be here, intended—though this seems so unlikely, so impossible— that I discover this wall that gives off a hollow thud when struck.

I dry off the cut and return to the bedroom. I kneel down to examine the place where I tumbled against the wall. There, at the bottom of the baseboard, is the little slit through which the mouse, flattening its body in that impossible way that is the special talent of mice, disappeared.

I look more closely at the slit. It is not a crack that has appeared from age or the gradual settling of the house but something made deliberately by some sort of woodworking tool. I run my fingers along the bottom of the baseboard. Sure enough, I find a series of such slits, perhaps eight or ten, along the length of the wall. They are perfect for mice to enter and leave, though I feel certain they were made for another purpose entirely.

I put my ear to the wall and hear faint scratchings on the other side. I knock once, twice, on the wall above the baseboard. The scratchings on the other side stop; my knocks echo in the room. I stand and go out into the hallway and then into the bedroom next door. I knock on the wall there; I hear the heavy sound and unyielding thwack of knuckles on plaster-covered brick.

Yes, I think, not knowing what to do with the knowledge. A false wall on the other side, in the bedroom I am inhabiting. A space in which mice now live.

I go back to bed, though I sleep very little, and fitfully.

II.
Hilde. Heidelberg, 1940

I'm amazed we managed to keep it hidden for so long, my working for the Arnholds, since it's illegal for gentiles to work for Jews. What Frau Arnhold said to me was true: to keep on doing so presented a serious danger for all of us. I left then and there, no lengthy good-byes—in fact, no good-byes at all.

I do not know what I am going to do. I worry about them; I miss them more than I could have imagined. I've never made friends easily, and with what's left of my own family so far away, the Arnholds are my life.

I know they will be all right. An important newspaperman like Herr Arnhold—and Frau Arnhold, on the boards of several prominent charities. How often did I serve the board members tea and Sacher torte when they gathered in the parlor? With their means, and their countless influential relatives and friends, the Arnholds will find their way clear of this mess. I am sure of it.

But what about me? I don't have influential relatives or friends besides the Arnholds—and they are now powerless to be of any help to me.

I'm not in the habit of eavesdropping, but some months ago—perhaps it is already a year now—I was polishing silverware in the kitchen, as I had done weekly in the six or more years since their marriage, when I overheard Frau and Herr Arnhold talking in the dining room, next door. Frau Arnhold said that they should pack and leave at once, find a way to get to England—or better yet, America. "That's out of the question," Herr Arnhold said. "We're Germans. I'll not be chased away by some crackpot, whose days are clearly numbered in any case. A temporary insanity—that's all this is. Besides, German is the medium of my trade."

Frau Arnhold's reply was caustic: "You need to be alive to use a language—even German." I had never heard harsh words between them; I was quite taken aback. And in truth, Frau Arnhold's vehemence had frightened me. If they were to leave, what would become of Christiane and me? I could not imagine how I would find other work. Besides, I had been with the family since I was no more than a girl myself. I began working for Frau Arnhold's mother, alongside my own mother—their head housekeeper for twenty years or more—at the age of sixteen. In those days I knew Frau Arnhold as Sarah; she was only two years my junior. When she married, at the age of twenty, I followed her to her new house.

Twelve years of happy occupation—six in the mother's house, six in the daughter's—despite the danger and fear of the past four. We somehow managed to keep those at bay, to carry on—I was going to say as if nothing was happening, but that wouldn't quite capture the truth of it. Life simply has a way of moving forward, even under the most extraordinary circumstances. In the midst of it all both of us fell pregnant, only five months apart, and then both of us had baby girls. And then ten months ago, when Hermann was sent off for training, I moved in with them, though I kept my own house to which I have now returned.

It is quiet here. Christiane is asleep. I feel so alone. What am I to do?

I will write tonight to my cousin in Bad Gandersheim. I met her just once, and she's only a second cousin by marriage. But her husband has a clerkship; perhaps he can find me cleaning work there.

I wonder if Christiane remembers her father. Ten months is a very long time in the life of a child not yet three.

I try to pray. For Hermann, lying in a grave somewhere in Poland. For our country. For the Arnholds, and all the Jews. To pray that I can find a way for Christiane and me to survive this madness. But I cannot pray. I stay for the longest time at the side of my bed, on my knees, as has always been my practice. But nothing comes. Only ashen words, empty of life.

Someone is rapping at my door. It's after midnight. Who can it be?

At first I am startled when I crack open the door, but then I realize that perhaps I've been expecting them all along.

I have never seen Herr Arnhold with such a look on his face, or Frau Arnhold. Even little Rachel seems altered, though she smiles when she sees me, pushes the door open, and runs into my arms.

I usher them in. They do not need to tell me why they are here.

"We had nowhere else to go," Frau Arnhold says.

I nod. "You will stay here," I reply.

Now Herr Arnhold speaks. "Just until we can find a way to get our papers." His tone is flat, and he doesn't seem convinced by his own words.

"Hilde, we should find someplace—"

"Yes?"

"To hide."

I look blankly around the parlor.

"The armoire—it's spacious. During the day you could stay in there. Then at night—"

Frau Arnhold shakes her head.

"Too obvious. And as for nighttime, that's when they come looking—" She doesn't say "for Jews." She doesn't have to.

I attended Rachel's baptism and afterward a luncheon. I remember helping the cook set out the platters; the thought of those little sausages, and of the crystal bowl overflowing with shrimp, now makes my mouth water. The whole family converted eight or nine years back, not so very long after I joined the household. Conversions mean nothing, though, in the face of the Nazis' racial-purity laws.

I think of Herr Arnhold's study, the twin busts of Goethe

and Schiller. I always liked that he had positioned them facing each other on a display table across from his desk, as if the conversation between two of Germany's greatest writers were ongoing, and Herr Arnhold, at his desk, drafting editorials that thousands of people would read, were a part of it.

Other, smaller busts were placed here and there on the bookshelves that covered three walls of the room. I dusted them on a rotating schedule. I particularly liked the sculptures of Heine—he was a fine-looking man—and Börne, who sat beside Heine on the shelf as he had sat beside him in deep if stormy friendship during the many years of their acquaintance.

It would be difficult to imagine a room more infused with the glory of German culture.

Calmly, in my head, I go through my house—bathroom and three bedrooms upstairs, parlor and kitchen and dining room downstairs. No crannies, no nooks, no secret little place.

"The attic—" I begin.

"First place they look," Frau Arnhold jumps in. "Hilde, it's presumptuous of me to say, but before we left, we talked it over with August, who is going to stay at the house and keep up the garden until we can return. He had an idea."

Now Frau Arnhold tells me about the wall. About building a little chamber of confinement upstairs, in one of the bedrooms. We would match the baseboard that runs around the rest of the room, placing some slits beneath it to allow for the passage of air. We would build in a removable panel through which they could on occasion—perhaps once a week—crawl out. We would seal it with painter's tape, and I could keep a little can of matching wall paint in the cupboard to paint over the tape each time I resealed it. I could move my dressing table in front of it, which would cover this panel completely. One piece of baseboard would also be removable; through this I would pass food and remove waste on a daily basis.

Frau Arnhold's voice is calm as she lays out the details, the same voice she used in the past to go over the weekly program with the cook, the junior housemaid, and me—the lunch and dinner menus and schedules of duties. In her eyes, though, is the plainest desperation I have ever seen.

Hermann kept a well-equipped toolshed at the back of our small garden. I go outside into the blackness, and turn on my flashlight only when I am in the windowless shed. I do a quick inventory.

It is as if, before going off to fight, Hermann had some premonition of how events would unfold, of this then unthinkable situation in which I now find myself. Nearly everything we need is on hand. After we were married, Hermann remodeled the house, which had belonged to his parents, both of whom had died long ago. He did all the work himself—papering, carpeting, painting, even building new cabinets for the kitchen. Neatly stacked in one corner of the toolshed is enough leftover baseboard for an entire wall, as well as a dozen or more lengths of wood suitable for framing and an adequate amount of plaster and lath. We'll need some paint, I calculate, and also some heavy glue, if I can find it.

In the toolshed I feel Hermann's presence so strongly that I swoon. I fancy I can smell him, too—his reedy scent, which always made me think of the forest. I feel my knees giving way, and I sink to the floor. I reach for the hammer on the shelf opposite me that Hermann held so often, so naturally. I picture him swinging it, whistling in that quietly cheerful way he had, glancing over at me with the faintest of smiles.

We tuck Rachel into the bed with Christiane. She promptly falls asleep, and then we set to work.

First, we plan the frame. We work very slowly with the handsaw to minimize the sound. Then we work with the plaster and lath to construct the extra sections of wall; this takes a very long time. Fortunately, the baseboard is cut into suitable lengths, so we do not need to use the handsaw again and once more risk attracting attention.

By dawn our work is done, down to the fashioning of the removable panel.

Upon waking, Christiane is pleased to have Rachel and her parents with us. Five months younger than Rachel, who is now a little over three, Christiane has known Rachel all her life. Frau Arnhold was always glad to pass along Rachel's beautifully made clothes.

When I explain to Christiane that she must not tell anyone the Arnholds are staying with us, that it is a secret of great importance, her little eyes grow solemn and she nods wisely. "Secret," she whispers. "Christiane tell nobody."

At around eight o'clock that morning Herr Arnhold hands me a large wad of bills. It is a significant sum, enough to last us all a long time. I hope, however, that poor Frau and Herr Arnhold and little Rachel will not need to stay trapped between two walls, like rodents, for a long time.

I do not ask questions, but I imagine that the plan for the new papers Herr Arnhold referred to is already in play—that in the very near future some powerful friend or colleague of his will knock on the door and hand me an envelope containing what they need to execute their escape.

The Arnholds retreat to the armoire (the new wall will not be ready until I can buy the few things we need), because we cannot keep the curtains drawn any longer; this is the hour I typically open them, and the neighbors do not miss a thing. We punch several holes into the thin backing of the armoire for air. I leave them with a jug of water, a loaf of bread, and a bedpan for their toilet.

I take my shopping bag, and Christiane and I head out. I visit three stores to find what we need. I feared we would return missing some critical item, but within two hours we are back at the house, fully equipped.

My ability to pray seems suddenly to have returned. I pray fervently for everyone I've failed to pray for in weeks. I pray that the papers will arrive soon, pray for the moment I'll be able to bestow one last embrace on this family that is closer to me than any real family I have left, and to wish them Godspeed.

III.
Christiane. Heidelberg, 1985

The next morning I rise early. I eat a piece of bread and drink two cups of instant coffee. I splash water on my face, get dressed, and step out into the mild autumn Heidelberg day.

I walk toward the city center. Above the hills in the distance the sun is still dragging itself upward, spreading wan streaks of white light through swatches of thin cloud. Around me the charming façades of two-hundred-year-old buildings, beautifully restored and maintained, lie about the dreadful events that took place here an eyeblink of fifty years ago.

I find a hardware store, housed in what must once have been the foyer of an elegant mansion. An impressive chandelier hangs from the vaulted ceiling, sending a shocking blaze of light out into the space.

A salesman approaches, and I stutter the names of the things I have come to buy. Finally I go behind the counter and point to the items I want. I eye a medium-size ax, but decide not to take it; it seems a suspicious item, and I don't want to draw attention to myself.

The clerk packs my purchases into a brown paper bag, and I pay.

I don't yet feel like returning home, so, clutching my bag of tools, I walk all the way to the old university, stopping to rest in front of Saint Peter's Church. I feel mocked by its idyllic beauty. All around me students carrying book bags wander and mill, exuding the unflappable confidence of young people raised in peace and destined for lives of privilege, success, and ease.

I cross the river and hike up to the Philosopher's Walk, where I sit for a long time looking down onto the city. The air is invigorating, and filled with the scent of a rich variety of trees: cypress and yucca and Japanese cherry, and numerous others I don't recognize. I gaze at the stone commemorating the German poet Joseph Freiherr von Eichendorff, who fell in love with Heidelberg in the early 1800s. I have never heard of him, let alone read his work, but I think about the expansive culture of which he was a part, and then think about how Germany thrust itself into its nightmare of destruction.

I head back down to the river, passing through residential neighborhoods boasting grand houses like the one in my haunting memory. I half expect to chance upon that house, as would happen in a dream. But this is not a dream, and I find no such thing.

I cross the Theodor Heuss Bridge and stop at an overpriced bistro for an early dinner. I order beef and sauerkraut and a Veltins beer, wanting to appear to be a tourist. This is silly, because I do not like beef and sauerkraut, and anyway, who do I think is watching me? Who do I think would care?

I leave the bistro feeling weighed down by the heavy, unpleasant meal, and fuzzy-headed from the beer. I walk the whole way home. Entering the house, I am aware of how very tired my legs are.

Still carrying the paper bag, I go directly upstairs.

I take out my tools and lay them on the floor. A good-size hammer, a crowbar, a medium chisel, three wrenches of different sizes, pliers, a screwdriver kit, a small handsaw, a package of sixty-watt lightbulbs, and a flashlight. I put aside the various boxes of nails, nuts, and bolts—items I bought to make my other purchases seem more normal. Looking at the boxes now, I feel foolish. The clerk in the hardware store hadn't exactly been squinting suspiciously at me.

I reach for the chisel, position it just above the baseboard, and give it a gentle tap. The sound echoes—loudly, to my ears—in the small room. I look around wildly. What am I expecting? The clattering of jackboots on the stairs? I hit the chisel again, harder this time, pleased with the little hole that appears in the wall plaster. I tap gently at the edges of a growing hole, chipping off small pieces of plaster and lath and placing them in a plastic bag. When enough plaster is removed, I use the crowbar to pry the remaining lath away. With this technique I am able to work quietly, picking away at the wall, though the work is slow and laborious.

Time has congealed; it no longer seems to be moving forward at all. The whole world has narrowed to this patch of wall, to the small movements of my hands, to the focus of my eyes on the plaster.

Some time later I find myself sitting on the floor, tools in my hands, staring at nothing. I don't know how long I've been sitting here, but I suddenly realize I am hungry. I put down the tools, sweep up with the brush and dustpan I found in the kitchen broom closet, and then go downstairs. I fix myself some eggs and sit at the kitchen table, which looks out onto a courtyard shared by several houses. When I've eaten, I rise and open the window to get some air. An incredible stillness pours into the room—the stillness of countless thousands of people undisturbed in their sleep.

I hear echoes. The past presses its shoulder to the present.

They chose to come at night—I've read this (hasn't everybody?). Chose to snatch people from sleep, breaking through the fragile, enclosing shell of dream life, with its promise of wishes fulfilled, or else of waking from nightmare back into the safety of reality.

My father was an officer, sent early on to command an infantry regiment on the front lines. I like to imagine that he volunteered for this post—that he signed up for the horrors of the battlefield rather than enter the ranks of institutionalized thugs. But the truth is that I have no way of knowing what my father did, or the circumstances of his death.

After washing the dishes I close the window and return to my work. Perhaps I'll find nothing but a small space between the walls, there for the purpose of housing wiring or pipes or providing some kind of soundproofing.

I retrieve the flashlight from among my recent purchases and kneel down by the hole I have made. I direct its beam into the space. I can't see much, but I can tell that the space behind the wall is considerably larger than would be an area given over only to wiring or pipes.

I go back to chipping and prying, lost in a trance brought

on by the repetitive, mindless nature of the work. I realize suddenly that the hole is now big enough to allow me to enter. I turn off the flashlight and, still holding it, crawl through the hole.

The air is thick with dust, and stale. As I make my way into the space, I am almost blind; only the faintest illumination comes through the hole from the dim ceiling light in the bedroom.

Several times I put my thumb on the switch of the flashlight, but each time I stop short of turning it on. I sense I am closing in on something fateful, on the truth behind that frantic determination in my mother's eyes when she blurted out this address—the kind of secret that can haunt a lifetime, that my mother, in the moments before death, suddenly felt certain she could not take unrevealed to the grave.

What peace could my mother's utterance have given her? And does such peace, if it is won, come only at the cost of robbing someone else—in this case, me—of hers?

Now, still on my hands and knees, I am struck by this thought: *Through much of my life I have been sleepwalking.* And here, in this frightening enclosed space, the dust thick in my nose, I am perhaps about to awaken.

IV.
Hilde. Heidelberg, 1940

Christiane has developed a fever. It came on very suddenly. She is so hot that I have removed everything but her underclothes, and have sponged her off with cool water several times in the past few hours. I will wait until morning and then send for the doctor.

I leave Christiane for the shortest time while I run to my neighbor, Frau Ballin, to tell her to phone for Dr. Ullrich. Christiane is not really alone, of course. But she might as well be, given the stark truth of the situation.

This is all so unreal. Can it be we have been passing the rudiments of life back and forth—food going in, waste coming out—for five months?

They did come out on occasion, though not as regularly as we thought they might, and then only to move like ghosts in the thick night. Even if there had been anything to say, the sound of voices, even whispers, has become too dangerous. I see them still—wafting through the space of the room, Rachel staying close by her mother's side, silent and gray, their movements an effortful slow motion in the darkness. As if they were not living people but only flickering images of themselves projected into the air.

For two weeks now I have not dared to remove the large panel.

Still no knock on the door from some friend bearing travel documents. Early on I was tempted many times to ask them, What plans did you make? What can we expect? But we've been reduced to silence, always worried that someone might hear, that the sound of voices other than Christiane's and mine coming from our house might arouse suspicion.

Eyes and ears are everywhere. Children are the most to be feared—especially the older ones, who will denounce their own parents to the Gestapo for expressing anti-Nazi sentiments.

Frau Ballin just left. She could not reach the doctor by telephone. Finally she went to his office. After waiting more than an hour, she was told that the doctor would stop by—if he could—at the end of his workday. Understandably, given the shortage of doctors, he is very busy.

It is two in the morning. Still no sign of Dr. Ullrich. Christiane is so hot—nothing I do seems to help, at least not for long. I fear giving her any more cool sponges; she's shivering from them, and at the same time her head is burning up. I wrap her in a light blanket, and then unwrap her. I just don't know what to do.

Three in the morning. Christiane's eyes have begun to roll back in her head. I am frantic. Aaaah—at last. The door. Someone is rapping on the door.

V.
Christiane. Heidelberg, 1985

My finger is on the switch of the flashlight. I hesitate. Finally I flick it on. I move the beam of light through the space and discover, once I see what is there, exactly what I now realize I was expecting to find.

Clothing, I see clothing, arrayed in piles on a makeshift bench fashioned of brick and old planks. The clothing has shape; it is threaded through with bones. Two skeletons wearing clothes. Collapsed onto each other as if they were huddled together in order that they might better approach their death.

I crawl closer.

I am upon them.

I rise to my haunches and pick up a woman's jacket. In the beam of the flashlight I see that it is blue.

Not two but three people died in this tomb. The littlest is here, beneath the woman's jacket; the little bones are wearing a dress—a girl, then. The dress is velvet, and the collar is lace. Maroon velvet, thick with dust. A bolt of recognition at the touch of it, and then a curdling confusion.

With no room to recline, they were sitting, these people, on the rough bench. Among the bones are liberal scatterings of hair. A swatch of dark tresses, brittle and coated with dust. Another pile of shorter, light brown hair.

I move in a dream; this cannot be real, this macabre archaeological find. Dazed, I move among the bones in this place of hiding that a young couple and a child clearly entered in the hope of eluding death.

The thought of that hope, lodged in the now empty spaces between their ribs, brings me to my knees. I allow my face to fall on the bench; my hands sweep at the plank, stroking the smooth leavings.

I touch something cold—something small and smooth, shaped, I think, like a heart. I fumble for my flashlight, but it falls to the floor and goes out. I find it and pull at the switch. It fails to work, somehow damaged by the fall.

The object seems to be a locket, and is attached to a chain. I feel around its contours, and snap open the latch.

I cannot see its contents in the dark, though I run my fingers over the filmy surface.

I want to tell my mother that I've found them, whoever these people are. I want to tell her she did not take her secret to the grave. I want to honor her heroism; perhaps she risked her life (and mine?) in harboring this family here, in this grim space.

Why, Mama, why did you feel that you failed me?

I don't know who they were. I have no hard evidence, but

I am certain now that the two of us were here, and that my mother built this wall. I do not know why she left our grand house, how she came to be here, or why she then left, as she must have. I am still on my knees; I have assumed the posture of prayer. I want to pray for these long-dead souls; I want to pray for the soul of my mother. I want to pray for myself. But I have no one to pray to, so I simply bow my head and weep.

Back in the bedroom I fumble in the dark to remove the bulb from the table lamp and screw in one of the new sixty-watt bulbs I bought with the tools, in what now seems like another life.

A memory rears up: I must have been about twelve. I am fumbling in the dark to find my lamp, which I knocked from my bedside table when I leaped from the bed, awakened by a surge of nausea. I rush to the bathroom. Stumbling down the corridor, flinging open the bathroom door, I make it just in time—flip open the toilet lid and heave out the contents of my stomach. The bathroom has two doors, as in many other prewar apartments on the Upper West Side. I lift my head to see that the second door, which leads into my mother's bedroom, is ajar. I see through the sliver that my mother, too, is awake; she seems to be crouching. I see only the crown of her head above the bed. She is praying, I suppose, as she often does.

She raises her head, and I find myself looking, through the queasy haze of my sickness, directly into my mother's eyes. I jump to my feet with the shock of it, for she is looking at me as if she does not know me. This is something different from the distance that has always existed between us. I am expecting her to call out—*Christiane, is that you? Are you all right?*—but she doesn't; she just continues to look right through me. I see then that she is clutching something, though I cannot see what it is.

Then she does say my name: *Christiane.* No inquiry, just my name. She utters my name a second time, and her face crumples; she clutches more tightly at whatever she's holding, and bows her head. I watch as her shoulders heave with grief.

I quietly close the door, rinse out my mouth, and creep back to my room.

I never mentioned this incident to my mother. But then, we failed to discuss a great many things.

Now I sit down in the comfortable chair by the bed. I closed the locket before leaving the tomb space. I snap it open again and look closely at the photographs.

What I see is not possible. And yet here it is, in my hands.

VI.
Hilde. Heidelberg, 1940

Doctor Ullrich has just left. He did not even try to disguise the truth.

There is little hope.

Cerebral meningitis.

He says Christiane will probably not survive the night.

I have no one to turn to.

I do not know what to do.

The doctor has gone. Christiane is in my arms. She has not been conscious now for several hours.

I pray she will open her eyes. I pray I will have a chance

to look one last time into her dear little soul. I want to tell her with my own eyes that no child has ever been more loved, that God will watch over her on her journey.

A mother should not outlive her child.

A knock. Who could it be? Dr. Ullrich again? Perhaps he has some medicine—or has realized his mistake. Not meningitis but something else—some other fever that is sure to break very soon.

No miracle medicine or new diagnosis. It is Frau Ballin. She is very distressed. The SS, she says: they're going door to door, tipped off that someone on our street is harboring Jews. They have pickaxes, guns; they are breaking into locked attics. They will tear down walls, Frau Ballin says.

How did she know? Who else has detected the truth?

She is wringing her hands. "You must leave," she blurts out. "Now. For Christiane's sake."

I am still holding Christiane. Frau Ballin looks down at her and puts her hand to Christiane's head; then she jumps back in horror. Only now does she see what must be in my face.

"It's too late," I whisper. "I cannot save her."

"You can save yourself," Frau Ballin says.

"Nothing of me will be left to save," I say, my voice dry stone transformed to sound.

Frau Ballin leans forward and presses her trembling mouth to my ear. She whispers, "The other child—the little Arnhold girl. Save her then, in Christiane's place."

Now my entire being is stone; I fear I am unable to move.

"They're at the end of the street. You have twenty minutes, perhaps twenty-five."

Frau Ballin pries Christiane from my arms, which have closed around her like granite.

"Your papers. Yours and Christiane's. And one change of clothes for each of you. *Hurry!*"

I move as in a dream—as in a nightmare. From a drawer in my bedroom I take my papers, from the closet a change of clothing for each of us. Frau Ballin, holding Christiane, follows me like a shadow. On an impulse I grab a little maroon dress, pull Christiane from Frau Ballin's arms—she is still wearing only her undergarments—and quickly dress her in it. I hand my child back to my friend. For a moment our eyes meet.

Then to the wall. I pull away the dressing table, peel off the painter's tape; recently dried paint comes away with it. I push on the panel; it falls inward. I reach for the flashlight we keep on the inside of the space. Frau Ballin is behind me. She crouches and hands me my child, limp now, and gasping a little for breath.

They are huddled on the makeshift bench we cobbled together that desperate night. Their eyes are hollow. Had I passed them looking like this on the street, I'd not have recognized my former employers. I'd have walked on, muttering a prayer for souls that seemed already gone from this world.

In Rachel's eyes, though—I see this as I approach her—a spark of life still shines.

Frau Arnhold's deadened eyes travel down to my arms, where Christiane lies, and something flickers in them. She turns her gray face to me and then takes my hand and squeezes it—so weakly that I barely register the gesture. She nods slowly, and with the other hand grips my upper arm. This she does with some strength; she seems to be pouring all that is left of her being into her grip. I wince from the pressure; she lets go of me and opens her weak arms to my dying child. She embraces her, holds her to her own wan cheek, whispers her name: "Christiane, little Christiane."

Now I reach for Rachel. Rachel turns wide eyes to her mother. For a moment Frau Arnhold's face is touched with an otherworldly brightness.

"Go, my darling," she says. "Carry me here—" and she lowers Christiane for a moment to her lap to free one hand, which she touches to her breast.

Rachel takes my hand, and together we crawl back toward the opening and out into the bedroom, where Frau Ballin awaits us. Before exiting, I turn briefly to glance at Frau Arnhold, who is fingering the velvet dress I quickly pulled onto Christiane. It was Rachel's dress; I remember how upset she was once when she soiled it while playing in the dry fountain that August had emptied to clean.

"I'll take care of your baby," I whisper.

A whisper comes back through the dank sanctuary that in the end was no sanctuary at all: "And I will take care of yours—"

I fear they'll stop us at the station, but they don't.

Now we must wait for the guard to come and check our papers.

We are on a train headed toward Bad Gandersheim.

Before we left the house on Kronenstrasse, I paused by the front door. I knelt and looked Rachel squarely in the face.

"Christiane," I said. She nodded a three-year-old's serious nod, and pointed to the wall.

I shook my head. "No," I said, taking her little hand with the pointing finger and turning it back at her. "Here. Now *you* are Christiane. That is your name, and you must answer only to that. Do you understand?"

"Me? Christiane?" she whispered, a puzzled look growing on her face as she pointed at her own little heart.

I nodded vigorously. "Yes, Christiane. Only Christiane. It is very important that you remember this."

Now it was her turn to nod, and this she did solemnly.

The guard is in the next car; I can hear him asking for papers.

I tell myself to remain calm. Rachel, bless her, is sitting quietly at my side, looking out the window. I have not wanted to say too much—I do not want to scare her. But children have a sixth sense. She knows the danger we are in; I can feel it.

At the station we waited for forty-five minutes to use the lavatory. Once inside, I changed her from the soiled clothing she was wearing into the fresh outfit I had brought for her— a dress that was also once hers, now slightly too small, but not obviously so. I brushed her hair and tied it with a ribbon I had grabbed along with the clothing.

"Your papers." I look up. It is a young man with a hard face. I hand him my papers.

He looks carefully from my face to the picture in my passport and back again, several times. He seems satisfied, and closes my passport. He looks at the picture of Christiane and then at Rachel. Something has stirred his doubt.

"Is this your child?" he asks briskly. "Her hair—in the picture it is curly. And more fair."

"Yes, sir. She has changed since that picture was taken, more than a year ago. At this age children change so in the space of a year. Especially their hair, don't you think? Why, my cousin in Frankfurt was born with hair white as snow, and now—"

"That's enough," the guard says curtly, snapping the papers shut and handing them back to me. But he seems to regret his shortness, because before moving on he adds, "Have a good journey."

I put the papers back in my bag and take hold of Rachel's little hand. Together we look out the window at the fields speeding by.

She never did open her eyes. I never did get my chance to look one last time into the eyes of my child. Perhaps she opened them after I left—to find not me, her mama, but Frau Arnhold, who looked nothing like the Frau Arnhold Christiane would remember.

I torture myself with this thought.

I only hope I have the strength to go on. I only hope I have the will to go on. For Rachel.

How quickly she took to answering to the name Christiane. Are all little girls so resilient?

VII.
Christiane. Heidelberg, 1985

I am holding the locket in my hand, staring at the two photographs within. On the left side is a miniature of a young woman who bears a striking resemblance to me—darker in coloring, but with the same arrangement of features: wide-set eyes and a narrow nose, sculpted cheekbones and a full mouth. She is more beautiful than I am or ever was, even in my youth. I attribute this to the common occurrence of similar features' arranging themselves in a more or less subtle or attractive way, as one often finds in families.

But when I study the picture I realize that, except for our

coloring, we're physically almost identical. The difference lies elsewhere. Even in this tiny likeness the woman in the picture exudes real charm, a kind of warmth I've always envied and admired.

My stomach is swirling with nausea; I fear I am going to faint. I close my eyes. The old memory rears up. That puzzled feeling again—only this time I am puzzled because I am wearing a beautiful dress of velvet and lace, and my mother is dressed plainly, over by the steps. This is new, entirely new.

Here, then, is the source of the puzzlement that has always dominated this memory, snapped, of a sudden, into clarity: I am in velvet and lace. And this is in contrast to my mother, who is crouched over the steps. What is that in her hand? A brush of some kind. Could she be brushing her hair? Here, outside? But the brush is large and has no handle. And what is that at her side? A bucket?

She turns, as she has turned all these years over and over again in the vibrant eternity of my memory. Shy, almost deferential, an affectionate, acknowledging look on her face. I smile and wave—not with a child's hot love for her mother but with something else: mild and peripheral affection, my attention more wholly absorbed by the pleasure of playing in the empty bowl of the fountain.

She is wearing a uniform; I register that now, for the first time. A simple blue shift protected by a crisp white apron. The uniform of a maid. I see now what she is doing. My mother is scrubbing the grand stone steps of the home.

And then this: *She is not my mother.*

I open my eyes and find that I am staring again at the pictures in the locket. On the right side is a photograph of a man; he is handsome and has fair coloring, not unlike my own.

I think of the two pictures, lying all these years in the dreadful tomb, facing each other in such darkness. I think of them facing each other this way through the years and the darkness, smiling right into each other's faces, closed within a heart of gold.

I turn over the locket. I see that the back is engraved. I hold it up to the light to read what is written. What I see is two names, in script: *Sarah. Walter.* And below this, an address:

72 Lindenstrasse.

I sit there in the now bright light of the table lamp, clutching the locket and listening to the silence of this Heidelberg night, so distant from another Heidelberg night in this same house, when a wall was not torn down, as on this night, but built. Same floorboards, same ceiling and walls—and time a mere flash from there to here.

I wait for the morning light. Finally I rise, change my clothes, and go to the bathroom to wash my face.

I glance at myself in the mirror. What I see catches me by surprise. I look different.

I swallow a cup of coffee and then leave, hailing the first taxi I see.

I give the driver the address, and then sit back in the seat and watch Heidelberg pass by. Beyond the Old City we turn onto streets that become wider and are soon lined with towering old trees whose leaves are beginning to change color. We pass by beautiful houses, taking a right turn here, a left turn there.

Finally the driver pulls up before a large, fenced-in property. We stop in front of the metal gate.

I pay the driver and approach the gate, above which I can see the top of the house, with its familiar outline. I reach up and ring the bell. Several minutes later the gate opens to reveal a man in his late middle years, dressed in gardening clothes.

"Please," he says politely, though within seconds his face fills with confusion and disbelief.

Beyond the gardener I see an impressive leafy garden, beautifully cared for. Trellises covered with creeping foliage, trees beginning to turn autumn shades, clay pots filled with a variety of plants lining the patio. A wrought-iron table and matching chairs sit beneath an ancient weeping willow; the table holds dishes and the remains of a breakfast.

"I'm wondering if I could come in," I say. My voice sounds strange, impersonal and far away.

"No one's here but me," he says, his eyes drifting across to the abandoned breakfast table. "I am the gardener."

I nod. He must see something in my face, for his own fills with compassion.

"I've lived on these grounds since I was a boy," he says. "You see, my father was the gardener before me. I'm sorry, miss. But could you be . . ." He hesitates.

"Yes?"

"It's just that you bear such a resemblance to the woman who owned this house, many years ago."

I am looking beyond the gardener into grounds that are large enough, I think, to seem endless to a two-and-a-half-year-old child. The gardener stands aside. Slowly I walk by him.

I hear it before I turn my head: the fountain, with its cascade of water. A sculptured child holding a large plate covered with fruit, the water spurting out from its hands.

I walk over to the fountain, sink down by its side, and cover my eyes.

Time skips backward—but no, it is different. There, I

wave to—I know she is not my mother. I wave to Hilde. "There is Hilde," I say. I raise my arm in acknowledgment.

Now I turn to see her, her dark hair bouncing a little around her lovely face as she hurries toward me. Now I am flooded with the hot passion a child has for her mother, that flash flood of feeling that makes the world vivid and bright.

"The fountain is dry!" I call out with fervor.

"Yes, my love. Isn't it fun?"

Her voice.

I run into her arms. She embraces me, kisses my cheek, strokes my hair. I smell her. She smells warm and kind; she has the scent of jasmine.

"Mama," I say. My heart is so full that I fear it will burst through my chest.

"Rachel," she says. "My sweet Rachel."

Rachel. My name is Rachel.

She laughs. It is the sound of sunlight, the sound of a happiness I have never consciously known.

"I see you have dirtied your dress! Never mind, little gosling. Hilde will clean it. It will be as good as new."

I turn again to see Hilde, by the steps. Our maid. Kind, devoted Hilde, who tried so hard to be a mother to me. Who, in saving my life, took away my past. Hilde, whom I had failed, and who in her dying moment believed that she had failed me.

I snuggle into the warmth of my mother's arms. I have found my home, and returned there.

The Porcelain Monkey

New York, 1990

I am troubled by the conversation I just had with Rinat, though also taken aback at how shaken I am. After all, it has been so many years; the stories—my own—about my wartime childhood in Berlin are of course not new to me. I suppose it is because I was listening with the ears of my daughter, home for two weeks from her graduate studies at Berkeley.

"The truth is," I said in response to her question, "I know very little about my own parents. That is why I've never spoken to you about them."

"Can you tell me what you do know?" she asked.

Those eyes—she had always been serious, old before her time. Even as an infant, she'd look out at me from the depths of those unnaturally blue eyes, eyes the color of cornflowers, as if trying to communicate some deep and ancient knowledge of mankind. *How can a child—a baby—be so knowing?* I used to think. But then, she was my first; *I will learn more about children,* I thought, *as more come along, God willing.* More did come along—five boys, about two years apart. And then, when I thought I was past childbearing years, I fell pregnant at age forty-five—bequeathed one last gift, my second girl, Leah, who is now sleeping upstairs.

It turned out that none of the others were, in fact, like Rinat.

She was also the only one with blue eyes. The others all have their father's deep chocolate eyes, the eyes of their Russian Jewish forebears.

When Rinat was about nine, after the birth of her fifth brother, I found her, one day, gazing into my dressing-table mirror, a frown on her face. "Why are my eyes so blue?" she asked.

"Recessive genes," I answered. "Your father and I—we both have brown eyes but we must each carry one blue gene. In you, both recessive genes came together."

I followed this up with a brief explanation of the principle of Mendelian inheritance. This seemed to satisfy her, though I did notice, from time to time, as she grew, that whenever Rinat caught a glimpse of herself in a mirror, that same frown would appear.

Rinat was always inquisitive, but she seemed to know instinctively to avoid asking me too much about my past. She knew I'd survived the War in the care of a gentile couple who'd rescued me and raised me as their own. My children did not ask what happened to this couple after I left Germany to come and study in New York almost thirty years ago. I did not mention them, and the children seemed to accept this. I wanted to let the past lie where I'd dropped it when I stepped onto the plane at the Berlin airport—I was twenty-one years old, my freshly minted arts degree in hand—to begin my new life in the New World.

I was up late tonight because Leah had cried out in her sleep. After I went to her the second time, I no longer felt sleepy, so I came downstairs to the small desk in the kitchen where I organize household affairs. I'd been sitting here about an hour when I heard the stairs creaking, and moments later, Rinat appeared in her bathrobe, her fair hair brushed and her face gleaming clean. Everyone else in the house was asleep—the eldest three boys back from yeshiva; the younger two boys, now both in secondary school; little Leah, finally settled; and, of course, Lev, my husband. This was my favorite time, when all the world—at least the little world I had made for myself—seemed at peace.

"I'll make some tea," I said to Rinat. "And there's some of that nut cake left."

Rinat smiled—a splash of sunshine across her usually serious features.

It does not worry me that Rinat has chosen to lead a secular life, though I know it upsets Lev. I also chose to live differently from the way I was raised. Why should she not cast about for a life that would fit the contours of her soul?

I'd said this to Lev when Rinat went away to college in the Midwest, where she discarded the long-skirted, long-sleeved garb worn by women in our community for T-shirts and jeans. He tried to be warm and accepting when Rinat came home during school breaks—then, she'd pull her old outfits from the closet out of respect for our practices, leaving her short skirts and tank tops in the suitcase under her bed—but it was clear that Lev was saddened by Rinat's break from our religious way of life.

I boiled water and made tea, then took out two parve plates and set a slice of nut cake on each. We sat at the kitchen table in the dim light thrown out by the lamp on my little desk. The curtains were drawn; I was aware of how precious this moment was: tucked away here, with my beloved far-seeing, deep-feeling daughter. I was about to ask her to tell me more about her thesis project, which she'd enthused about earlier at dinner, when she blindsided me with her question about my real parents.

I reached for safe words.

"My mother had dark eyes and dark hair. I don't remember her smile."

No, not safe words after all. But these were the words that came.

"Yes," Rinat said simply.

I tried again.

"I don't remember my father."

I corrected myself.

"I never knew my father. He must have been killed—earlier."

Rinat raised an eyebrow. Panic surged through my chest.

Packed away. It was all so carefully packed away. Airtight. Twenty-eight years. More. Even Lev had never tried to pry open the seal. Why was she doing this? And why now? What, exactly, was Rinat expecting to hear?

"Darling," I said as kindly as I could manage, given the sudden loud thumping in my chest. "I was only three years old when I lost my parents. Not much more than a baby."

"Three-year-olds have memories," she said quietly. "Maybe not completely verbal memories, but impressions. Sights, sounds, smells."

I closed my eyes, tried to catch hold of a sight, a sound, a smell. I felt only blackness.

I opened my eyes, shook my head.

"I'm sorry," I whispered. "It's just too difficult for me."

The sudden flash of anger on Rinat's face came as a shock.

"It's difficult for me, too," she said, her voice still quiet, though I detected a sharpness in it. "It's my history, too. Aren't I entitled to know something about the blood that runs through my veins?"

The blood that runs through her veins.

A wave of nausea passed through me.

"Mama. Please," she said, imploring now, the anger gone.

I nodded. Again closed my eyes. Waited for the nausea to pass.

"I'll tell you what I know," I began. "I am in my mother's arms. I am cold, and very scared. *Scared* is too mild a word. I don't have a word for the feeling. I see goose bumps on my mother's shoulders and arms. I see she is very distressed to be so exposed.

"We are walking with the others—there must be hundreds of us. All women and children. In front of us is a very old woman—I can see her old, wrinkled skin. It is like thin paper with lacy blue veins underneath. She is trying to cover her private parts with her hands, like everyone else, except the women holding children, like my mother; their hands are not free.

"It is silent. No one is talking. No one is allowed to talk. We are walking along a concrete path toward a big room. Finally, we reach the door, which is open. My mother stops suddenly. I look at her face. Her eyes are wild—she looks like a wild animal. She shouts something. There is a guard. He has a kindly face. There have been other guards, but their faces were not kindly.

"I feel my mother pushing me out of her arms. She is pushing me into the arms of the guard. His uniform is rough, scratchy, I feel it up against my naked skin. I grab on to his neck. I can feel my mother's panic—she wants me to go to this man, I can feel it, so I grab on to his neck.

"I am in his arms, but I hear his voice—very loud, in my ears. 'No, madam. You must take the child, too. She must also be deloused.' He thrusts me back at my mother.

"But my mother has gone limp. As he passes me over to her, I see her eyes—they are not her eyes. They are not my mother's sparkling, loving eyes, flashing with life. They are the eyes of a corpse. Her arms, they do not reach up for me. They are hanging at her sides like rope.

"I crash to the ground. I hear a loud crack. A pain shoots through my head. I feel blood rushing out, through my hair; it is sticky and warm. I am crying. I am scooped up, a hand is over my mouth. I am made quiet. I am in a close, dark space—perhaps inside the guard's jacket. I am warm, it is quiet.

"That is all I remember. My next memories are of being a little older, three and a half, maybe four. Playing in our apartment, waiting for my papa—I called him Papa, the man who saved me, the guard. I called his wife Mama, though I never loved her as I loved him. She was a cold person; I tried to keep out of her way."

Why was I telling Rinat all this?

I did not, in fact, recall all the details I was telling my daughter; I had reconstructed the narrative from the story the man I'd called Papa had told me when I was twenty-one, a little younger than Rinat is now. Though it has come to feel like a reality I lived through, down to the shadings of fear, the expressions on faces, the sight of goose bumps, and the grim feel of a cold wind on naked flesh.

Talking about it—for the first time, ever. It left me shaking. Rinat reached over and clasped my hand.

"Thank you, Mama," she said, her voice back to the gentle, soft voice I knew so well.

But why, then, the frown? That same perturbed frown I'd seen so many times, over the years, when Rinat had been unaware of my gaze.

I've been sitting here for some time now, since Rinat went back upstairs.

It is cold in the kitchen. My eyes are itchy and dry; I don't usually leave my contact lenses in for such a long period. But I cannot get myself to rise. My body is leaden, sunken into the chair.

Perhaps Leah will awaken again. I train my ears on the darkness upstairs but hear only silence and stillness up through the four floors of our brownstone—the darkness pouring on upward, through the ceiling, up into the deep blackness of the wintry night sky.

Berlin, 1978

I am walking the streets of my childhood.

I have never before spent a night away from my six children. But Lev is an adept father, he will manage; and the older ones will help the younger. I thought I would feel bereft, but instead, I feel oddly calm and removed, as if the life in New York I've so carefully constructed, child by child, Sabbath by Sabbath, a world distant, has been peeled away to reveal this old reality, suddenly sprung to vivid and dominating life.

Even my modest, uniformlike clothing—usually a haven, the way I carry my bounded world with me—feels clumsy on my body: the skirt reaching almost to my ankles constraining, the long-sleeved blouse too hot for this warm day, the scarf tied around my head too tight.

For a moment, I see myself as others perhaps see me—a caricature, a "type," a woman who lives by rules and regulations rather than by the thrust of her own idiosyncratic meanings.

I walk the streets with a Jew's memory: the sound of German sticks in my ears like scraps of barbed wire; in my own throat it is brittle and familiar, a hateful home.

How could all of this not make me think of my father?

He is everywhere: on every street corner, in every store, in every German sentence I utter or hear.

My father is still in the nursing home, still receiving the care I pay for biannually from New York, with the funds he had accrued in his seventeen years as a government official after the War. My bank handles the transaction; I prefer not to have to think about him, about the fact that he is still alive. Though living partially paralyzed in a nursing home is not much of a life.

I do not plan to see him.

Here I am, at our old café. Ten minutes early.

Bertholdt is early, too. There he is, hardly changed, sitting at the table we used to sit at together, sipping an espresso. He sees me. I approach the table, and when he stands to greet me, I dispense with the laws of modesty by which I usually live, and lean across to offer my cheek. He brushes against the scarf I wear to cover my hair. I smell his familiar scent, close my eyes, for a moment tumble back through time.

I felt the electricity between us the moment I first saw Bertholdt, sitting in the introductory art history class. 1958. I had just begun attending the university; I was seventeen years old. Bertholdt, his roguish smile, his eyes sparkling with intelligence and humor. It all came rushing back. The feel of his touch when we first made love in his ramshackle student digs. Nights and days, bleeding into each other. The nights, languid and fiery; the days, traipsing through museums, drinking coffee, talking, laughing, touching, always touching each other. And me—on fire with everything. Love, art, ideas, and love again, whether tangled in the sheets with Bertholdt or staring together in wonder at a canvas or sculpture.

I sit down. Bertholdt looks at me with the eyes of our old love.

"Suzana. My goodness, you look beautiful."

I look back with the smile of a stranger, then reach up self-consciously and touch a finger to my head scarf.

"Beautiful," I say. "I don't think so. But thank you."

He asks about my trip. I make the appropriate polite remarks.

"So," he says, scanning my face in the way of a lover— deeply, peering beneath the surface. I feel the stranger-smile falling from my lips.

"So," I breathe.

"You've changed," he says, suddenly looking puzzled.

I laugh. "Of course I've changed! I'm an Orthodox Jewish matron, now."

"I don't mean that," he says with no sign of humor. "Your eyes—"

I blink once, twice, three times.

"It was a very long time ago," I say kindly, fiddling with the place mat on the table. Bertholdt reaches across the table and places his hand gently over mine. The kiss, his hand; this is the first time in fifteen years that I have been touched by a man other than my husband.

"Not so very long," Bertholdt says. His eyes are sad.

I wait for a moment so that the shadow of the past might slide away.

"Six children," Bertholdt says. "I can hardly believe it. My little Suzana—the mother of six children."

"I can hardly believe it myself," I say. "Right now my life in New York all seems like a bit of a dream."

"I know what you mean," Bertholdt says.

"I've been Shulamit, now, for quite some time," I say gently. "Suzana sounds like someone else's name."

"Shulamit. Of course. I'm sorry."

For a moment, we're silent. Then Bertholdt speaks.

"Thank you for coming. It means a great deal to me."

"Aaah—that troublesome porcelain monkey," I say.

The West Berlin Senate is mounting an exhibition, titled— dubiously, I think—"Prussia: Taking Stock." Bertholdt, appointed chief curator, has found that though the Senate members assured him autonomy, they have tied his hands on the question of the porcelain monkey, one of twenty that had been owned by the great eighteenth-century thinker Moses Mendelssohn, which Bertholdt very much wishes to include. Too ugly, they say. And too pointed in its message of centuries' old anti-Jewish sentiment.

I have come to impress upon the Senate committee the historical significance of the monkey, given my specialty: Jewish artifacts in German cultural history. It is not a specialty that boasts a great many members.

Looking at Bertholdt now, I wonder why the monkey has taken on such critical importance to him: that he would go to such lengths to track me down and have me come all the way here on its behalf.

Of course, I think. How could I have been so stupid? The

monkey, a symbol of the mistreatment of Jews by Germany that long precedes this century. Mendelssohn, at age fourteen, made to enter Berlin at the gate reserved for cattle and Jews, required to pay the same livestock tax the farmers paid for each of their entering beasts. It must be this: the monkey is part of Bertholdt's own digging out from the trough of historical remorse. And also, of course, a link to me, now that I, too, am a Jew: a link to our lost past.

Looking into Bertholdt's troubled face, I see that he needed to see me.

He hails the waiter, orders an American coffee for me and another espresso for himself.

"I was quite taken aback at the Senate's position," I say. "For heaven's sake, it's 1978."

"You shouldn't be surprised. There's a lot of it going around. That it's time to move beyond the mea culpa. That we have to embrace what is good—no, glorious—about our German heritage. The Senate Committee is convinced that putting the Mendelssohn monkey on display is just another act of chest beating. *Look how badly we treated the Jews, even in 1759! Aren't we all villains!* And you won't be able to argue for the monkey on aesthetic grounds—the thing's so damn unpleasant to look at. You're going to have to walk a tightrope."

"That's a pretty tall order," I say. "The monkeys are significant only because they belonged to Mendelssohn. And they belonged to him only because he was forced, as a Jew, to buy them."

Now, finally, Bertholdt smiles.

"Perfectly logical, of course. But you'll sniff out the angle. If you can't do it, nobody can."

"Do you already have the monkey?" I ask.

"Yes. I had it sent two weeks ago. I took the liberty of not informing the owners about the Senate roadblock."

"I'd like to see it," I say.

Bertholdt drains his espresso and stands. "Right. Then let's go."

I take one last sip of my coffee and rise. Bertholdt throws a bill on the table. As we leave the café, I am aware of his hand resting lightly on my arm, steering me, as he used to do in that familiar, proprietary way.

We step out into the sunny morning. Bertholdt drops his hand from my arm. We walk side by side in comfortable silence.

I am thinking about Moses Mendelssohn: thinking about the day he went to the Royal Porcelain Works to purchase the quota of expensive porcelain imposed by the king on all Jews in Berlin, a condition of their being permitted to marry. The couple was not allowed to choose the items they might want; Jews were given defective pieces or items that wouldn't sell.

I see Mendelssohn driving along a street much like this one with Fromet, his betrothed, in a cheap hired buggy. The day I picture is gloomily appropriate to the occasion: sunless, misty, cold. He sits in the carriage, a full head shorter than his plain bride, hunched beneath the hump on his back and looking out from luminously intelligent eyes. I picture them drawing up to the Royal Porcelain Works and disembarking from the dingy cab. The driver waters his horse as he waits for his customers to return. Moses and Fromet approach the clerk in the warehouse, who smiles derisively as Mendelssohn, a lifelong stutterer, attempts to voice his request. Fromet stands by, her face touched with the anticipation of a young bride to be who, contrary to the fates of her friends with their arranged marriages, is very much in love.

"Would it be possible," he begins, and then catches on the

next word and must start all over again. "Some dishes, perhaps. Or soup bowls."

Fromet takes over.

"We throw ourselves on the beneficence of His Royal
Majesty, King Friedrich, to grant us some tableware to fulfill
the requirement that Jews, on their marriage, purchase three
hundred thalers of Royal Porcelain."

Three hundred thalers. A full twelve months of Mendelssohn's wages for long hours of labor in the warehouse of his
employer, Isaac Bernhard, protected Jew of King Friedrich.

"The beneficent king," the clerk replies, "in his infinite
God-given wisdom, will bestow on you such porcelain as he
sees fit for a Jew."

The clerk ushers the bride and groom toward a storeroom
at the back of the warehouse. He seems to take pleasure in
sorting through his dozens of keys to find the one that will
open the lock.

Inside, the lighting is inadequate, and the storeroom so
crowded with life-size porcelain statues, it is at first difficult
to make out what they are, though it is evident that each of
the many pieces is identical.

"Your monkeys!" the clerk exclaims. "Make their acquaintance. You will grow fond of them in time, I am certain of it.
No one would have them—but you will, Herr Mendelssohn."

The clerk leaves them for some minutes to examine their
new "purchase." Twenty life-size monkeys of such garish distaste it is a wonder they were conceived at all, let alone put
into production.

On their wedding day, the Mendelssohns take possession
of their monkeys. The husband treats his ugly new house-
mates with a certain irony. Many years later, his famous
grandson, the composer Felix—a Christian, thanks to his

parents, who converted so their children might enjoy the opportunities denied to Jews—keeps one of the offending monkeys in his studio, beside the piano where he composes his magnificent works for the Church.

The angle, I say to myself over and over to the rhythm of our brisk walking. *What on earth is the angle?*

By the time we reach the museum, I think I have it.

"Okay," I say to Bertholdt. We halt at the base of the wide steps.

"It's simple, really. It is 1759. One of the greatest German thinkers of all time—they called him 'the German Socrates,' after all—takes possession on his wedding day of twenty porcelain monkeys from the Royal Porcelain Works. Is it not of historical interest that these porcelain creatures adorned his house? And that they passed through the generations— one of them presiding over the music room of Germany's brilliant, beloved composer Felix Mendelssohn?

"We avoid mention of the porcelain quota. Instead, we focus on the generational link of German genius, of the contributions made by grandfather and grandson to the German cultural heritage, in two entirely different fields of endeavor. The monkeys, handed down, were witnesses of both."

Bertholdt looks unconvinced, but he nods.

"Perhaps you can bury a reference to the porcelain quota in the label on the vitrine," I add.

"It may be the best we can do," he says.

We climb the steps and go through a side entrance reserved for museum employees. We take a winding back corridor and come to a halt before a locked door, which Bertholdt opens with an antiquated key.

Inside, he flicks on the light. The room is large and crowded with artworks. He guides me to the far wall, to where two vitrines stand side by side. One contains the garish life-size porcelain monkey, and the other a small and very pretty monkey figurine. Bertholdt points to the pretty figurine.

"This is the one the Senate wants to include as a sample of Royal Porcelain from the period. Nothing, of course, to do with Mendelssohn or Jews. Someone on the committee tracked this one down at the Hohenzollern Museum."

I look at the sweet little figurine, then turn to the Mendelssohn monkey. "It truly is awful," I say.

"Yes, isn't it. Imagine—twenty of them, all crowded into his small house. Bumping into them at every turn."

Bertholdt and I had spent so much time together, years ago, in places such as this—in this very museum in fact, though not, of course, in the curatorial rooms. We stand quietly together, looking at the monkeys.

"Do you remember that book I gave you?" Bertholdt asks. "Wasn't there a reproduction, in there, of a painting of Mendelssohn?"

That art book—the book that changed my life.

"Yes, I remember," I say. "A lithograph by the French painter Maier."

The past; it would not, after all, slide away.

"Do you ever think about how things might have been, if we'd stayed together?" Bertholdt asks softly.

I might have stayed, had my father not suffered his aneurysms. Had I not been in the position of clearing out his apartment, which is when I found my mother's hatbox, with its disturbing contents. I might still be here, living an altogether different life in Berlin, with Bertholdt.

"I had no choice. I don't think I could have lived other than how I have lived."

I see, from the corner of my eye, that Bertholdt is biting the left side of his lip, an old habit I remember well.

"You never explained it to me. Not really."

Explained. How could I have explained?

"I just knew I had to leave. It's not that I didn't love you. I did. In a way, I still do."

Bertholdt turns to look at me. His eyes are glistening. Pleasure and pain, I see them both in his eyes. He seems to be waiting for something more.

"It was bigger than I was," I say quietly.

"What was bigger than you?"

"I don't know. Being German, I suppose."

My answer surprises me, but Bertholdt nods.

"It was when I became involved with Judaism that it started making sense. I knew that I was working my way home. Converts often have that 'aha' moment—they stumble across something that points them toward an ultimate, personal truth. For me, it was a few words in Genesis: when God says to Abraham, 'Go forth.'

"I used this when it came time to present myself to the Rabbinical committee. They ask one question: Why do you wish to become a Jew? I answered with these words from Genesis, and then offered two further readings of the statement. One, from a thirteenth-century sage: 'Go to your self, know your self, fulfill your self.' You see, I had to leave my life here—my life with you—so that I could go to my *self.*

"A sixteenth-century Kabbalist adds another twist: 'Search and discover the root of your soul, so that you can fulfill it and restore it to its source, its essence.' "

I can see that Bertholdt is listening intently. Suddenly, I feel ridiculous.

"I'm sorry. This all sounds a little abstract, doesn't it?"

Bertholdt looks bewildered. I wonder if he is about to cry.

"It's funny, isn't it," he says—not crying, but with a tremble in his voice. "You went on a mission to restore yourself to your essence. And it looks like you found what you were looking for. And I—I feel as if the life I was supposed to live was snatched away."

Bertholdt reaches again for my hand. I allow him to take it.

"I don't mean to blame you. Truly I don't. It's just that I've not found it easy—not found it possible, to be honest—to love again."

He squeezes my hand slightly. "I've never stopped missing you," he says.

We're both, now, looking at the vitrines. The room echoes with the past, our pasts in among the rest. We stand there for some time in the cool, windowless space.

"Poor monkey," I say softly. "Dragged into all this."

I failed, this morning, with the West Berlin Senate. They were firm in their resolve. Moses Mendelssohn's monkey will be returned to its present owner; the pretty Hohenzollern figurine will be displayed instead. I am to fly back to New York this afternoon. Back to my children, back to Lev, back to the life I have made.

I have an hour and a half before I need to head to the airport, where I will return my rental car and board the plane.

I decide to take a drive.

I find myself driving toward Lake Tegeler.

I turn onto the familiar driveway leading up to the baronial mansion that is now a nursing home. I pull into a parking space and turn off the engine.

It's a beautiful spring day. Sitting in the car, with the windows rolled down, I hear the chorus of birdsongs coming from the crowns of the trees, and breathe in the heady scent of the flowers lining the driveway: jasmine, gardenia, honeysuckle, lilac.

I look up at the imposing building, up to the window on the third floor where, sixteen years ago, I last saw my father. He is still here, my father, still in the care of nurses and aides. Perhaps still in that very room where I last laid eyes on him.

I will not go in to see him.

I don't know why I've driven here.

I turn on the ignition. The driveway is wide enough for me to make a clean, easy arc. I head back down the hill and out onto the highway.

I am thinking of my children. I have been away for almost two days; it will be another twelve hours before I am back with them. It seems an eternity.

I unroll the window, put my foot to the accelerator. I feel the road unfurling beneath the wheels of the car. I know that I will never come back here, to Berlin, to Germany.

On a whim, I reach up and remove my head scarf. My hair flies up around my face. I brush it back with my hand.

Berlin, 1962

For three days now I've done nothing but rifle through my father's possessions. Numbing work, though also agonizing, if there is such a thing as agonizing numbness.

After taking my father to the nursing home that is to be his new residence, I returned directly here, to my childhood home on Friedrichstrasse, and set about sorting and packing things up.

I organized, shuffled, compiled, taking time to devise the right categories and then assigning objects to their salient places. It was only after the first long day at this task that I allowed myself to recognize the pointlessness of much of my effort. I knew that, in the end, I would discard most of what I was organizing. But I also knew I had to see the thing through.

I began with the living room, then went to work in my father's study, a sunny room with a porch that leads out onto the small courtyard. My father had loved this private space; as a child, I often watched him from my bedroom window, where I spent long hours reading or playing with my dolls. Through the window, I would see him at his desk, attending to paperwork. Every so often, he would rise, step onto the porch, then light one of the thin, strong-smelling cigarillos he smoked throughout the day, surveying the little garden he had fashioned from two dozen or more potted plants, which he tended early each morning before setting out for his job as a senior official in the Taxation Department.

Now, I clear my father's filing drawers into boxes, which I label and stack in the front hallway. Next, his books, the volumes I'd looked at and fingered as far back as I could remember: Goethe, Schiller, Lessing, and others my father had purchased in more recent years—Rilke, Schnitzler, Mann. I remove, too, the framed copy of Heine's "Die Lorelei," which Father had placed on a shelf beside a photograph of me as a child, about thirteen years old, dressed in running gear and receiving one of the many medals I had won as a sprinter before I gave up my budding career.

The last item packed, I survey the eerily emptied room.

I turn and make my way to the bedroom.

After my mother died, my father rid the house of all

traces of her: her clothing, toiletries, the various ornaments and collectibles she had accrued in her forty years of life. So when I stand on a chair to check the high shelf of the armoire, I am surprised to see a large hatbox, covered in floral paper. The sight of the box sets off flashes of visceral memory which I cannot describe but which hold the texture and feel of my early life.

I reach up and take down the box. Inside, facedown, is the framed photograph I know instantly the moment I turn it over. I have not thought about this photograph since my mother died four years ago, when I was seventeen. It is a picture of my mother in her peak of glory, standing alongside the rest of the Olympic track team, her two medals, one gold, one silver, hanging around her neck. Her youthful face glows with triumph. I don't recall ever having held the picture in my hands; I had seen it always only from a distance, through a cut-glass door, on the uppermost shelf of the dining room breakfront.

Berlin, 1936.

Now, holding the frame for the first time, I peer closely at the photograph. I see with some surprise that my mother's face is beautiful—very beautiful, in fact. No sign of the grim, resentful mother I knew. All my memories of her involve a recoiling from her coldness, her selfishness, from the anger that oozed from her like a toxic, oily liquid. Her life had not turned out the way she had planned—the way I could see now, in this photograph, she had hoped; and she had never forgiven us, never forgiven the world, for this fact.

Giving up my own future career as an athlete when I was sixteen—a year before my mother's death—was a savage blow to her. Through me, she'd been given a chance to reclaim some of her former glory; I would run in her athletic footsteps, bring honor, again, to her and her beloved Fatherland, though this was, of course, no longer a term that was used. I never felt her love, but I felt her longing for my success, intuited her plans for my life. Which is why I put a quick end to it all—in some ways, I see only now, at my own expense. But giving up the pleasures of running (it was in my blood, I was born to it) was a small price for the deeper reward of dealing a blow to my mother. I never looked back, though I have at times been acutely aware of the silent ache of my unnaturally curtailed body.

I discovered other interests; I turned my efforts to the study of art, which has its own satisfactions.

But there is something else, here, in this photograph. Something I'd not noticed before. There, on my mother's arm: fingers. A man's hand in a sort of embrace. Not my father's: I know the details of his hand the way any child who loves her father knows the shape of his knuckles, the length of his fingers, the quality of his clasp.

I remember, now, one of my parents' rare arguments; they had lived together in a kind of enervated resignation, which was, while loveless, generally without rancor. So the few heated, angry exchanges they had stand out; this argument was about the very photograph now in my hands.

I must have been about nine years old. I am lying in bed, struggling with the sleeplessness that has plagued me for as long as I can remember. I sit up when I hear my father, usually accommodating and calm, raise his voice. I creep to the door, open it very slightly, and put my ear to the crack.

"I don't want to have to see it there, day after day," my father says.

"You're jealous!" My mother, sneering.

"Don't be ridiculous."

And now my mother, with intensified scorn. "Just because you didn't make the team—"

My father's voice, again: "Are you really that ignorant?"

Then, the closing of a door. They are in their bedroom; one of them has decided to close the door. They continue to have words—I can hear raised voices—but I can no longer make out what they are saying.

After the fight, the photograph remained in its place until my mother's death. I no more noticed it than I noticed any of the familiar objects in our apartment; they were simply the contours of my daily existence.

But then it disappeared—possibly on the actual day my mother died.

She had succumbed quickly to her illness. Cancer of the stomach. Not a lingering, painful death, but a swift and sudden abandonment of life. Diagnosed one week, she was gone the next, as if my mother had decided, in her already advanced state of resignation, that there was no point putting up a fight.

Now, a spear of pain lances the numbness that has overtaken me since I began packing up my father's life: that my mother had not bothered to try to stay alive for me. What use was I to her, after all, having put an end to her chance of rewriting her own lost dreams?

For the first time, I notice the width of the matting around the photograph—too wide, really, for the size of the picture. The balance is wrong. I turn the frame over, push away the little silver levers holding the backing in place. I remove the heavy, velvet-covered board, then slide the photograph from the glass. I turn over the picture.

There is my mother, her eyes shining with pride, the faint smile on her lips, looking into the camera toward her glorious future, looking toward it still, even from the grave. There she is with her fellow athletes, all of them shimmering with their own prowess, with the promise of a greater Germany, enthralled with the booming might of the Third Reich.

Those fingers clasping my mother's arm—they are, of course, attached to a hand. Now, I see what the wide matting has been hiding, all these years. Standing beside my mother, the star of Germany's 1936 women's Olympic track team, warmly clasping her arm, is my mother's beloved Führer himself.

Hitler presided over the Berlin Olympics as if anticipating a future world reign; this was well known. He attended every awards ceremony in which there was a German medal winner, as if their athletic victory were advancing the might of the Third Reich. Why should I be surprised, then, to find him clasping the arm of my mother?

I return the picture to the frame and set it down on the bed, then reach into the hatbox and withdraw three notebooks. Each is bound in fine kidskin dyed a pastel shade: one dusty purple, one pale blue, the third rose. Each bears the words *My Diary* and is embossed, on the spine, with my mother's name.

I begin to leaf through them. They are filled with my mother's childish, sloping script. Each entry is dated. The writing appears to mature as time passes through the pages, which together cover a period of just over five years and include my mother's Olympic victories, her pregnancy with me, and my birth.

Her sentences are choppy, flat, uninteresting. And sticky with self-absorption. Her entire world seems to consist of nothing but her own little sphere of self-important fantasy.

I skim through the first book, stopping here and there to

get the gist of the passage of her days, skipping over long, tedious passages about the mundane. I put down the first book and leaf through the second, then turn to the third.

Toward the end of this final notebook, I fall into a long section that suddenly grabs my attention.

It is the story of my beginnings.

I sit down on the floor of my parents' room, which is covered with the same soft, taupe carpeting on which I took my first steps, and flip through the pages. I have trouble actually reading the words—they spring out at me like plump, troublesome insects baring pincers or poison stingers. Every now and then, a fragment of meaning lodges in my brain.

Hysterical declarations of allegiance to her Beloved Fatherland. Teenage ecstasies over her Führer. Her pining protestations of love for her hero-heartthrob are truly sickening.

1940. Germany will not be stopped.

Page after page. A patch of warm sunlight moves slowly across the room. The past jumps up at me, through the insectlike scratchings of my mother's script.

What's this? What strange honor is my mother frothing about? It seems to make no sense; I have trouble understanding the words. I read the passage over once, twice, three times. And then, the meaning breaks from the page.

My mother is to be sent to a special "camp"—a place to which only the purest Aryans are invited. She is to be matched with an equally pure thoroughbred. For the purpose of breeding.

A genetic experiment: to populate the Third Reich with perfect, Aryan specimens. An Olympic champion, pride of her race. To be matched with another athletic purebred.

A resortlike retreat in the country. Delicious, wholesome meals.

Meeting the other young people.

Being matched with my father. When she first sees him, her heart "leaps" and she "jumps for joy," along with other weary, romantic clichés.

Four nights, in one of the beautifully appointed "marital chambers," though there has not, as yet, been a marriage.

Conception.

I am so proud. I am to contribute a perfect child to our glorious Fatherland. I am serving our Führer. I tremble to think of it. I hope it will be a boy.

Toward the end of the final volume, my mother recounts her difficult labor and, then, a sour note of disappointment.

She's so ugly. Wrinkled and skinny. I'd expected a plump cherub like you see in paintings. I told Matron to take her to the nursery and give her to the wet nurse. I had wanted a boy. Perhaps we will be luckier next time.

Reading my mother's words feels like a blow to the gut. I have long since peeled my mother from my life; even at her funeral, I felt little emotion. It surprises me that the sentiments of a shallow twenty-three-year-old who never, as a mother, meant much to me, would have the power to wound me as deeply as they do.

There are no entries, now, for three months. And then:

We are to try again tonight. I pray we are luckier, this time.

From here on, the entries are sparse, and terse. Every month, a simple line:

Menses today. Disappointed.

And then, a long gap.

I am to be paired with another man. I know the fault lies with Hermann. How could it not? I conceived the girl so quickly. I think I hate him. All these wasted months.

Another long gap.

They say I can try two more men, and then I must leave. It is not my fault.

And then, the diary's final entry.

I have been told I must leave. I am so ashamed.
Hermann and I are to be married.

I cringe at the thought of my father deciding to marry this woman toward whom he had so little feeling. I know, however, why he did.

I was the light of my father's life, as he often used to tell me. He married my mother to be with me.

I close the notebook and sit for a long time on the taupe carpet. When I began reading, the sun was streaming in through the window, warming my back and forming patterns on the carpet. Now, dusk is hanging in the room and I am beginning to feel cold.

I place the diaries back in the hatbox, noticing for the first time, that there are a few small objects in the bottom of the box. I reach in and retrieve three items—all toys from my early childhood, playthings I'd not seen in fifteen years or more. I finger the items—the wooden top, and two toys my father had made for me from salvaged items: a spool, a length of old wire.

And now, another memory, snatching away the present, pulling me back.

It is 1945, I am four years old. I am playing with the wooden top my father brought home for me one day, perhaps two years earlier, in the thick of the War. A small wooden spinning top with an unusual shape: a three-dimensional rectangle that narrows to a cone. To get it to spin, one grasps the small stick protruding from the top of the rectangle and gives a quick flick. Each of the four faces of the rectangle has some symbol painted on it, but they have been concealed by thick splotches of black ink. I remember peering at the sides, trying to make out the hidden symbols, but the ink covering them is too dark, and I can discern only a curve or a line here and there.

There was such scarcity of all things—we were surviving on a diet of old potatoes cooked in lard, and a weekly ration of the dried beef my father had stockpiled early on in the War. I own several toys my father fashioned from nonessential items: a sardine tin attached to a piece of string serves variously as a princess carriage, a pet dog, or my royal servant; a wooden spool with a cheerful daubed-on face is my beloved clown. My prize possession is a little statuette of a bicycle fashioned of wire. It is a marvel of detail: seat, handlebar, spokes and chain, even a tiny lever with which to change the gears.

The wooden top is my first treasure not made by my father. It feels like a small piece of the wider world—of a world without war. When he gave it to me, it was wrapped in a piece of newsprint and tied with a fragment of twine.

I am sitting on the tile of our hallway, spinning the top. The radio is crackling in the background. My mother is sitting in the brown armchair in the adjacent living room, crying loudly and uncontrollably. I have never seen my mother cry before, so I stop spinning the top and turn to look at her. Her hair is untied from its usual bun and hangs limply around her face, which is splotchy and distorted. I hardly recognize her. This doesn't particularly trouble me. It is my father who fills the world with life.

I look across to the old velvet sofa where he is sitting. It has been some weeks now—I could not say exactly how long—since he has ceased putting on his uniform and disappearing for days or weeks on end, to attend to his soldierly duties. One day, he was just suddenly with us in the apartment all day long. Of course, this delighted me no end.

I cannot understand what is being said by the radio announcer, though I can hear that there is alarm in his voice.

"What is it?" I ask. "Papa, what is the man saying?"

But before he can answer, my mother wails, "Our Führer is dead! They have murdered our Führer!"

Now my father unslumps from the couch, stands, then walks slowly to my mother and leans over her. He takes her by the shoulders. In my memory, I see him shaking my mother—though surely this cannot be true, as my father was the gentlest, most patient of men.

"Nobody murdered him. Do you hear? He took his own life. He held up a gun and shot himself."

My mother shakes her head back and forth; her stringy hair flies up around her head.

"No!" she wails, then starts to thrash her arms and legs. "He wouldn't leave us. He wouldn't!"

Her eyes are wild. It is no longer my mother.

I hear my father's voice—deep, loud, stern. "He killed himself. Do you hear me? We've lost the War. It's over."

My mother is shrieking. In slow motion, I see my father raise his hand and slap her so hard across the face that the force of the blow knocks her into a lumpy heap in the armchair. She is suddenly quiet. She is looking blankly at my father. Tears still flood from her eyes, but she no longer flails or shrieks. A large red patch in the form of my father's hand grows on her cheek. My father turns and walks past me, enters the bedroom, and quietly closes the door. He does not look at me, he does not acknowledge me in any way. I am alone with my mother, who is whimpering quietly in the chair.

I turn back to my little wooden top. I pick it up and spin it, then watch as it furiously twirls, slows, and topples onto its side.

I haven't seen this toy for so many years; I'd wondered, on more than one occasion, what had happened to it.

It was in my second year of studies at the university—almost three years ago now—that I came across a photograph in the beautiful book on religious artifacts that Bertholdt had given me. As I flipped through its glossy pages, the picture jumped out at me. There, beside an engraved silver rod with a gold tip, which the notation identified as a "yad," was a wooden top exactly like my own, though the sides were of course not inked out; I could see clearly the sinuous lines of Hebrew letters, one on each face of the three-dimensional rectangle. A dreidel—the ceremonial toy that Jewish children play with during Chanukah, the festival of lights.

I stared at the picture for a very long time. And I resolved to ask my father where he had obtained the dreidel he had given me, surely a contraband object in Nazi Germany, 1943.

The opportunity to ask him, however, never seemed to arise. Or should I say, I never worked up the courage to ask.

That same book contained a reproduction of a lithograph that seized me with its dark complexities. Seated at a table, in an elegant late-eighteenth-century drawing room, is a short man with a large head and misshapen back. He peers out from dark, intelligent eyes, which emit a deep steadiness that seems to flow into the room.

Above him hovers a tall man with fair coloring—his friend, the writer Gotthold Lessing. The hunchback is Moses Mendelssohn, known in his day as both "The German Socrates" and "The Jew Mendelssohn," one of the greatest thinkers in the history of the Western world. Across the table from him is a man of impressive bearing: the physiognomist Johann Kaspar Lavater, famous in his day, who is attempting to convince Mendelssohn that he must, as a great German thinker, convert to Christianity, the only legitimate religion.

It was this lithograph that drove me to make a study of Mendelssohn's life. He never did convert, though many of his children and grandchildren did. At his death, of his fifty-six descendants, fifty-two were Christians, including his famous grandson Felix Mendelssohn, who composed some of the greatest church music ever written. For most of these descendants, the funeral of their grandfather was the first—and last—Jewish ceremony they ever attended.

I put the toys my father made for me back in the hatbox and close the lid, slipping the wooden top into my pocket. I carry the hatbox into the hall and place it on the discard pile.

*   *   *

I swing my car onto the curved driveway of the nursing residence. The series of cerebral aneurysms my father suffered some months ago, at the young age of fifty, have left him paralyzed from the waist down. He has patches of slack muscle elsewhere, such as the left side of his face, which hangs on the bone like overcooked meat. His mental faculties, however, appear to have been spared. His eyes are lucid, and he can speak, though haltingly, and with many distortions. If I concentrate, I can understand what he is saying.

The sight of the mansion up on the hill overlooking Lake Tegeler—once the home of James Simon, the legendary "cotton king," art patron and adviser to Kaiser Wilhelm II—arouses conflicting emotions.

I pull into a parking space and turn off the engine. Below me, the lake sparkles in the high noon sun; a family of ducks paddles about in the water, and several couples with young children stroll upon its banks.

I sit there for a while, looking down at the pleasant scene. Below me, the strollers by the lake have moved on to other diversions. I get out of the car and lock the door. I haven't eaten for some time, and now my stomach swishes with acid, which rises unpleasantly in my throat.

I climb the grand steps and enter the foyer, whose chandelier, despite the bright sunlight pouring in through the massive leaded windows, is fully ablaze. I am greeted by the receptionist. She presses the buzzer to summon my father's nurse, who appears some minutes later—fastidious in her starched uniform and cap, like all the nurses here, though exceptional in her jittery, slightly overbearing friendliness.

"Your father will be so happy you've come," she says, clasping both my hands in hers.

I try to smile back, then follow behind her on the journey through the mansion that will deposit me at my father's door.

The house's original artwork was plundered by the state twenty-five years ago, when the Nazis seized the mansion, and everything in it, from the son of James Simon, himself a prominent citizen. In what seems to me a misplaced attempt at restitution, the present owner tracked down the identities of the paintings—which are still to be found either in private collections or in Berlin's museums—that had once hung on the walls. At considerable expense, this man procured high-quality reproductions of these original works and hung them throughout the house. I find myself cataloging the paintings as we wend our way up the curved stairway and along first one ornate hallway and then the next. Here, the van Gogh, now two Courbets. A lesser Gauguin—I've never had a taste for Gauguin—and then a long hallway in which I recognize a Pissarro, a Cézanne, and two works by Vermeer. An entire hallway is dedicated to works of the German Impressionists, some of which were commissioned by James Simon himself. They all stare back at me in their eerie falseness, as if aware they are claiming to be something they are not.

On the wall outside my father's room hangs the house's single Goya. I pause to examine it as the nurse reaches down to open the door.

"Here she is," the nurse exclaims as she strides into the room. "Let's get some air, shall we?" She hurries over to the bay windows and flings them open.

My father turns to me. The left side of his face hangs loosely; I flinch at the sight of him.

All my happy memories from childhood involve my father. They are simple memories, no different, I should think, from those of any other child who has grown up in an ordinary home with at least one loving parent. There was the War, of course, and after that, the chaos and shame of defeat. But a few daily pleasures shone through: a game my father played with me when I was a tot, in which he sat in a chair cross-legged, and I balanced on his foot as he swung it high and low, high and low, while singing "Die Lorelei" in his pleasant tenor. *Ich weiss nicht, was soll es bedeuten.* I do not know what haunts me, this nameless, sorrowful pain." His face would glow with happiness and love; I would fix my eyes on him as he swung me thrillingly up and down. Behind him, the portrait of his father also swung up and down with the motion: his father, in full military dress, who distinguished himself in the Great War and was later rewarded with a prestigious government post. I would throw my head back and laugh, and my father would laugh with me.

Other memories—of me tearing around the apartment, my father having pushed all the furniture back against the walls. "My little cornflower comet," he would say. Later, he'd time me. After doing two circuits of the entire apartment, I would fling myself into his arms, demanding to know the reading, enthralled at the prospect of beating my own best time.

"Nurse, if you don't mind," I say, "I'd like to have some time alone with my father."

The nurse seems a little put out, but after fussing over my father for a minute or two, she leaves.

"Papa," I begin. "I've been sorting through your things. I'll bring you whatever I think you might want. The rest I can store at my place."

"I don't need more than I have here," my father says haltingly, stretching out each vowel in a way that is painful to hear. "Get rid of it all."

Papa is looking out the window at the sloping lawn that leads down to the lake. I can still see the family of ducks, though from this distance they are no more than moving gray-green splotches.

"I found a hatbox, at the top of the armoire. It had some things in it of Mama's."

A pause.

"You can get rid of that, too."

"Diaries. Her diaries, from a long time ago."

Nothing.

"Did you ever read them, Papa? Did you ever read what Mama wrote?"

"I didn't have to read them. I lived it. Besides, she wasn't much of a writer."

There is something sinister in the sound of my father's distorted speech.

"I read them," I say. "As much as I could bear to read."

Another pause. My father's lips are working soundlessly as he attempts to formulate words.

"It doesn't make any difference," he says. I am puzzled by his response. How could the truth about their pasts—about how I came to be—make no difference? I reach into my pocket, pull out the little wooden top.

"This was in the hatbox, too," I say, walking over to my father and putting the top in his hands. He looks down at it blankly, and then his face curdles with distaste, as if I'd handed him a slimy, dead fish.

"Your wooden top," he says. "You loved that wooden top." He reaches up and hands the toy back to me.

"Where did you get it?" I feel a cloud of confusion coming over me.

Papa looks at me blankly.

"I don't know, I don't remember."

"You do remember. I know you do." I don't know why I say this, I know only that he kept the toy for a reason, that the sides have been inked out, that the wooden top holds some kind of secret.

Now my father whispers, his words unnaturally drawn out.

"It is not your business to know" is what I think he says.

I take a step toward him.

"It *is* my business. You made it my business."

I see something in my father's face that I don't think I've ever seen before: hatred.

"All right then. I'll tell you. I'll tell you where I got that little top that you so treasured."

My father begins to talk. That hesitating, awful speech, filled with pauses and stuttering repetitions.

As he speaks, images pop up before my eyes. I see everything, as if the past were happening all over again.

"I was the keeper of the doors," he begins. "That was my job."

My father's job. His contribution to what was going to be the glorious ascent of the Third Reich.

He tells me for the first time where he worked: at the Ravensbrück concentration camp, not far from Berlin. His job was to usher new arrivees, who had been selected for extermination, to what were referred to as "showers" or "delousing chambers." Mostly women and children, and the elderly. Naked, all of them, shivering from the cold. My father's job was to close the door and stand guard while the "delousing," achieved with Zyklon B gas, took place. My father was to wait until the last of the screams and the choking coughs ceased. Then, he would call members of the Sonderkommando, the Jewish slave force, themselves slated, some months ahead, for death. They would come and open the doors and set about removing gold teeth and fillings and any valuables hidden in body cavities before transporting the corpses to be burned in the crematoria.

Day in, day out, my father stood by the doors. When it came time for the Sonderkommando to take over, he would walk to the officers' mess to take his main meal of the day. Sometimes, he would squirrel away a treat to bring back home to me on his next leave—something that would keep, like a piece of dried fruit or a spoonful of sugar he would wrap carefully in paper and seal at the edges with wax.

On one particular day, as my father was ushering the naked people through the door, uttering the scripted lies that were supposed to reassure and impart docility—how long the showers and delousing would last, where they would go to retrieve their clothing—a woman suddenly pulled away from the faceless stream and my father found himself being forced to look into her face. Her dark hair had been hacked short, and she had fierce eyes. A young woman, perhaps twenty-four or twenty-five, who was holding a little girl.

The women were usually separated from the children and then assigned to work duty, my father says matter-of-factly. But when the women would not give up their children, the children were sent along with the mothers to the "showers."

"The little girl looked to be about your age," he says. "You were two and a half—I remember thinking that the little girl must be about two and a half, like you. Then all of a sudden, the woman practically threw the child into my arms. 'Take her.' She said it very quietly, I almost couldn't hear her. 'Take my baby.' The little girl stretched her arms out to me and clutched on to my neck."

My father is no longer talking to me. He is looking right through me, as if I don't exist.

"How could I not think of you?" he is saying again, to the window. I have the ridiculous feeling that my father is talking to the family of ducks paddling about down there on the lake.

"I peeled the girl's arms from my neck and handed her back. But something had happened to the woman. Her arms were hanging at her sides. I expected that the mother would take the child. It all happened very quickly, but the next thing I know, the girl has fallen to the ground. I hear a cracking sound. I look down to see that the little girl has cracked her head on the concrete floor; there is a lot of blood. She starts to cry. This attracts the attention of a nearby guard.

"I am down on the ground. I pick up the little girl. Again, she clasps me around the neck."

My father turns back to me. The good side of his face wears an expression of bewilderment. He is looking at me, but he is still talking to himself.

"I wasn't thinking," he says. "One of the guards grabs the girl from my arms. 'What are you doing?' he asks. His voice is calm, like that of a schoolteacher about to explain a lesson. 'She's hurt herself,' I say. The guard says, calmly, 'Resume your duties,' and places the child in the arms of an elderly woman. The girl is crying. Her hair is matted with blood. 'But I thought—the infirmary—she's hurt herself,' I say. The guard is now getting annoyed. 'What difference does it make?' he asks. The old lady walks into the chamber; the little girl is still crying, reaching her arms out for me.

"I do what I am told. I resume my duties. It is only later,

when it is time to call the Sonderkommando to open the doors, that I notice something on the floor, in the corner. I lean down and see it is some kind of top. A wooden top. The girl must have been holding it and let go of it when she fell. It must have rolled off into the corner without me noticing.

"You had so few playthings. So I put the top in my pocket and walked to the mess for lunch. It was a very cold day. I remember putting my hands in my pockets to keep them warm and holding on to the little wooden top. I remember thinking how happy you would be to have such a toy.

"And you were happy. You gave me a dozen kisses."

For a moment, my father's eyes flicker—with happiness. My father, the man I had adored as a child, whose visits and tenderness and embraces I had lived for.

I open my mouth to speak. My voice is a croak.

"When did you black out the letters on the sides? They were Hebrew letters, weren't they."

My father looks puzzled.

"I don't know," he says woodenly. "I don't remember. Maybe in the barracks, maybe at home."

I take one step backward, a second, a third. I am shrinking back, away from my father, away from his words. I find myself standing pressed up against the wooden door. I am still shrinking back, but there is nowhere further to go.

"Papa," I groan. My papa, my beloved papa.

"I am nobody," he says.

What is he saying?

I feel my hand on the door handle behind me, feel myself turning it, pulling the door open. I move with the moving door, then find I am in the hallway. My head, the world, all of it I know, is a hurricane. I feel myself swaying as if in a squall.

My hand is in my jacket pocket, I am clutching the dreidel.

I see the little dark-haired girl, see the terror in her eyes. See her crashing to the concrete floor.

I am running through the elegant halls of the old mansion; I do not see the fake Courbets and Vermeers and Manets as I pass by, though I know they are there.

I see the little girl's hand instinctively unclutching as she falls to the ground, the dreidel clattering as it rolls into the corner from where my father—the keeper of the doors—will later retrieve it, later, when the cries have been silenced, before he begins his casual stroll to the officers' mess, where he will take his simple though nutritious lunch.

I am speeding through the hallways. I sense eyes turning my way; someone, I think, calls out to me.

I take the little girl in my own arms. Tears slide down my face.

"I will rescue you," I whisper, clutching the little toy she surely treasured as I had.

I am in the parking lot, I am fumbling with my key at the door of my car.

I am in the car. I check the rearview mirror before backing out of the parking space, catch sight, in the glass, of my blue, blue, cornflower eyes.

I swipe at the tears on my cheeks.

"I will give you back your life," I whisper as I roar down the steep driveway and out onto the open road.

New York, 1990

An hour or more has passed since Rinat went back upstairs. After she left, I turned off the lamp on my kitchen desk. I have been sitting here all this time in the dark. It is very cold. The heating is on a timer, which drops the thermostat down through the thick night hours and comes back up again only at 6 a.m., in time to heat the house by 7 a.m., when I normally rise and rouse everyone.

Now I hear, again, the creaking of the stairs. I wait, I do not turn. I know, from the sound of the tread, that it is Rinat.

"Mama, I can't believe you're still sitting here! It's like the Arctic."

She sits opposite me, as she had earlier when I told her the story she'd asked to hear. "Why have you not gone to bed?"

My eyes are dry. I blink once, twice. My contact lenses have been in for almost twenty-four hours and are very uncomfortable.

My husband has never said anything about the fact that I wear contact lenses, which are considered an unacceptable vanity within our close-knit religious community. But people slide things by—I have friends who attend all-women's exercise classes, and others who dye their hair, though in public their heads are always covered. The contact lenses have been my slide-by.

When I first met Lev, I explained that my special kind of astigmatism could not be properly corrected by eyeglasses. He accepted this. I was new to the Jewish religion at that point. Lev was—and still is—proud of my having come to Judaism from the heart, as a convert: of my having mastered the complicated rituals and practices and been a model Orthodox Jewish mother and wife, while also to some extent keeping up my own career as an art historian. I suppose that, at the time, he saw the lenses as a remnant of my old life, before I became a Jew; and later, he probably just forgot the matter entirely.

I was always understandably self-conscious about the prospect of Lev seeing me put the lenses in or take them out. So I made a point of waiting until he was asleep before removing them; and, as I arose very early, I would slip them in before he was up.

Amazingly, I managed to keep the truth from him for almost five years. Although perhaps not so amazing, given the laws we live by—given the possibility, within our customs, of maintaining a self-contained and demure distance, even in matters of the greatest intimacy.

We had always made love only in the dark; I had always retreated to a private space, closing my eyes to Lev while also giving him as much of my being as was left for giving.

Only once did he catch me.

We had made love, and I waited, as always, until I thought Lev was asleep before rising to wash. This, too, I typically did in the dark.

I don't know why, that evening, I switched on the night-light in the bathroom. I had taken out my lenses and was closing the faucet when I looked into the mirror to see Lev reflected, behind me, shadowy in the dim glow. He was looking at my eyes. His own looked startled.

What he did next surprised me. Quietly, he flicked off the switch on the night-light. I felt his arms about me, gently, from behind; he lay his head on my shoulder. He cradled me, that way, for some minutes. Then, in the darkness, he guided me back to my bed. Our room has two full-size beds, to allow for separation during those days of the month when the Family Purity Laws proscribe any kind of physical contact between husband and wife—when I may not even pass Lev a glass across the table—but also for comfort, together, in one of them, during the rest of the month, when lovemaking, especially on the Sabbath, is a mitzvah. In the thick of that night, Lev climbed back into the bed with me and held me, in sleep, all night long. Held me in comfort and acceptance, though I can't imagine he knew the full extent of what it was he was silently accepting.

I have never forgotten that night. I have never stopped feeling grateful to Lev for that moment.

The whole idea of the contact lenses seems in a way absurd, when looked at in the cold light of day. But I've learned that logic plays little role in such matters. For me, there is no cold light of day. At least none that makes any real sense.

After I read my mother's disturbing, callow diary, after I saw my father that last time—asked him, finally, about the dreidel—the desire rose up and bit me in the throat, a desire that perhaps to others would seem an aberration. I could no longer stand to catch sight of myself in the mirror because of the unnaturally bright blue of my eyes, eyes that were the result of a bizarre bit of genetic planning in a dark hour—my dark hour—of history.

That is why, after leaving my father's room in the nursing home that day—I knew I would never see him again, and indeed, I never did—I drove to the ophthalmologist and made my inquiries about the new contact lenses, still in the early days of development, that could change the color of your eyes. The transformation I sought, it turned out, was the easiest to effect (and the least requested): blue to brown—in my case, cornflower blue to dark chocolate. Nazi eyes—with the slip of a finger—turned to Jew.

Rinat's face is blotchy, and her eyes are puffy and swollen. She has clearly been crying.

"What is it?" I ask.

"It's not true, is it. The story of how you were rescued. The kind German soldier who saved you."

I feel a rise of panic, and then, my head clears.

"It is and it isn't," I say quietly to Rinat, who is looking at me with a strange, frozen expression.

"There *was* a little girl," I continue. "She was about to enter the gas chamber, and her mother tried to push her into my father's arms. But my father didn't save her. The little girl went to her death."

I pause. It is so very quiet in my sleeping house. So dark, so cold, so quiet.

"*I* saved her, though," I whisper. "I found a way to give her back her life."

"Mama, what are you talking about?" Rinat is looking at me as if I have gone crazy. "Why is it all such a secret?" Now, there is accusation in her voice. "Can't you face the truth?"

The truth. Which truth does she want to know?

"Perhaps I can't," I say.

"And what if I can? What if I have more—"

"More what?"

"More—guts—"

Rinat has never spoken to me this way before. There she is, this daughter I know so well, with all her shadings and kindness and complexity, this girl who has felt the suffering of the world since she was a very small child.

"I'm sure you do have more guts than I have," I say quietly.

"Well then—?" Her eyes well with tears.

"Let me go and wash my hands," I say crisply. Now, Rinat looks baffled. I rise, walk—in a dream—over to the kitchen sink, and carefully wash my hands.

"Come," I say, and Rinat rises, too. I take her arm and guide her through the dining room and out into the hallway.

I open the door to the powder room, flick on the light, and together we enter the cramped space.

I take the contact lens case from my pocket and set it down on the rim of the basin. I reach up and remove one contact lens, then the other, putting each in its little cup in the case. We both look into the mirror—my eyes, unmasked, at last—I look from her blue blue eyes, across to my own, and back to hers.

"You see," I say, "I have blue eyes, too. The same color as my mother's. My father also had blue eyes, though his were a darker shade. They were matched partly for the color of their eyes, my mother and my father."

Rinat looks stunned. She is staring at me, in the mirror, can't take her eyes from my face.

"I was a runner as a child. When I was fifteen, I was in training to be an Olympic athlete. I loved to run from the very moment I learned to walk. I used to streak around my parents' apartment. They called me 'Cornflower Comet.' A ridiculous nickname, but that's how it was.

"I gave up running a year before my mother died. I did it to spite her. I never loved my mother. In fact, I think it would be true to say I hated her. I didn't know exactly why I hated her at the time. It was only later, when I learned the truth about her, that I understood."

"And your father?" Rinat's voice comes out a croak.

"It was more complicated with my father. You see, when I was a child, he was my whole world. He gave me many reasons to love him."

Rinat reaches a slender hand up to the glass, touches the place where my own eyes are reflected.

"I found out the truth about him, too. A very bad truth—worse even than my mother's."

She looks so sad, Rinat: so very sad.

"I couldn't bring myself to hate him," I say. "I tried to, but I couldn't. So I left. I left and never saw him again."

When Rinat speaks again, her voice is very low.

"Why would you disguise your eyes like that? What have you been trying to hide all these years?"

"What have I been trying to hide." It is a statement, not a question; I make this statement to myself.

"I don't know—them, my parents. My origins. My country. Myself."

When I received notice from the nursing home, some years ago, of my father's death, I instructed that he be cremated. That there be no funeral, no grave, no gravestone. And that all remaining funds in his estate be sent to the Simon Wiesenthal Center.

I tell none of this to Rinat. I look at her and sense that she knows these things without me having to say them, wonder again at how this child of mine, now a grown woman herself, can know the things she knows. It's as if the secrets of her parents and grandparents are sidling up against her own soul.

Finally, exhausted, Rinat says, "Mama, I'm going to bed." She doesn't kiss me before leaving, or embrace me, as she usually does. She simply turns, and climbs back up the stairs.

I listen to her fading footfalls.

Leah has awoken again. I hear her crying. Now I climb the stairs, too, pass the rooms of my other sleeping children, pass my own room, where my husband is snoring gently, then enter the nursery at the end of the hallway.

By the time I reach Leah, she is whimpering quietly. She suffers from bad dreams, as I did as a child. I lift her from her crib—at almost three years old, she still likes the security of the crib, though she will be ready soon for a toddler bed—and take her in my arms. She cradles her head in my neck, sighs with deep relief, places her thumb in her mouth and gently sucks. I listen to her sweet suckling grunts and make the soothing sounds that mothers the world over make to settle their crying children.

Leah's other little hand is closed into a fist; perhaps she fell asleep clutching the dreidel I had given her to play with earlier. I hold her, rock gently, close my eyes, hold her close, this dark-haired, dark-eyed little girl to whom I had, miraculously, already well into middle age, given life.

For all the dark-haired, dark-eyed little girls who didn't get to live their lives. And to those of us who did, and who must try, in some way, to make up for their loss.

The Lamp

I.

Miriam. New York, 1987

I jolt awake with a distinct feeling that something is awry. I look at the clock. Five a.m. I pick up the phone by my bed and dial my mother's number. The phone rings emptily: on and on and on. Finally, it cuts off. David lies asleep beside me. I jiggle his arm.

"Something's happened to my mother," I say. He mumbles in his sleep and rolls over.

I get out of bed, pull on a T-shirt, sweater, and pants, and slip into my shoes.

"I'll call you," I say and head out.

Usually I walk the twenty blocks down to Seventieth Street, but today I take a cab. The streetlights hang above me; they cut glaring bright spheres from the night.

I know when I turn the key in the lock that it is too late. I can feel that my mother has gone out of the world.

I find her in bed, curled on her side. She has a faint smile on her lips.

On the bedside table is a manila envelope. I pick it up and see it is labeled in my mother's neat hand with my name and, beneath that, "Important Papers." I reach in and draw out a few stapled sheets of paper. The first page lists my mother's investments: several savings accounts and a dozen or so treasury bonds. The next page contains the details of two life-insurance policies, the first of which dates back to 1946, the year my mother and I, a child of two, arrived in the United States from Germany. The third page is headed "Cemetery Plot." It names a cemetery I've never heard of—Beth-El, on Forest Avenue in Paramus, New Jersey—the number and location of the plot, and a telephone number.

The final page contains the following instruction: "Please call the Chevrah Kadishah. Give them the cemetery information. They will make the necessary arrangements." A number and address follow.

Chevrah Kadishah. The name rings a bell, but I don't know who or what they are.

I flip back to the first page and see that my mother has scribbled something in pencil in the lower right corner. "Take care of the lamp." Beneath this, she has written the date, May 7, 1987, and her signature.

May 7 was yesterday.

I scramble to make sense of it all. My mother, lying in bed last night, must have had some thought regarding the lamp: I know which lamp she means. Not wanting to forget the thought, to be neatly typed up later—or perhaps even intuiting that there was something wrong with her, that she may be lying down to meet her death—she rose, retrieved her envelope of important papers, and scribbled the note.

I take the papers and go into the living room. I sit in my

favorite chair. It is a heavy, comfortable chair, covered in velvet that was once red. All these years it has sat before the wide, uncovered window, facing the sun, which burns high over the Hudson, and it has faded to a dusty pink.

I pick up the phone and dial the number for the Chevrah Kadishah. The phone is answered by a man with a slight accent. I tell him my mother, Ruth Tuschak, has died, and he says something back in a language I don't understand. I think it is Hebrew or perhaps Yiddish, I can't tell which. His voice is sincere and kind. I say thank you—I assume he has offered me ritual words of condolence. He asks for the address, which I give, and he says he will have someone here within the hour. I say nothing more. I am holding the phone, waiting for him to say something further.

"You need to call the police," he says gently.

"Yes, of course," I say.

"Tell them we are on our way. The police officer will know to wait."

"Good, fine, thank you," I say.

"I wish you long life," he says.

I hang up the phone.

My mother has thought of everything. My mother has always been thoughtful. She did not, however, leave instructions for how I was supposed to go on with the world feeling this way: empty, lifeless, and gray.

I look around the room. The apartment is so full of her; she is everywhere. The room is filled with the sound of her movement, her sure, steady stride. Every object holds her glances—eyes filled with appreciation or worry, or happiness, or dread—holding her in the cup of their being. Looking at everything, I feel her memories and secrets, though I do not know what they contain.

There were always only the two of us. I used to think we were two parts of the same person. We read each other's moods, and there was a deep kindness between us that I didn't see between other mothers and daughters, whose relations, even when loving, seemed more complicated and fraught.

It makes no sense—that my mother would want the Chevrah Kadishah to tend to her body, that she'd bought a plot in a Jewish cemetery.

There is always some hidden spot. It hadn't occurred to me that in my mother's hidden spot was not only the trauma of living through the Second World War in Germany, of surviving the bombing of Dresden, her birthplace, all of which I knew about only in a cursory way, but also that she endured and survived all this as a Jew.

I know so little about my own beginnings. I know I was born nine months before the bombing of Dresden, in the basement of someone else's house. That my mother was helped by an elderly woman who perished in the bombing. That a year after the War ended she came to New York on a boat, carrying a small suitcase and a lamp, and that I, a toddler of two, was at her side.

I asked, once, about my father. I was seven or eight years old. We were sitting over breakfast at the kitchen table and I blurted it out: "Who is my father?"

My mother put down her teacup.

"You have no father," she said, a fierce look on her face.

"But, Mama," I protested. "Everybody has a father."

She took me hard by the shoulders. "Listen carefully," she said. Her eyes were angry. My gentle mother, always so patient, was looking at me with naked anger in her eyes.

"We have everything we need—right here. We have a

home, I have work I enjoy doing, you go to a good school. We want for nothing. Nothing!"

I was frozen in terror. I did not recognize this agitated woman.

"You have no father and never did. The world is this way. This is the best of the world, not the worst. Do you understand?"

Tears dripped down my face. I did not understand what she was saying, but I nodded—my first lie—that I did. I looked at this stranger and wondered where my beautiful, kind mother had gone.

I had, though, heard what she said, if I'd not fully understood her meaning. And in my own little soul, I found a way to honor her words as true. I put all thoughts of a father from my mind. She was right; what more did we need? Together, we had everything we could want.

They come within minutes of each other—the police officer and the Chevrah Kadishah. We complete all the paperwork. My mother is put on a stretcher, covered with a sheet, and wheeled to the service elevator. It is early, still; no one is about but the porter, who works the service elevator, and the doorman, both of whom I've known since I was a child. They offer their condolences.

I watch as my mother is packed into a green van and driven away.

I realize only now that I have not called David. David does not know that my mother is dead.

I go back up to the apartment, sit down in the faded chair, and dial my own number.

David picks up on the third ring. I hear activity in the background—the kids getting ready for school.

"Mom has died," I say awkwardly.

"Miriam? Is that you?"

I clear my throat. "Yes, David. I found her in bed. She looked peaceful, you know? They just took her away."

"Don't move," he says. "I'll be right there."

I hang up the phone.

I look at the lamp on the side table next to the chair. Of course, this is the lamp my mother was thinking about as she lay in the bed last night, the lamp she has asked me to take care of for her. The lamp she brought with her from Germany, more than forty years ago.

I realize now, looking at it, that this lamp has always filled me with a vague dread. I touch the heavy gold base, run my hand up the ornate shaft, which has a floral design worked into the metal. It is iron, I think, covered in gold leaf.

I finger the opaque, pinky beige shade. When lit, the lamp gives off a soft, luminous light that is ghostlike and otherworldly.

I will never know what this lamp meant to my mother, or why she brought it all the way here. Why she has asked me to take care of it; what link it held, for her, to her past.

I will never know who she really was. Who her family were, what happened to them. Why she hid from me the fact of her—or my own—Jewishness.

The pale morning sun has risen over the river. It spreads cool white light over the still surface of the water.

It is the first morning sun I have known without my mother in the world. It is unfamiliar and uncommonly cold, not a sun that seems capable of warming the world.

II.
Ruth. May 7, 1987

I have thought about her so many times, that young woman I glimpsed, through a gap in the side of the cattle car. She had such a thin face, a face that had seen too much suffering. And yet there was serenity in her eyes. She was going to her death and she surely knew this; and her baby would never be born. Did I imagine it? That in her eyes there was also the tiniest pinprick of joy?

That night, as I stood in the field, breathing in the sweet spring breeze while the train rumbled by, carrying not cows to their death but people, I put my hand to my own belly and felt the flutter of newly formed hands and feet in miraculous, liquid movement. Perhaps, when our eyes met, the young woman also had her hand on her belly; perhaps she, too, was thinking of that safe watery place in which her baby felt the pleasure of its own movement. Perhaps her quiet joy was in knowing that her baby would never be wrenched from that glorious place into this world.

It's hard to believe that this happened so long ago. That my unborn baby of then is now my Miriam, who has just had her forty-third birthday.

I knew it that night—knew that that moment would stay with me always. How is it one knows, even in extreme youth, the instances that will define one's life?

Did the woman also know the effect she would have on me? That because of that one brief moment, my own life—the life of a stranger—and that of my baby would be saved?

The evening I was sent from the house of Frau Stieglitz in disgrace I wandered the dark streets, though it was after curfew. I didn't care. I had nowhere to go; I had come to the end.

I walked as the moon rose in the sky, keeping to the back streets, slinking along in the shadows of the houses and apartment buildings I passed, hoping I might simply disappear.

Then, I heard footsteps. I ducked into a side alley and pressed myself up against a building. Several large garbage cans were stored in the alley; I positioned myself so that I was partially hidden by their bulk.

The footsteps sounded louder: two, perhaps three, sets of jackboots, not in regimental step but sloppy and noisily out of kilter. Drunken soldiers. My heart pounded in my ears. *What does it matter if they find me?* I thought. *What can they do? I cannot be made at the same time to carry a second baby fathered by a Nazi. Perhaps they will beat me, and then slit my throat. Well,* I thought, *what of it? A better fate than that of the woman in the cattle car. Better to go quickly, in an alley.* We had all heard stories—hundreds of thousands of Jews, perhaps more, along with all kinds of other prisoners of the Third Reich, sent to places of slavery and death. I myself had seen dozens of children being thrown onto trucks for deportation. Children too terrified to cry. And when the toss missed its mark and a baby crashed to the street, its head splitting open and gushing its contents onto the ground, there would be a crude laugh from one of the soldiers, or else an expression of disgust at having to clean up the mess.

The footsteps, they were almost upon me. Yes, I decided it would be better to step forward and meet my fate head-on. Two soldiers, maybe three. I would be unable to hide it any longer; they would know I was a Jew.

And then, in my mind's eye, I again saw her face, the eyes of the woman in the cattle car. As I stood there, in the alley, I wished I knew her name, so that in my own moment of death,

I might commemorate her and her never-born child, say a prayer, perhaps (to what? To whom?) in their names. *I will join you,* I thought. *My baby and I will join you both.*

I was readying to step out into the street. I could hear the soldiers talking in loud voices. One let out a drunken laugh.

Miriam.

The name popped into my head. *I will call her Miriam,* a voice inside me said.

But something stopped me from leaving the alley and placing myself in view of the soldiers. The idea of sacrificing myself suddenly seemed like a betrayal of this woman, to whom I had given a name.

She had not chosen to hasten her own end. A flash of intuition told me that it had been a long, brave journey to that moment in the cattle car—that she had many times, and against the odds, heroically warded off death. That the serenity I saw in her eyes in that briefest of moments had come only when escape was no longer possible.

I felt like a coward. A threat only, and I had been ready to give it all up. Did I not owe it to her—to the woman I had named Miriam—to do everything in my power to live? To give birth to this baby in my womb as she surely had no chance of birthing her own?

I felt a twinge of misery at the thought of how my baby was conceived. But then another thought swam into my mind: *This baby is wholly mine.* I was free to love my baby as fully as any woman had ever loved her child. What, after all, was the brief moment of conception in the face of a long life?

In that alley—it was cold, I was shivering—I was suddenly filled with a love so fierce, it took hold of all of me and made me shake. A love that was as big as all four of us—Miriam, her baby, my own baby, and me. Still pressed up flat against the wall, I turned my head to see the soldiers pass. There were two of them, though they made enough noise for three. The heels of their boots thudded against the pavement, and clacked off into the distance.

When I had my baby in the basement of Frau Wanzl's house, nine months before the house was destroyed in the bombing, I was not surprised to find it was a girl. I had known it would be from that night in the alley. I named my baby Miriam.

Now, I walk to the kitchen to dial Miriam's number. I feel an uncomfortable pressure in my chest. I make a mental note to call my doctor in the morning for an appointment. I am late, this year, with my checkup.

The phone is ringing. Miriam picks up.

"Darling," I say.

"Mother!" She always has delight in her voice when she hears it is me. We chat for a few minutes, she tells me about her day and what the children are up to: Matthew is at a soccer game, Celia is at choir practice.

"And you, Mom? How's everything?"

A strange feeling washes over me—a gray sadness that somehow has a peaceable glow.

"Darling—" I feel suddenly choked up and find I am unable to speak.

"Mom, what is it? Is everything all right?"

I manage to take two deep breaths, in and out.

"I just want to say how proud I am of you. No mother on earth could have a better daughter."

She is silent a moment.

"I love you too, Mom," she says quietly.

Now, I have a terrible, panicky feeling I will never see my daughter again, never again see her fluid, graceful movements, or look into her soulful, sensitive eyes. This child of mine, given to me in such a dreadful, roundabout way. The child I fought so hard to nourish and birth. The child for whom I stayed alive so that I might love her with every ounce of my being. Whom I named Miriam for a woman I glimpsed, once, whose name I did not in fact know.

And now I realize something else—another gift from the woman whose name I did not know. That if I never set eyes on Miriam again, it is all right. Did I not hold her in my arms, moments after she squeezed from the womb? Did I not know every joy possible in loving her and watching her grow?

"Hug those beautiful children for me," I say.

"I will."

"You're the best mother in the world," I say, as I have said to Miriam many times. "You know that, don't you?"

Miriam lets out a relieved little laugh. "I'm not so sure about that," she says. I can hear that her moment of concern about me has passed. "But if I am, it's because I learned it from you."

I hang up the phone and go back into the living room. I sit on the faded chair by the window—the chair that has been Miriam's favorite from the time she was a little girl. I think of the countless times it has held her dear form, of the thoughts she must have had while sitting here, looking out at the river: the dreams she dreamed, her sorrows and sweet childish joys.

I look out at the moon, which tonight is bulging and fat. I look out at the moon for a very long time. I drift off into a half sleep, aware of the growing pressure in my chest.

III.
Ruth. Dresden, 1940

We are hurrying through the streets. I feel the pressure of my mother's hand; she is gripping my hand as if she might steal it away from my body to keep for herself.

It is dark; I feel the danger pressing in on us. We take the back alleys. I am impressed by my mother's knowledge of all the twists and turns. We walk between and behind tall buildings, stumble across piles of garbage. I hear scuttlings, and from time to time catch sight of a small glinting eye attached to a speeding blur of fur.

Tomorrow, my family reports for deportation. My mother, father, two younger sisters, Anna and Barbara, and Shmuel, my little sunshine brother who last week turned four.

I, too, had packed the one small bag permitted each person. I was singing to Shmuel when I heard my mother and father whispering urgently to each other in the corner of the room. After Shmuel had fallen asleep, my mother came to where I was sitting on the mattress I share with him and sat beside me.

"Ruthele, do you remember Frau Wanzl?"

Frau Wanzl, the milliner, for whom my mother had worked five or six years ago, when Jews were still allowed to work for gentiles. I had been about nine when I last set foot in the store; I had a clear memory of a plump woman with a plain and not unkind face.

"Yes. I remember her store, too."

"I'm going to take you there. Tonight."

I'm not yet fifteen. I need my family—Mama, Papa, the girls, Shmuel—and they need me.

"But, Mama! I want to stay with you."

She reached up and stroked my hair.

"Perhaps she'll take you in," she whispered.

"What about Barbara and Anna and Shmuel? Why can't we all go together?"

My mother looked down at the floor, then back up at me. In recent years, I had often seen pain in her face, but never a pain like this.

"She could never take all of you," she says.

"Why me?" I ask. My voice is very tiny.

"You are the eldest. You don't need taking care of—you can help her." My mother again touches my hair.

"Your hair, your eyes. The others are so dark."

When she next speaks, it is into the blackness. "You might have a chance. If Frau Wanzl is willing to take the risk."

We sit for a while on the mattress. Then my mother rises, picks up my small suitcase, and hands it to me. She says nothing, only looks at me with all that pain and nods in the direction of Shmuel.

"Kiss him," she says. "Say a prayer for him."

What prayer can I say for a little boy I love more than life itself? Who fills the world—even this awful world—with delight? How can I kiss him good-bye?

I shake my head, tears fly from my eyes. But my mother presses my shoulder and I lean over Shmuel and kiss his warm cheek. He exhales, with parted lips, and I catch the sweet scent of his little-boy-sleeping breath.

Now, my mother leads me to the dining room, where Barbara and Anna are folding the tablecloths and sheets we cannot take with us and putting them neatly away in the linen cabinet. They look startled when they see what is in our faces.

"I'll be back soon," my mother says to them. "Kiss your sister."

They have learned there is no questioning the things that happen, and they lean forward to kiss me good-bye. I look into their dear faces, though I cannot bear to. I have learned to do things I cannot bear to do.

My father presses both my hands in his.

"We will find you," he says steadily. "When this madness is at an end."

And now here we are, hurrying through the streets.

Finally, we arrive at Frau Wanzl's store; it is bolted and locked. We go around to the alleyway beside the building where there is a little door, and my mother gives three sharp raps.

Some minutes later, we hear muffled footsteps on the stairs and the door opens.

It is Frau Wanzl. She is wearing a dressing gown and has rollers in her hair. She looks alert; it appears we have not awoken her.

She glances furtively up and down the alleyway and then ushers us in. We climb the narrow stairway to her apartment, which is above the store, and enter the kitchen. We sit at the small kitchen table. Frau Wanzl does not seem pleased to see us.

"This is Ruth," Mama says. Frau Wanzl is flustered.

"With her coloring," my mother continues, "she could be your niece."

Frau Wanzl's face is closed. Her eyes look ungiving.

"I'm sorry," she says. "I am alone. I am struggling just to keep myself. And harboring a Jew . . . you understand. It's a serious offense."

I see my mother reaching into herself; I have seen her do this many times. She is reaching into herself to gather all the strength she possesses.

When she speaks again, her voice is coaxing and calm.

"She can help you," my mother says. "She is a capable girl—she can sew, cook, clean."

Now my mother puts her hand into her blouse and pulls something from her undershirt. It is a huge wad of bills. She slides them across the table to Frau Wanzl, who looks down at the crumpled bills with some surprise, then across to me. She is eyeing me, now, with some concentration.

"I do in fact have a niece who lives in Pilsen. A year or two older, I'd say. I see what you mean about how the girl looks."

Minutes later, I say good-bye to my mother and watch, from the door of the kitchen, as she goes back down the stairs. I study the way her body moves—the roll of her shoulders, the way she dips with each step, the distinctive swivel of her hips. I have known these movements all my life. I feel the world slamming shut.

I do help Frau Wanzl. I sweep and clean and cook what food we can find. She also teaches me to work on the hats, though she has few customers.

I do not know how much money my mother left with Frau Wanzl. Of course, money leaks its value daily. But it was a huge pile of bills—perhaps my parents' life savings. Enough so that the closed look in Frau Wanzl's face changed when my mother slid the notes across the kitchen table.

1943

It has been almost two and a half years that I have been here, with Frau Wanzl. The story my mother suggested—that I am

Frau Wanzl's niece from Pilsen—has worked without a glitch.

I feel like I am floating through someone else's life.

Frau Wanzl does not treat me unkindly, though I would not describe her as warm. She seems like a person who lives for her dailiness; she cares about her hats and what she will eat for lunch, and she remembers her husband, killed early in the War, with some happiness. She seems only to nibble at life, the way she nibbles at the dried crusts I serve her for breakfast, which she smears thinly with preserves she bottled years ago, when fruit and sugar were plentiful.

She still has a dozen or more jars of those preserves; she allows me the same amount she allows herself, having calculated that her supply will easily last—even with two of us—beyond the end of the War, which she feels certain is near.

I believe Frau Wanzl is grateful for my company. She does not have a great need for talk, but when I move about the place, while she is sitting and sewing, the radio crackling in the background, a calm lifts from her, like the feeling you get when walking through a forest.

So when one day Frau Wanzl comes into my room—it is late at night—and tells me that the money has run out and that she is going to have to place me as a domestic in someone's home, I am surprised.

"I met an old customer in the market the other day. She says she could use a girl. I told her about my niece and she seemed quite pleased." She says "my niece" as if she is talking to me about someone else. As if, together, we are deciding the fate of this hapless young girl who is not me.

"You'll be paid in room and board. There is a great shortness of money, as you know, even among the well-to-do."

The next morning, I pack my little case. Frau Wanzl puts

on her best Sunday dress, a gray silk. She fishes something out of her armoire—it is all the way in the back, packed in a wooden box. It is a dress, too large for me, and very old; it has a musty smell and a dated cut. She shakes it out and helps me into it. It is made of fine green satin, with little flowers dancing all over it. She tightens the belt, which gives it some shape. I look in the mirror on the front of the armoire and see how thin I've grown. But the dress looks pleasing; it picks up the color of my eyes.

"There," she says. "You look very pretty."

She smiles. I think it is the first time I have seen her smile—really smile—in the time I have been with her. She pats my arm. My heart squeezes a little. I am not sure what to feel.

"This was mine," she says, "when I was a little older than you. I was always on the plump side, but it will serve nicely."

"Thank you," I say, realizing that this is a gift of considerable meaning for Frau Wanzl.

"Perhaps you can take it in a little, once you're at your new place," she says. "Here, let me give you a needle and some thread."

Frau Wanzl removes several items from her sewing box, which she wraps in a small square of brown paper she takes from the kitchen drawer.

I put the little packet into my suitcase, and together we head out into the street.

It is a long walk. We pass shops and apartment buildings and parks. We pass the department store and government buildings. Then we turn onto streets that have large town houses. This is where the wealthy live. I have not been so far from Frau Wanzl's house in the time I have been with her. Though our covering story has given us no problems, I do not have papers. I have not wanted to take the risk of being stopped.

The house of her former customer is grand. I have never been in such a grand house. We climb the stairs leading to the front door, and Frau Wanzl reaches up and raps with the brass knocker. The door is opened by Frau Habich, who smiles tightly at Frau Wanzl and looks me frankly up and down.

"Well, Frau Wanzl, you were right! She is a pretty and well-presented girl. Come in."

Frau Wanzl declines to enter. She seems to want to deliver me quickly so she might hurry home to resume the quiet ticking of her days.

"Really, I must be going," she insists when Frau Habich presses her at least to come in and see the children. Frau Wanzl bestows a second real smile, and then hurries back down the steps, turning in the direction of her home.

"Thank you," Frau Habich calls out after her.

And I am here, in my new place of employ.

I notice, as Frau Habich ushers me in, that there is something greedy and off-putting in the way she continues to eye me up and down. She shows me to the small servant's room off the kitchen, which is where I will sleep, and then takes me upstairs to the nursery to meet the children.

The children are sweet—Klaus, age five, and Margret, almost seven. They greet me politely and then eagerly show me their toys.

I meet Herr Habich later that evening. He is wearing the uniform of a Nazi officer; from the various stripes and decorations, it appears that he holds a high rank. He looks at me with some distaste, though I see something else glimmering in the back of his eye.

Frau Habich earlier explained how she wished me to serve their supper, which is to be on the table promptly at nine, a half hour after Herr Habich returns home. She was very particular about which side to serve from, and the way in which I was to clear things. When I am in the kitchen, after the meal, I hear them talking in low voices. I have the feeling they are talking about me.

The next evening, after Herr Habich has returned home and I am serving their supper, he addresses me as I set down his plate, though he looks at his wife when he speaks.

"It is customary in our house for a new maid to take on a name we give her. We like to think that her old life has disappeared, and that she is now a part of our household."

His tone is the strident, commanding tone of an officer, speaking to an extreme subordinate.

"From now on, you will be known as Karla. Karla Morstin."

"Yes, sir. Karla Morstin," I say.

I learn very quickly to do exactly as I am told and to keep out of Frau Habich's way. She is moody. When in good cheer, she hums about the place and leaves me to my work, apparently unaware of my existence. When the wind turns sour, she sniffs me out and follows behind me in search of transgressions, which she invariably finds. Then, she treats me to an angry torrent of abuse. Once, she denied me dinner and locked me in my room.

The children, though, are lovely, and always happy to see me.

I am living as a shadow. I am waiting for the heavy night to lift, though I can't imagine what I will do when it does. Do not shadows disappear in the full light of day?

*   *   *

I am serving dinner; tonight, there is beef.

Herr Habich seems in a spirited mood. He is looking for someone to taunt.

"Excellent potatoes," he says, piling a second serving onto his plate. "Perhaps your grandmother taught you to make potatoes?"

I am circling behind him in order to serve Frau Habich some meat. I no longer marvel at the delicacies Herr Habich is able to get in these times of terrible scarcity. His position and influence in the Party assure him of whatever he wants.

I have noticed several new paintings on the walls. I don't know much about art, but they seem very beautiful and unusual, like the works of famous painters. I visited the Zwinger museum many times when I was a small child, when Jews were still allowed to do such things. I must have been about eight the last time we went—a very long time ago. But I remember the paintings, the way something beautiful shone out from behind the canvas and into the world. Herr Habich's new paintings have this same quality—magical, otherworldly, and yet, at the same time, realer than real.

I am certain the paintings are stolen. They don't call it thievery, though. When things are taken from Jews, it's called "reappropriation."

"Where was your grandmother from?" Herr Habich is still talking. His voice is slimed with ill intent.

I place a slice of beef on Frau Habich's plate.

"All my people are from Pilsen," I say. "They are milliners. I was to apprentice with my aunt, but with so little demand, now, for hats . . ."

I trail off and head back into the kitchen with the plate of beef. I place the platter on the counter and stand for a moment, trying to collect myself. I am trembling. The sight of the beef sickens me; five or six slices sit in a watery red pool with an edge of congealing fat.

I hear Frau Habich's voice, floating in from the dining room.

"It's a beautiful lamp, really. Thank you, my dear."

"I'm glad you like it."

"It will go perfectly over my writing table. I do believe that's the perfect spot."

"Yes, that is the perfect spot."

Herr Habich is always bringing his wife gifts. I saw the new lamp on the hall table, earlier. For some reason, the look of it upset me.

I take in two or three breaths and find I am no longer trembling.

I turn to begin tending to the dishes when I sense I am not alone. Herr Habich is standing right behind me. I didn't hear him come in; he must have been walking on cat's feet.

He is standing so close to me—too close—but I am up against the counter and therefore cannot take a step back. His breath is hot and foul smelling.

"Go ahead," he says. "Help yourself to a slice. You must be hungry."

"Thank you," I say. "I ate earlier, with the children."

"Just a little tidbit, perhaps?" He leans across me, picks up a fork from the counter, spears a rare morsel—it is almost raw—and holds it up to my mouth.

My stomach churns at the sight of it.

"No, really," I say. "I'm not hungry." I hear the trembling in my voice.

"Is there something wrong with our meat?" he whispers coldly. "Is it unclean?"

I open my mouth, he thrusts the fork in violently, the chunk jabs at the back of my throat, and I gag. I manage to remove the morsel with my teeth and begin chewing.

"There," he says. "That's better. I like it when girls do as I say."

I concentrate on getting the meat down. I fear I will choke on it. My mouth is very dry, but I am afraid to move in order to get some water. I am chewing and chewing. He is looking at me now with a horrible leer.

Finally, I swallow.

"There. You see? You really should do as I say."

He moves in even closer. He reaches up suddenly and grabs hold of my left breast—with such force, it sends a ray of pain shooting through my body. I stifle the scream that rises in my throat.

"Now," he says calmly. "I'm going to find out if there are other ways you can be of use to me besides cooking my potatoes and meat and cleaning my toilet. Tonight, if I find you have locked the door to your room, I will have you arrested."

Arrested. What is he saying?

"I don't like Jewesses as a rule, but you're a particularly fine specimen. You hardly look Jewish at all. Perhaps you have some mixed blood."

Now he twists his clenched hand and the pain in my breast intensifies. Then, he lets me go.

"I trust you enjoyed your scrap of meat," he says, turning to leave the room. "Feed the rest to the dog."

I look after him at the swinging green door. I watch until it is still, and then go about cleaning up the kitchen.

Later, I lie in my bed waiting.

I do not know what to do.

There is nothing I can do, so I just lie there and wait.

Perhaps, I think, I can return to Frau Wanzl's. No, she seemed to want to be rid of me, once the money my mother gave her was used up.

I will find another position, I think.

But then the reality hits me like a slap to the back of my head.

I have no papers. The ones I had, stamped all over with *Jude*, were of course no use; my mother destroyed them the night she took me to Frau Wanzl's.

I hear the kitchen clock chime. It is two o'clock in the morning.

The door handle; it is turning.

Herr Habich enters. He is wearing his dressing gown. It is dark, but the curtain on the small window is open; there is sufficient moonlight for me to see the ugly gleam in his eye. He locks the door from the inside and approaches the bed.

"I've known all along," he says matter-of-factly. "Unlike some of my colleagues, who have a deep and personal revulsion toward Jews, I find I am indifferent to the fact of their being racially inferior, at least when it comes to physical matters. In fact, the filth of them excites me."

He is upon me now. He sits on the bed and reaches over to the neck of my nightdress. He pulls on the ribbon and it falls open. "It was no trouble to get you falsified papers—I have them safely tucked away. So keeping you here poses no danger to me. When I saw you—you really are very beautiful, even for a Jew—"

My nightdress is open, now, all the way to the waist. He pulls it from my shoulders.

"I'd have been a fool to turn you in," he mutters. He is no longer aware of what he is saying or doing. He falls upon me.

I feel I am being devoured.

When he is finished, he rises, fixes his dressing gown, and leaves without another word. I hear him turn the key from the outside.

There is no way to run away; there are bars on the window, and now the door is locked. Besides, where would I go? If I did hazard returning to Frau Wanzl's, Herr Habich would only find me there and turn me in.

I clean away the blood as best I can with one of the kitchen rags stored in my room and then stand by the window, looking out at the sky.

I remember my father's words. *We will find you. When this madness is at an end.*

I have waited so long for that time. For almost three years I have been a shadow, moving through a world that is no longer real. All this time, I have soothed myself with the thought that the real world is going on somewhere else. That I must wait only until I can find it again and resume my real life. I imagine it sometimes, this other world. I see my father there, and my mother. Of course, also Barbara and Anna and Shmuel. The children are growing up without me, but we will catch up with each other when the time comes. I see Mama stirring soup on the stove, smiling as she talks about her day. Papa is by the fireplace, reading one of his beloved books. Later, he will gather the children at his feet and read to them from an adventure story or a volume of fables. Every now and then, one of them turns to the window or stares up at the ceiling; they are listening for me, or thinking of me, wondering how I am faring in this shadow world of mine, wondering when we will all be together again.

I am still standing by the window of my little servant's room, looking up at the black sky. I stare into its darkness, and I know something I've known all along but not wanted to face.

There is no other world. Mama is not stirring soup on the stove; the children are not gathered around Papa as he reads by the hearth. No one is listening for a sound or echo of me, or imagining our joyous reunion. No parallel world, only this one. I will not resume my life; I will not rejoin my family. This is all there is of my life. Nothing but blackness, reaching into the heavens, and me, standing here, alone in this little servant's room, alone with the tearing pain between my legs and the memory of the crushing pressure of Herr Habich on top of me.

Herr Habich comes the next night, and the night after that. Each time he stays for less than an hour, and when he leaves, he locks the door from the outside.

I think about the false papers. Somewhere in this house are the papers. They are my only chance.

All my housework is done on a precise schedule, the rooms dusted and cleaned on a rotating basis. Each day, I am alone in the house for an hour or two at most. It is then that I snoop, sticking to those areas of the house I would have reason to enter on that particular day.

I suspect the papers are in Herr Habich's study. The problem is that the study is always kept locked. I clean and dust it only once a week—on Thursday morning—and I am always accompanied by Frau Habich, who settles into the reading chair with a magazine.

The first Thursday after Herr Habich begins his awful nightly visits, I enter his study with a new sense of purpose. I take stock of the various places papers might be stored. There are many possibilities. The filing cabinet is fitted with a lock. The rolltop on the escritoire is kept open—unlikely, then, to contain anything important. I decide that the papers must be in the filing cabinet.

Weeks pass.

I am stuck. I have searched every room, but for the study; the papers must be there, but Frau Habich is always with me when I clean the room, and at all other times the door is locked.

On one of the days that Herr Habich leaves before dawn, Klaus awakens with a high fever. His eyes are rolled back in his head and his body is limp. Frau Habich looks panicky when she tells me she must take Klaus to the hospital. She tells me to wait until it is time to wake Margret and get her off to school myself.

I help her get Klaus into the car, and then watch as she drives away.

I go immediately to the study and test the door. I am in luck. It is unlocked.

Herr Habich must have gone in to retrieve something before leaving for the day. It is Frau Habich's job to see that the room is locked, but today, distracted by Klaus's illness, she did not follow after her husband and lock his study door.

As I suspected, the filing cabinet is locked. I go through the rest of the room quickly. I work like a practiced thief.

Nothing. No papers. They must be in the locked file drawers.

I awaken Margret, help her dress, and give her some sausage and black bread for breakfast. I walk her the three blocks to school and come directly back to the house.

When I return, I find Frau Habich in the hallway, looking distraught. She informs me that Klaus is very ill and must stay in the hospital, then tells me to pack two bags, one for him and one for her. She writes a note to her husband, which she seals and leaves on the kitchen table, takes the two bags, and hurries back out of the house.

That evening, Herr Habich sits alone at the table as I serve him his supper.

Later, when Margret is in bed, he comes to my room earlier. His wife is spending the night at the hospital with Klaus. The look on his face is even more unpleasant and leering than usual.

The plan I devise is a dangerous one. But I have very little to lose.

I succumb in my usual way, only this time, instead of deadening myself and disappearing to a blank, distant place, I remain alert. I keep my eyes open.

To my disgust and alarm, I see that he, too, keeps his eyes open. Eyes that are despising and full of contempt. He is particularly rough, squeezes and twists my breasts so hard the pain tears through me. I fear I will not be able to stifle the scream that is full in my throat.

But then, finally, he closes his eyes. He grunts the most dreadful insults. *Pig slut, swine Jew, filth, manure.* The insults seem to incite his lust. He bucks and pounds at me; I feel the hard bedframe beneath the thin mattress pressing up painfully against my spine. I see stars, then feel my eyes rolling back in their sockets. I will myself not to faint; I cannot faint, this is my opportunity.

I reach with my right hand to the box by the bed where he has placed his ring of keys. Carefully, silently, I feel for the smallest one, the key that might fit the lock of his filing cabinet. My fingers are like deft little creatures, they pluck at the keys—here, one of about the right size. The key ring is the kind that latches open. I maneuver the little key to the joint of the opening and press as hard as I can with forefinger and thumb down on the latch. It clicks open. I slip off the key and press the latch closed again.

Not a minute too soon.

He lets out his finishing grunt and rolls off me.

He is up, buttoning his pajama pants.

He says nothing, leaves the room and locks the door behind him.

I must do my search tomorrow. He may notice the key is missing, but then again he may not, depending on what his day holds. I must return the key to the ring tomorrow night when he comes.

Herr Habich leaves a little later, today, in order to take Margret to school, as Frau Habich has still not returned. I wait about half an hour, to be certain they will not return for something forgotten, and then make my way to the study. Slowly, I turn the handle.

The door opens. Perhaps Herr Habich does not himself have a key to the study, or else it simply did not occur to him to lock it, given that it is not his habit to do so.

The little key is lodged in my brassiere; I feel it against my skin.

I hurry inside the room.

The key slips easily into the filing cabinet lock. It clicks open. I slide out the top drawer and begin examining its contents, starting at the back and flipping the files forward. Here, in the middle. An envelope that looks crisp and new. A name penned on the front.

"Karla Morstin."

I put the envelope into the front of my dress, close and lock the drawer, and return quickly to my room, where I slide the envelope under the mattress. I go back into the kitchen to collect myself. I am grateful I am alone. I would not be able to hide the thumping of my heart, the shallowness of my breathing, the rush of freedom that has surely risen in my face as a bright, hot flush.

Frau Habich returns in the afternoon. It turned out not to be meningitis, which was what the doctors had feared, but something less dire. She tells her husband that the boy will be able to return to school in a week or so.

That evening, when Herr Habich comes to my room off the kitchen, I replace the little key on the ring with ease.

I have not had my menses since Herr Habich began his nighttime visits. It has been almost two months, too long for this simply to be irregularity.

The very next day, Herr Habich packs a trunk and bids farewell to the family. He has been sent to a posting some hours away. I hear him promise his wife that he'll have regular home leave, twice a month.

I lug the trunk to the hallway and set it down by the door. Herr Habich looks at me coldly, but when he speaks, it is to his wife.

"If she gives you any trouble—any trouble at all—get rid of her."

I avert my eyes. I fancy I feel a quickening in my belly where this man's child is pulsing to life.

I have the papers, but I have nowhere to go.

A week later, Klaus returns to school. Frau Habich puts on a good dress and tells me she's going shopping. She's gone for some hours. When she returns, she comes directly into the kitchen and stands before me in her turquoise wool coat. I am peeling potatoes. She has an odd look on her face.

"I visited Frau Wanzl's shop today," she says. "I thought I would buy myself a new hat."

"How is she?" I ask.

"Are you not in contact with her? Come to think of it, I've not seen any letters going in or out of the house."

"The mail is not the most reliable, these days," I say. "Understandably, of course."

"She's your aunt," Frau Habich says.

"Yes," I mutter. "We were never very close."

"She is no longer there. The shop is boarded shut. The apartment is empty."

"Oh," I say. "So many people are leaving, now." My voice sounds weak and unconvincing.

Frau Habich's face is hard; she seems to have come to some decision.

"She's not your aunt, is she," she says.

I do not answer.

"My husband assured me your papers are in order, and there is no question of racial impurity. But I don't like having a liar in the house." She pauses, seems to be thinking something over. "You'll stay until I can replace you. But I won't have you around the children. Understand?"

I am still holding a peeled potato I was preparing to slice. Frau Habich leaves the kitchen.

There is no reason to stay any longer. Perhaps I was lingering only because of the children. In any case, what was I expecting? That a plan would suddenly present itself just as I needed it, in time for me to leave before Herr Habich's return?

I wait until Frau Habich goes to pick up the children from school, then pack my few belongings into my small case and leave through the front door.

I head toward the outskirts of the city. It is early afternoon. I randomly choose a direction and start walking. I walk a very long time. I listen to nothing but the sound of my footsteps on the concrete and keep my eyes steady, my shoulders square. Whenever I feel a little surge of panic, I repeat to myself, over and over: *My papers. I have my papers.*

It is almost dark by the time I reach the suburb at the edge of the city. It is a small, modern development, not far from the railway tracks.

I turn onto a neat street, stop before a white house, and ring the doorbell. A woman answers the door. I say I am looking for a domestic position in return for room and board. She shakes her head and turns me away.

I go up one side of the street, then down the other, repeating the words which quickly become automatic. I see many different kinds of faces—tired, angry, suspicious, or scared. I also see faces that are simply empty.

Finally, in the middle of the third block, a thin woman, with unwashed hair and several small children around her, similarly unkempt, tells me to come in. She moves about in a cloud of anger; I can almost see it, like dust, around her head.

"Your papers," she commands, holding out her hand. I draw the envelope from my blouse and hand it to the woman, who removes the papers and scrutinizes them. Satisfied, she hands them back.

"There's not much to eat, you'll have to get used to that," she says as she walks me through the small, untidy house.

"You'll have to keep all this clean, do the laundry, and take care of the kitchen and garden. Any mistakes, and you're out."

We come to a rough storeroom attached to the back of the house.

"You'll sleep here," she says, pointing to a mat on the floor that is covered in dog hair. "Put your things down. You can still get in a few hours' work."

Her name is Frau Stieglitz. Like those of most of the women around here, her husband is off fighting in some distant place. She doesn't speak of him—or of anything else, besides issuing instructions.

How many months have passed? I feel less well every day. As my belly swells, I feel my strength draining away. At night, I collapse on the mat in the storeroom and fall into a dead sleep.

I have two blouses; one is billowy and loose. I now wear only this one, as it hides my changing shape. Once a week, I wash it out and hang it from the wood rack. By morning it is almost dry. I put it on damp; as I go about my work, the heat of my body dries it completely within an hour.

Tonight, I cannot sleep. It is a warm night; a breeze carries with it the feel of another place, another climate, another time. I rise from my mat and walk to the small window, then stand up on my toes and peer out. A three-quarters moon glows fuzzily through a light patch of cloud. I open the window and breathe in the softness of the faraway place and feel an urgent desire to be outside so that I might feel the breeze all around me.

I open the storeroom door and step out into the unruly garden, which grows the precious onions, potatoes, and carrots we harvest and store in wooden bins in the basement. Frau Stieglitz uses a quarter of the potatoes to brew a wine I've not been allowed to sample but which gives off a pleasant, earthy scent.

I walk through the overgrown grass, with its tall raggy weeds, and come to the barbed wire fence that separates the Stieglitzes' plot from a wild field leading down to the railway tracks. I stand for a time up by the fence, breathing in the soft air, which delicately fingers my face and hair.

I hear the rumble before I see the train in the far distance. The breeze is now coming from behind me; it seems to be urging me forward. Carefully, I climb over the wire fence, which catches the back of my nightshirt as I jump, tearing a strip of the worn fabric away. I remove the strip of soft cotton and wind it around my wrist to keep for some future use.

Now I am in the field. The grass is strawlike and pricks my feet, but somehow I register no pain. I walk briskly toward the railway tracks, as if heeding some supernatural call. The train is winding its way along the distant tracks, winding its way toward me. I am going to meet it.

The clouds glide about, forming and re-forming against the black sky. I look up and see that the moon is unmasked, now a bright and incomplete disk, nakedly glowing.

I run, the prickles underfoot a distant irritation. I am thinking only of the train curving slowly toward me.

I reach the tracks and watch as the train crawls forward. It is a cargo train, pulled by a strong black engine. I count the cars. There are seven; they are old and made of wooden planks. Cars for transporting livestock. I listen but hear no bleating or lowing. The train seems to be slowing. I fancy I hear the engine straining, as if the train is in some kind of trouble and coming to a halt.

It is almost upon me. The moon is like a cold white sun in the black night sky. *Wake up,* the night seems to say. *Wake up into this strange black day.*

The train trundles past. The planks of the cars are ill-fitting and old, showing gaps in places; here and there, a plank is missing altogether.

I see, now, that arms thrust out from the gaps. Ragged dark sleeves sprouting thin desperate hands and, here and there, the gleaming of eyes.

I have never before seen such eyes.

The light seems suddenly to swarm as if the moon has let loose beams of streaking vermin. I bat at the buzzing streaks of light, then succumb to a great dizziness and fall to my knees. I regain my balance and find I am staring at a large gap in the middle of one of the cars—a plank or two gone missing—large enough to see a woman's face, almost in its entirety.

Our eyes meet.

Everything freezes—the moon, the breeze, my body, the train. Everything but her eyes, which move the length of my body, up and down. Her face disappears; she has straightened up. I see the side of her; a piece of clothing is raised. I see what looks like the curve of a pregnant belly.

Her eyes, again, at the gap.

I raise my own nightshirt, reveal to the sky and the night—to the eyes of the woman in the cattle car—my own swollen belly.

And then, the train is gone. It has picked up speed. The rumble grows louder and the train heads off toward its destination.

*   *   *

One evening, not very much later, I am washing linens in the trough outside my room when Frau Stieglitz comes up behind me. I hear the angriness in her step before she even speaks.

"Turn around!" she commands.

I turn around. Suds drip from my hands to the concrete floor.

She leans forward, seizes the hem of my billowy blouse, and yanks it upward, all the way up, revealing my worn, ill-fitting brassiere and the full contour of my belly.

"Get your things and get out," she says in a rageful voice. "I won't have a slut in my house."

I dry my hands on the dishcloth and walk toward the storeroom. It takes me a few minutes to collect my belongings and pack them in my battered case. A few more minutes, and I am out on the street.

I walk in the direction of the city. The sun is setting, and I walk toward where it has stained the horizon orange and pink.

I put one foot in front of the other and walk. I must keep walking, I say to myself. There is nothing more of my world at this moment but steady, and ceaseless, movement.

The streets are dark; I am back in the city. I am wandering past tall buildings, winding in and out of alleyways, perhaps the very alleys through which I hurried with my mother the night she took me to Frau Wanzl's. That seems like the life of another person, a person who lived long ago, who perhaps has died and is buried, somewhere, deep beneath the ground.

The cold bites at my toes. The moon is a new sliver, lolling about in the sky, not caring to give off much light.

Here, the sound of soldiers.

I know what to do. There is nowhere for me to go, now, but downward, into the darkness.

But then—I see her face again.

What is her name? I wish I knew her name.

Miriam. I will call her Miriam.

The soldiers, I hear them. Come, soldiers, come and take me away.

Miriam.

My feet do not move.

I am here, still, by the wall.

The soldiers have passed.

I step back out onto the pavement. I look up and down the street.

I know this street. My bearings snap clear, as if a fog had been hiding the map and now lifts, revealing the clear and distinct lines of the streets and their names.

My feet move of their own accord. I am walking now with some strength.

My feet are taking me back to Frau Wanzl's.

It is still dark when I reach the millinery shop, though at the horizon I see a shadowy band of gray. The place is shuttered; scraps of paper and piles of old leaves cover the sidewalk.

I go around to the side door. A length of wood has been jammed beneath the handle. I manage to dislodge it. The door opens easily; I see that the lock has been broken. Inside the shop, all the hats and materials and display stands are gone; there are only bare shelves and a dusty floor. I go to the door at the back leading down to the basement.

It is pitch-dark and very musty. I make my way down the stairs by feel. When I get to the bottom, I feel along the wall.

My legs bang into an object here and there. I trip upon a cardboard box. It is empty. In the darkness, I lift the box and tear it open so that it is a flat sheet. I put the cardboard down on the ground and sink to the floor.

All of me is a wound of tiredness. I close my eyes, and the darkness floods into me.

When I awaken, I find I am looking into the eyes of an elderly woman. She is holding up a kerosene lamp, which gives off a circle of yellowish light. She leans over me and looks at me quizzically. I look back, and she smiles.

"So, you have found my sanctuary," she says. "Good. We will be friends."

The woman's face is deeply wrinkled. The arrangement of creases and folds has the strange effect of making her seem young, rather than old.

"I'll heat some water for tea," she says, pointing in the direction of a small burner. "Our hostess was kind enough to leave a good supply of kerosene. She was very planful, who-ever she was. Her basement was well-stocked when I arrived."

The woman's name is Mathilde. She tells me nothing of her past. I tell her nothing of mine.

She sees immediately the condition I am in.

"I find bits and pieces, during the day," she says. "No one minds me. Last week, someone gave me a sweet bun."

She looks down at my belly. "Don't worry," she says. "I'll see you get what you need."

Mathilde has salvaged items from upstairs; she has turned the basement into a comfortable home. Later I, too, slip upstairs and bring down some bedding and a few pieces of old clothing I find in a box in Frau Wanzl's armoire.

Frau Wanzl left four jars of her preserves. She probably could not fit them into whatever luggage she was able to take with her. She also left a mound of dried corn ears and a small bin of flour. These are the basis of our supplies; we go out each day to try to obtain whatever else we can.

Time slithers along, poisonously unnoticed. I don't know when the baby will come. My belly is not very large, but I have always been thin, and there is not much food for us to eat. I begin to sense, though, that the baby will come soon.

1944

The time has come. I am grateful Mathilde is here; I am grateful that I am not alone.

She must have done this before. She seems to know what to do.

The pain is coming from outside of me. The earth has cracked open and flings itself up to join with me, dragging me into its burning core. I do not scream, I only sink into the tearing of the earth and clutch onto Mathilde's arm when it floats into my field of vision.

The earth slides and my belly slides with it, the small mountain of my belly slides downward, away from me, and the baby squeezes into the world. I look up to see that Mathilde has the baby by one leg—she is holding it upside down and slapping its back.

"You have a baby girl," Mathilde says, and her face is lit up like a bright sun.

Miriam, I think. *My little girl's name will be Miriam.*

*   *   *

No one troubles us. We are two women, living in the basement of Frau Wanzl's house.

Mathilde helps with the baby. She takes care of her when I go out to search for food.

Our supplies are dwindling. Only one jar of Frau Wanzl's preserves remains.

It is early in the morning, not long after dawn. I come across an abandoned store. It has the familiar broken glass display window, the yellow paint on the unbroken section—*JUDEN!*—already peeling.

No one stops me as I climb in—there is no one much about, in any case. The shelves are empty; everything has a thick coating of dust.

In the back storeroom, I find seven jars of pickles in a box tucked behind a filing cabinet. It is a significant find.

The weeks pass. Perhaps the snake that time has become will slither us out of this life and into another. Or perhaps it will just curl in on itself. Perhaps there is to be no other life than this.

February 1945

I awaken to the air-raid sirens. We are well-acquainted with them, but tonight, it is different. Every air-raid siren in Dresden and for miles around is blaring. It is a crazed, atonal orchestra.

The baby has become accustomed to the sirens; they do not wake her. I sit up on my mattress and strain my eyes through the darkness to Mathilde's mattress. I crawl over to it; with my hands I feel that her blankets and sheet are pulled back and that her bed is empty. She has probably gone upstairs to use the bathroom and will return any moment, now that she has heard the wild screeching outside.

The pounding begins. It explodes over us, beneath us. The baby wakes, and I see from her contorted face that she is screaming, though the sound is sucked up into the pounding.

I take the baby in my arms. I try to put her to the breast. She will not be soothed. She flails her arms and legs, her head thrashes back and forth, tears fly from her eyes. I try to cover her ears; she pushes away my hands with her tiny little fists and pounds at the air.

I place Miriam on the mattress, where she continues to thrash about.

Mathilde has still not come down the stairs. When will Mathilde come?

The earth shakes, everything in our basement home rattles. I hear the sound of objects falling and pray that nothing will fall on the baby and me.

Miriam has stopped flailing. She is lying still now, her tears spent.

I lie down on the mattress. I take my baby in my arms. I close my eyes and wait for the world to extinguish.

The apocalypse is over.

The world is destroyed.

But I am still here. My baby is in my arms. My baby and I are still here.

I don't know how long it has been since the fusillade ceased. My nostrils are filled with the acrid, burning smoke of the end of the world.

A stench of ash pours into the basement. It has been pouring in, now, for an age. I am surprised it has not suffocated us.

The baby has awoken. Slowly, I rise. My limbs are so stiff—my knees and hips seem to be locked. I do not know how long I have sat here, in the corner of the basement.

I place some flour in a bowl, add a dollop of preserves and water from the jug, and then vigorously stir. I feed the pasty liquid to the baby, who slurps it up happily. Then, I remove the wet cloth from her bottom and wrap her in a fresh, dry one. I slip her into the sling I have fashioned from an old yellow tablecloth I found my first day in the basement and go up the one flight of stairs to the street.

I manage to push the door open, though this takes some doing; rubble is piled up around it. Frau Wanzl's shop is in ruins. The apartment above is no longer there. All around me, nothing but ruin. I don't know how to make sense of what I see.

Last night, the little basement dwelling I share with Mathilde existed within a city I have known all my life. Today, that city is gone.

Mathilde is gone.

My face is wet with tears. The feel, on my skin, is foreign, as if these tears are some secret communication from another life—from someone else's life. I do not remember the last time I cried.

I pick my way through the smoldering rubble.

I see that it is day, though a strange kind of day. The sky is deep gray. The sky is smoke and soot and the residue of countless burnings.

All around me, strange people-ghosts walk in slow motion: silent, gaunt. Aliens, with soot-blackened faces and red-rimmed eyes: as if they have all been made up for a play and are wandering about, looking for the stage.

We are no longer people of this earth.

Smoke billows from everything. I walk by one ruined house after the other. Tremendous, scorched heat ripples into the air. I can't sidestep the heat, it is everywhere. I push the baby's head deeper into the sling and shield it with my hand.

I don't know what I look like. Perhaps I, too, am one of the ghosts.

It seems I have been walking forever. Nothing is familiar; there are no landmarks, nothing that would tell me where I am going. I follow my feet. The baby sleeps.

I seem to have some kind of homing device; it has taken me toward a part of the city that is damaged but not destroyed. I look around me. Many houses, here, have survived; some are completely intact. Here and there, a house is in ruins, but not completely; in the rubble, I can make out familiar objects. I see a grand piano, its lid torn off and lying beside it like a huge broken wing. I pass countless bed frames, piles of charred furnishings, mountains made of roof tiles and broken bathroom fixtures. I see sculptures of metal that are beautiful in their way, though they are grim beyond all reckoning.

Here, this street is familiar. Now, another.

I move in a trance. I walk from street to street. I am circling around something familiar, moving toward a destination, but in a maze, taking twists and turns to reach its center.

I am standing before a partially ruined house. The top floor is gone, the ground floor is also mostly destroyed, though parts of rooms remain. I see where the kitchen was; oddly, the sink has remained in place. I know this kitchen, I know this sink. I stood for many hours before this sink, washing dishes. It is the house of Frau and Herr Habich.

I pick my way through the rubble. Maneuver, by instinct, toward the place where the stairs lead down to the basement.

I move aside bits of wall; here is what looks like the back panel of a cabinet. The stairs are somewhere around here, I know it.

Yes, here is the opening.

I drag away a large piece of wall and see that the stairs leading down are undamaged. I take them carefully, holding my arms protectively over the baby, who is bundled around my waist.

By the bottom of the stairs is a kerosene lamp. I pick it up; it is heavy. I shake it a little and it swishes loudly. On the shelf above I find a stack of a dozen or more boxes of matches. I light the kerosene lamp, and the details of the basement spring into view.

The Habichs have set it up to be a self-sufficient living space. Two large mattresses, big enough for all four of them to sleep; stacks of food supplies—cans, bags of dry goods, a huge tin filled with dried beef. A bookshelf full of books and the large wooden toy trunk that was formerly in the nursery.

In one corner is a table with four chairs. On the table is the lamp I remember with the unusual shade. I walk over to the table, lift up the lamp; the cord dangles limply to the ground.

I am wondering how I can get some of these supplies back to Frau Wanzl's basement. I know I cannot stay here. Even if I felt it were safe—what is safe, now? The world is in ruins— I would not be able to bear it, being surrounded by all their things: all these objects, exhaling the stuff of their lives.

I imagine that they survived, that Herr Habich received advance notice about the bombing and whisked them all to safety.

I am looking, again, at the lamp. I am struck by an odd certainty: that this lamp needs to be rescued. That I need to take it out of this place and bring it back with me.

I rise, stuff some boxes of matches into one pocket and a handful of the dried beef into the other. I slip three cans into the sling along with the baby, and pick up the lamp. I take the sheet off one of the mattresses and use it to make a bundle of more foodstuffs, choosing carefully, as even if I could find the house again, the street is full of looters; the supplies will quickly be gone.

The baby is stirring in the sling. She lets out a robust, hungry howl. I place the lamp and the bundle I have fashioned on the table, sit in one of the chairs, and give the baby my breast. I do not always have milk, but now she sucks, and I feel her pulling the milk from somewhere deep within my body. She suckles fiercely and happily, and the milk flows.

IV.
Ruth. May 7, 1987

I am sitting in Miriam's favorite chair, looking out at the moon, which tonight is enormous and perfectly round. I drift off into a half sleep, aware of the growing pressure in my chest.

I hear familiar voices. I am stacking plates in a sink, lost in my own thoughts, not really listening to the voices floating in from the dining room. The water is cold, and the block of soap does not readily work up suds. Familiar voices from a long-buried past. That's what it is in my chest—not a problem with my heart but only fear from the long-dead and distant past.

I run the old rag over and over each plate until the grease works loose and the plate comes clean.

Frau Habich's voice floats into my awareness.

"Such an unusual lamp. It will go beautifully on my writing desk."

And now, Herr Habich. "I'm glad you like it, my dear."

"The shade—it is unusual. Is it some kind of animal skin?"

Herr Habich gives his mirthless laugh.

"Yes, as a matter of fact. It is."

"I've not seen anything quite like it before. It's so strong and yet so thin. It's almost transparent. What kind of animal is it?"

"Swine," Herr Habich says. He is chewing. He must have taken a bite of the strudel I earlier set before him. "Jewish swine."

I tumble through colors and images and sounds. I see the woman with the thin face there, in the cattle car; I have flown into the car myself. I am with her; we are together. She lifts her blouse, and I see her swollen belly. The child is near ready to enter this sorry world. She rests a hand on the mound; I see, in the sliver of moonlight that shines in through the crack in the wooden planks, that her skin emanates a rosy, pinkish glow.

"My baby," the woman in the cattle car whispers. She is talking to herself. Perhaps she does not see me; perhaps she does not know I am there.

"Sweet baby, perhaps we will meet in another world."

Her head is bowed, she is talking to her unborn child.

"Perhaps, there will be a better world—"

"Miriam," I breathe, and now I am smiling into the face of my own baby. "Miriam," I say again, aware that this baby is no longer a baby but a grown mother with teenage children of her own.

I jolt back to full wakefulness.

I was back in the house of Herr and Frau Habich.

How is it one can hear and not hear? I must have heard what they said, all those years ago. And yet in my half sleep, it was as if I were hearing the words for the first time.

I remember the way my skin glowed when Miriam was growing within me. Now I recognize the unearthly glow I have known all these years in the light of the lamp. It is the same glow: the glow of a life, springing from nothing, blooming from the heavens within a woman's womb.

One heard so many awful facts, after the war. Facts about what the Nazis did. I learned to block them out before I even fully understood what they were. Now, I remember hearing that the Nazis made things from human bones and teeth. That they made lampshades from human skin.

My lamp—the shade. Someone's skin. Someone like the woman in the cattle car. Someone like her. Someone like me.

I rise, walk over to my filing cabinet, and remove the envelope that contains my important papers. I scribble a note in the corner of the first page—tomorrow, I will type it out fresh—then walk into the bedroom and put the envelope down on the bedside table. I change into my most comfortable nightdress.

In the bathroom, I splash water onto my face and brush my teeth. I stand for a few moments looking into the mirror.

I look down at my body; I remember the youthful, smooth flesh. Now, my muscles and skin hang loosely from the bone. If I close my eyes, I can feel myself back into that young body; I would not be surprised if I were to open my eyes and find myself again as I once was.

For a moment, I feel a plunging sadness: that I never tasted romantic love. But then, every life has something that is not to be, some hard little seed, lodged somewhere within whose fate it is to lie dormant.

I have, though, known motherly love. I gave birth to

sweet little girl, held her in my arms, took care of her, loved her, watched her grow.

How I rejoiced when Miriam found David. How I rejoiced to see their love.

It is dark; I have turned on only the night-light. But I can see the look in my own eyes. Not sadness, but something else. Yes, it is there. That same serenity. And a tiny pinprick of joy.

I walk back to the bedroom and climb into my bed. I have never had curtains on my windows: I like to see the sky. From my bed, which is up against the window, I lie looking at the black sky with its bloated moon, and feel proud of the life I made for Miriam and myself. I feel my heart squeezing within my chest—squeezing tightly around this life of mine, which has been wondrous, in spite of everything. I close my eyes but continue to see the moon, which floats with such equanimity over everything, and drift, very calmly, into sleep.

V.
Miriam. May 9, 1987

I am here, in New Jersey, at the Beth-El cemetery. I have come to bury my mother.

My mother has not been alone since I found her yesterday; the Chevrah Kadishah have one of their members sit with the deceased every moment, so that they will not be alone as they approach the grave. Though she lived most of her life, as far as I know, without religion of any kind, my mother's lifeless body has been tended as the body of a Jew. I cannot know what the idea of this must have meant to her—and of having a Jewish burial, and being laid to rest among Jews—but it must have meant something. My mother was

not a capricious person; I have no doubt that she thought long and hard before drafting up the instructions in her "Important Papers."

The rabbi, appointed by the cemetery to conduct a service, instructed me earlier about the tradition of relatives dropping the first few shovelfuls of dirt into the grave. He has finished his words; I pick up the shovel. It is very heavy. I load it with fresh dirt, then allow the dirt to slide into the grave. For a split second, there is the almost imperceptible sound of heavy grains swishing through air, and then the dirt thuds onto the bare pine of the coffin.

I am peering into the closed blackness of her grave, which soon will be sealed forever from any sights or sounds of this earth. I feel I am peering also into another grave, one that my mother fashioned for herself while she was still alive. Perhaps there are graves that must be dug if the living are to go on living.

Yesterday, I was greatly troubled by the thought that I'd never know the significance of my mother's lamp. I felt shut out, once and for all, from really knowing her.

Now, though, looking into her grave, I feel something else. That my mother had every right to keep hidden whatever she needed to hide. Today, I will also lay to rest the secret of the lamp, here, in this Jewish cemetery, where my mother deemed she belonged. When I visit her grave, I will honor her secrets, along with her memory.

I know no Jewish prayers—in fact, I know no prayers of any kind, except for the Lord's Prayer, which I learned as a child at school. I do not know what to say, though I feel a sudden desperate need to say something. I hand the shovel to David, then lean across to the rabbi.

"What is the prayer?" I ask urgently. I don't intend this,

but it comes out almost as a shout. The rabbi hands me a small pamphlet he's been holding beneath his prayer book. I take the pamphlet and see the words on the top: "Kaddish. Prayer for the Dead." Beneath are the words—in Hebrew, no doubt, but rendered phonetically in English.

David is settling his shovelful of soil into the grave. Through my tears, the words on the page are swimming, but I manage to make them out. I begin reading. My voice is still too loud. Everyone around me falls silent. I stumble over the unfamiliar words; my voice is shaky and gravelly and harsh.

"Yisgodal ve yisgodash shemay raba."

Mama, I know you can hear me. Mama, from your double grave, hear the words of your people. I am doing my best to give them voice.

I stumble through the prayer. I look into my mother's grave.

Mama, are they my people, too?

PART II

Paper II

Dark Urgings of
the Blood

I.

Even in the early morning, the sun splashes through the high windows, with their beautiful mahogany moldings, filling the hallways with light. I wonder if the architect calculated this, studied the patterns and direction of the light and planned each angle to maximize its infusion into corridors and rooms. I picture him camping out on these grounds, more than a century ago, sitting patiently for hours on this or that incline, wandering the hundred and fifty acres of gently sloping land in a trance, lugging the various tools of his trade, one thought only guiding him: *How can I capture the light?*

Or perhaps it was sheer happenstance. Perhaps the architect gave little thought to the light, beyond the most obvious and momentary consideration. Perhaps rather, he was going for grandeur, sequestered in his office surrounded by floor plans and models of English manor houses. Perhaps what gripped him was the idea of re-creating here, in the New World, a haven of aristocratic gentility: rooms in which trouble or hardship have no place, in which luxury and comfort promise everlasting ease and whisper of immortality (will not this equipoise of elegance endure forever?). Perhaps the exquisite inpouring of light—clean white in the mornings, as now, hot yellow in the afternoons, and later luminous moonlight—was no more than fortuitous accident?

I have had these thoughts a hundred times. I make a mental note to look up some details about the architect, who feels somehow like a personal friend, though he is long dead. I can't help wondering what he was thinking, as he set about designing this kind of a setting as a hospital for the insane.

But I am distracting myself from what I am about to encounter, and here I am, already at the locked door to the unit. I pause, holding the key, and quickly go over the few facts I have in hand.

Dvorah Kuttner, a woman of thirty-two—my age, in fact—mother of a two-week-old infant and six other children ranging upward in age to thirteen. Not so unusual for a Hasidic woman, though still astounding to me, being as yet unmarried and childless. I flash on Ronald, so quietly eager for us to get married; it is I who hesitate, though I'm not exactly sure why. Another image floats to mind: young Hasidic families on their way to and from synagogue. I have seen them many times driving through Williamsburg or Crown Heights on a Saturday. I crane to see the fresh faces of the young women, their expensive wigs as well-tailored as their Sabbath outfits, pushing strollers or prams, often also pregnant, and surrounded by children of all ages, two or three only if the woman is very young, more if she is older. I marvel at how neat and well-behaved the children appear, how serene and in control their young mothers, and feel a strange ache as I watch them pass, a confusing shimmer within that I've never fully analyzed. Now, standing here, readying to interview my new patient, Dvorah—who, in the throes of a psychotic postpartum depression, is unlikely to resemble this image I have of harmonious control—I realize that what I have felt at those times is longing. I can no more imagine feeling the sense of preordained destiny I see in those fresh-faced women on their way to recite ancient prayers than I can imagine how Dvorah must now feel, on the other side of this locked door, tied, as she is, by her ankles and wrists, to the metal posts of a bed. Dvorah, who was put in "four-point restraints" after she extracted a small chunk from the shoulder of a young female mental health worker with her teeth. "She's tiny," I was told thirty minutes ago in my morning briefing with Dr. Finkelstein, our unit chief. "Tiny and tough."

I turn the key in the lock.

The unit has that heightened, oddly festive feel always evident after a dramatic incident. Staff and patients alike wear a distinctive expression—an excited and slightly shamefaced glow of self-importance that comes with having witnessed some dreadful, gossip-worthy crisis. I nod professionally to each person I pass, respond "Good morning" to their "Morning, Doctor."

I head directly to the Quiet Room.

Kevin O'Malley, a mental health worker, is sitting on a chair in the corner. Dvorah is struggling against the restraints. Her eyes are hard and feral, but as I approach her, they seem to melt to a liquid stillness: mirrorlike and yet slightly tremulous, like the undisturbed surface of a lake.

"Dr. Erick, this is Dvorah," Kevin says in his unruffled voice.

"Hello, Dvorah," I say.

"I told them I couldn't be touched," she says. "Not by a man." Dvorah's voice is deeper than one would expect from the look of her—she's slender and feminine, despite the heavy scowl on her face.

"No one will have cause to touch you if you refrain from attacking people."

"It's against Jewish law," she says. She hisses when she speaks—it seems to come from the back of her throat.

"So is violence toward others," I say.

Dvorah's scowl deepens. She looks away.

I turn to Kevin. "Why don't you give us a few minutes alone," I say.

He rises. "I'll be right outside the door," he says good-naturedly. He leaves the door ajar.

"Okay," I say. "Let's start at the beginning."

"There is no beginning," Dvorah quips back. "Only the eternal return of the same."

Fine, I think. Nietzsche. They told me she was educated in both Jewish and secular studies. Unusual for a Hasidic woman. And Dvorah, with seven children. Seven children! From a distance, you might suppose her no more than a girl of nineteen or twenty.

"How about your date of birth. Let's start with that."

"I turn thirty-two next month," she says. A softening in her tone.

"I'd be happy to do the math on the year," I say. "If you hand over the date."

"Twenty-fifth."

I write it down. April 25, 1960. A few months before my own birthday.

"They tell me your name is Deborah," she says.

I see a shadow of triumph on her face.

"Yes, but we go by surnames and titles here," I say. "Makes things easier."

"Dr. Erick, then."

"That would be right."

I clamp down on my own reactions, as experience has taught me to do. Dvorah has that hair-trigger emotional responsiveness that is common among inpatients in psychiatric hospitals; she is watching me in that hyperalert way I've come to know so well—watching for any chinks in the professional armor that might create a personal opening.

"I'm glad they sent you," she says. The pitch of her voice seems to have risen; the hiss is gone. As if she's coming up from some underground pit, as if she's scratched her way to the surface and can now freely breathe. "It was meant to be."

The shadow of triumph is gone. In its place, I see a wispy sadness. Now, spread-eagled on the bed, her hands hanging limply from her bound wrists and head turned sideways, she looks at me steadily and long.

I feel a prickling at the back of my neck. I return her gaze.

Something passes between us. This happens, sometimes, with patients, though not very often. A kind of mutual recognition. I have learned that these are the patients I can most help, though at some cost to my own peace of mind. I sigh quietly, inaudibly, I think.

"Tired, Doctor?" Dvorah asks. Not inaudible then, my sigh. I remind myself again that patients like Dvorah do not miss a thing.

"No, Dvorah. I'm not tired," I say. "I was just thinking about how I might be most helpful to you."

"I'll tell you how," she says, twisting her wrists where they hang tied to the posts of the bed. "You can take me out of these barbaric chains."

"They're not chains," I say. "They're cloth restraints. And we'll take you out of them when we can be sure you won't try to injure anybody else."

"You have my word for it," she says.

I hear a note of desperation. Tenderness surges through me; she seems so small and suddenly looks so perplexed, like a child punished by a capricious and unjust parent. I rise from the chair and approach the bed. I reach down and touch her forearm.

"Really?" I say gently. "Do I have your word? If you tell me your word is worth trusting, I'll have Mr. O'Malley undo the restraints."

"Yes," she whimpers, tamed, now. "I promise."

"Kevin?" I call out. A moment later, Kevin reappears. I gesture to the restraints. He looks dubious, raises an eyebrow.

I nod. "Go ahead," I say. "Mrs. Kuttner has given her word."

"Could a nurse do it?" Dvorah whispers. "I'd prefer to have it done by a woman."

"Call Nurse Harmon," I say, and Kevin leaves to get the nurse.

"Thank you, Doctor," she says, and for a moment, I glimpse a different Dvorah—nicely dressed, her wig neatly brushed: pushing the pram with her newborn on the way to synagogue, surrounded by her other children as if moving within a little moving forest, all six of them saplings that have sprung up around her and been granted the miracle of motion.

*   *   *

I am sitting in my attic office, which overlooks the vast, sloping lawn that leads down from the main hospital building to the road. The binder for Dvorah Kuttner is open, but I am having trouble writing my daily notes. Usually, the words gush from the pen, but today, I feel uneasy. The diagnostic terms and stock phrases that help us organize our thinking fly through my head, but they seem like locusts intent on picking my living, breathing patient to the bone.

All through medical school, I felt the pull of psychiatry, though I held it at arm's length, telling myself it was not a real medical specialty: too airy-fairy, not hands-on enough for someone as practical as I thought myself to be. I could read psychiatry as a hobby, I thought, keep my interest alive in a way that would serve my patients in whatever more legitimate medical specialty I chose; at the time, I was toying with cardiology.

All of that changed during the six-week psychiatry rotation of my internship year at Montefiore Hospital, deep in the Bronx.

The chief psychiatrist was a tall, husky man of Greek heritage with an impressive, laconic bearing. His dark eyes shone with both kindliness and intelligence: there was also a backnote of sadness. I felt from the first that he was taking my measure. Not so as to analyze or condescend, but out of an organic fascination with human nature. He was what some would call a healer. He was also a researcher with the utmost standards of rigor, and the supernatural energy of a committed scientist.

It was Dr. Theophilus who turned my ignorant notions of psychiatry on their head.

My first day on the unit, my three fellow interns and I trailed Dr. Theophilus on his ward rounds. The first patient

we saw—a Mr. Husani—was locked into what was euphemisti-
cally termed the Quiet Room. A handsome man in his forties, Mr. Husani had dark hair and strong features, and was
suffering what Dr. Theophilus called "a full-blown manic
episode." His first day on the unit, Mr. Husani had attacked
an orderly, who had required a number of stitches to his
hand. Mr. Husani was placed in the Quiet Room, dressed
only in a hospital gown—no underwear, no socks or shoes,
nothing with which he could do himself harm—while the
staff waited for the antipsychotic and mood-stabilizing medication to take effect. When we saw him, he had been in there
for two days. Every thirty minutes, a nurse or orderly would
check him by standing before the thick glass window cut
into the door or else entering, accompanied by another staff
member, to try to engage the patient. Between two of these
thirty-minute checks, the patient had drunk the contents of
his urine bucket and then somehow managed to tear the
untearable hard plastic container, slicing open his face with
the jagged edge.

Mr. Husani believed he was God, and had been sent down
to earth to free the poor. He was angry to be kept by the hospital staff from his mission, which was why, he explained, he
was behaving as he was.

He was now on suicide watch, which meant that someone
was stationed at all times before the glass window. This put a
strain on the staff, Dr. Theophilus explained, but everyone
pulled together to see that everything got done.

I felt badly about stepping up to the window to "view" the
patient, as Dr. Theophilus invited us each to do. How could
I not recall the ogling of a poor, trapped beast in his cage at
the zoo? It was part of our training, though, I reassured
myself. Besides, it was my first day on the rotation; I wanted

to create a good impression. Flouting the unit chief's suggestion would have been out of the question.

I gestured to the other three interns to go first. After the third of them stepped aside, I approached the glass oblong and peered through. There was Mr. Husani, crouched in the corner, staring angrily at the glass. He was scowling and sullen both; his jaw worked agitatedly, as if he were struggling with a stubborn bit of gristle.

I looked him directly in the eye and held his gaze. His jaw stopped working; something in his face softened. Slowly, he unfurled from the floor and took a few tentative steps forward. I felt as if he were looking at me across a great divide from a distant and terrifying shore, and as if, terribly alone, he had given up all hope of ever again finding companionship or succor. I had the urgent, irrational feeling that this grown man was a child, placed in my care, and that I had to find a way of reaching him and taking him under my wing.

I also had another feeling: that the place he was inhabiting—treacherous beyond all imagining—was a place I had been to, perhaps in another life, perhaps in my dreams. That it was a place from which I had escaped, so that somehow I might help him, too, break free.

Slowly, Mr. Husani approached the window. Now he was up against me, his face pressed to mine, the two of us separated only by the double-paned glass.

His eyes were rimmed in red and very deep. I caught my breath.

I *did* know this place. At least, I had glimpsed it.

As a child, I would sometimes lie awake at night, engulfed by a black feeling that snuffed light and joy. Heart racing, I would lie trapped in my bed, gripping the sheets, certain I must flee some appalling, imminent danger. But where would

I go? Me, a little child? What would I do, alone in the predatory dark? I would close my eyes and listen to the thudding of heart and hissing of blood, sounds that seemed to come from an ominous reality that existed secretly, silently, behind the bright, freshly painted scenery of my daily existence. It was only a matter of time, I felt certain, until the walls of my waking life—days of contentment and play, the adoring faces of my parents—would crash in on me and I would tip into the terrifying pit that lay just on the other side.

Finally, sleep would come, and I would awaken to billowing curtains and streaming light, to tenderness and warmth and delight.

But I would not forget the pit; it throbbed within my happy world, as near, as distant, as inescapable as my own beating heart.

Now, gazing into Mr. Husani's eyes, I was flooded with those old feelings I had known as a child.

Mr. Husani reached up to the glass with his right hand and delicately drew two fingers down the length of it: a stroke, through the glass, to the side of my face. In his eyes, that awful depth—and pleading—and the faintest glimmer of hope. I held his gaze for a moment longer and then, almost imperceptibly, nodded. A faint smile for a moment touched his lips.

I stepped away from the glass to find Dr. Theophilus looking at me intently.

At the end of rounds, Dr. Theophilus dismissed us for lunch and then casually asked if I might step into his office briefly before joining the others in the hospital cafeteria.

In his office, Dr. Theophilus invited me to sit.

"I thought I'd assign you to Mr. Husani for the duration of the rotation," he said. "He seemed to respond to you."

"Thank you," I said. "I'd like that."

"Mr. Husani is what we call a tough case. He has not, as yet, responded to anyone."

"Oh?"

Dr. Theophilus paused.

"Are you considering going into psychiatry?" he asked.

"No. Well, maybe. I don't know, I haven't decided."

"If you'd like to discuss it with me at any point, I'd be happy to do so."

That was the end of my audience with Dr. Theophilus. I left his office full of heated and conflicting emotions: confused, excited, tremulous, alarmed. But within all of it, I felt alive: terribly, heart-throbbingly, elatedly alive. More alive, in fact, than I'd ever before felt.

Yes, I thought, as I walked hurriedly down the corridor. *Psychiatry. Of course! What could be a more natural fit?*

In the six years since that day, I have learned to ride the waves of confusing, ecstatic, gut-wrenching emotion that assail me still, in my work. One of my greatest satisfactions has been the mastery that has come with taming these inner tide swells and undertows and being able, therefore, to help others who are at the mercy of their own.

I close my eyes and try to still the feelings leaping about within. But they won't settle and come into focus as they typically do. I open my eyes again and stare at the blank sheet in Dvorah's binder, shaky with the discovery that my usual control over my own reactions and emotions seems to be letting me down.

Dvorah has been in the hospital now for two weeks. She is guarded and still seems delusional, but is no longer dangerously impulsive. I decide she is ready to start meeting with me off the unit. So, today, I collect her and accompany her to my office.

I sit in a hard-backed chair, and Dvorah sits opposite me on the low blue chaise longue. She seems particularly quiet; perhaps she is unsettled by the change of setting.

We have been sitting for some time in silence.

"It happened after each of them," she says finally.

"What happened, Dvorah?"

"The baby got to come out, only I got plunged far down, beneath the earth."

I nod, as therapists do a lot in sessions with their patients.

"It was never quite so bad as this time, though," she continues. Again, that gaze—as if she were trying to climb out of her own skin and into mine. "You've no idea what it's like, having so many children. One after the other."

"It must be very difficult."

"*Difficult* is not the right word." There is a trace of scorn in her voice.

"Understating it, huh?"

"I'd say so."

A long pause.

"How is my baby?" she asks in a voice so tiny, so light, she might have been a baby herself.

"He's doing very well," I say.

"I've been trying to figure out why it was so much worse with this one."

"I'm not sure there are reasons for such things," I say. "Postpartum depression is a biological event."

"Biology has its reasons."

"Perhaps," I say, feeling dogged on this point. "But the body does things sometimes for no particular reason."

"I don't believe that," Dvorah says, her voice still tiny, her gaze becoming more searing with each moment. "There *are* reasons," she says. "For everything. Surely you believe that. It's your stock-in-trade. Etiologies. Causes and effects. Feedback loops. Otherwise, what would be the point of the medications you dispense? Or psychotherapy, for that matter?"

I pause for a moment to collect my thoughts.

"You're right, I do believe that certain events are connected—that you have suffered a postpartum depression because of biochemical events set off by your pregnancy and the birth of the baby. But I see this as a description of what has happened to you, rather than an explanation. I don't think there are mystical causes lying behind the fact of the hormonal swings."

This does not feel quite right, being so didactic. And yet, I feel I must address Dvorah's questions head-on.

"How do you explain, then, that we are both named Deborah?"

"Your name is Dvorah," I say.

She looks irritated. "That's the Hebrew version of Deborah. You're just trying to sidestep the issue."

"What issue, Dvorah? What am I trying to sidestep?"

"The fact that I've come here for a reason."

"What reason is that?"

"What reason do you think?"

I feel like I'm playing chess with a skilled and tricky opponent. I'm aware of feeling cornered. My mind leaps to alertness.

"I feel like you're trying to corner me," I say.

"You'd know more about cornering people than I would," she says blandly, though I see a hard nub of suspicion in her eyes.

"Do you feel cornered by me?" I ask.

"It's not me I'm worrying about."

"Who, then? Who are you worrying about?"

I watch as her face transforms. It's like watching rapidly moving clouds rearrange themselves in a stormy sky.

"The children," she says. Her face crumples. "How could you do it?" she says in a strangled voice. "How could you?"

"What, Dvorah? What have I done?"

"The children," she whispers. She bows her head and quietly weeps.

I glance at the clock. We've been in the office for twenty minutes. Long enough, I think, for her first real session.

"Come," I say, quietly. "It's time we returned to the unit."

Dvorah rises obediently, still crying.

Together, we take the stairs down and walk along the main hallway toward the unit.

It is an unusually dull afternoon; a wan light slants in through the huge windows and hazes to gray before hitting the varnished floorboards. It is the first time I have ever seen the hallway so dim.

I go directly from work to the Greek restaurant, three blocks from Ron's apartment, where Ron is already seated and sipping a glass of wine. He looks bright-eyed and cool, though he has just come from a busy day at the legal aid office where he has a difficult caseload. I sit opposite him, feeling ragged and soiled by comparison.

"Hard day?" he asks, raising the bottle of Greek wine on the table and leaning over to pour me a glass.

I nod. "One of my new patients," I say, bringing the glass to my lips the minute he puts down the bottle. "I could use this," I add, taking a long sip. "It's going to be a difficult treatment."

"How can you tell?"

"There's a feeling you get."

"You'll figure out the best approach." Ron reaches over to take my hand. "You always do."

I look into his face and marvel at the optimism that seems to hover about him. It was this quality that drew me, electrically, to Ron, the day I first set eyes on him at the conference on the legal rights of psychiatric patients. Sighting him across the room, I was struck by what I can only describe as a lightness to his being; he seemed to emit hope, as if he were wholly unencumbered by any knowledge of the darkness that had plagued me since I was a child. We had our first date that night and have been together ever since. I have been proven right about the freedom of spirit I sensed that first day; though he is serious by temperament, and approaches his work with intensity and rigor, his soul radiates a sunniness that I find a great relief.

Usually, Ron's reassurance would be as soothing as the smooth wine I am sipping, but for some reason, today it unsettles me further. Looking into his face, I feel an odd shudder of dread, the kind of feeling one has when watching a movie in which the characters, involved in a happy moment, have no idea of the lurking danger.

"I hope you're right," I say, trying to affect some cheer. When I take my next sip of wine, I realize I have withdrawn my hand from his.

"My father's brother came to me after the baby was born."

This is the second week we've been meeting in my office, and already Dvorah seems to feel comfortable here.

"Where does he live, your father's brother?" I ask.

"Where does he live?" My question seems to surprise her. "Why, he doesn't live anywhere! At least, not anywhere I know about."

"You said he came to you."

Dvorah jabs at her temple, once, twice.

"Here, in my head. He came to me while I was nursing the baby in my room. Of course, I tried to protect the baby. But he was very persuasive."

Eight days, I count back in my head. Eight days since Dvorah started on the new mix of medications. She is clearly less agitated, though the delusion seems still in full swing. I'm praying that we've hit upon the right cocktail. Otherwise, it could take many more weeks.

"At first, he had to force me to put on the uniform. He must have had it specially made; it fit like a glove. But I got to like it. It came to feel—I don't know, right. I didn't want to take it off. That was when the problems began. How could I, in good conscience, wear the uniform and at the same time take care of the baby? The baby was suckling at my breast! I didn't know what to do. I decided the best thing was just to stop feeding it. Let nature take care of things."

"Can you tell me a little about your father's brother?" I ask.

"What is there to tell?" she snaps. "He was who he was. He must have had his reasons."

"For what?"

"For doing what he did."

The usual cat and mouse. With Dvorah, more than with other patients in my experience, I feel I must tread carefully. She seems to want to tell me what is troubling her—the details of her delusional system—but she is also quite paranoid and readily moved to rage. It's important for her to feel she has an ally in me, of this I am certain, and so I find myself reluctant to press her. Evoking her wrath and making an enemy of myself would leave her feeling frighteningly alone.

I decide to go at it from a different angle.

"Did you ever meet him?" I say. "I mean, anywhere other than here," and now I point to my own temple to indicate the mind.

"Well of course I didn't. How could I have? Once he got off the boat, he made a point of disappearing."

"Where was he from?"

"From the old country, of course. Same place as my father. And quite an old country it was! Old and decrepit and just about ready for the grave. I'm sure, Doctor, you'd agree."

I see she is going somewhere. I wait.

"Bad at some things, good at others. The occupiers brought in their own tailors; they were particularly good at making uniforms. I'll tell you this much, the Germans are good with a stitch."

Dvorah seems momentarily amused by her own round-about way of talking. Then, her gaze hardens to a glare. Her eyes seem to be boring right into me.

"Why am I telling you this? You, of all people? You'd know more about this than I would. After all, I was kept in the dark."

She looks away.

"I still have it," she continues, after a time, reverting to that disconcerting, back-of-the-throat, hissing whisper. "The uniform. It's hidden in my room. Just see if you can take it from me."

"You don't want me to take it?"

"Just try."

"Why do you like having it?"

She looks at me with a lost expression.

"Why, it keeps me safe," she says.

"From what?"

"That's a stupid question, Doctor," she says.

Her eyes glint with suspicion. "I thought you were different," she continues. "I thought you were on my side."

"What would it be for me to be on your side?" I ask.

She does not appear to have heard me.

"You have a uniform, too," she says. "I know you do—over there."

Dvorah points to the closet across from where she is sitting. I rise, walk to the closet, and open the door. The top shelf holds several boxes of files. Hanging on the rod beneath is my spring jacket; a silk scarf is tied around the neck of the hanger.

"What do you see?" I ask.

"Your jacket," Dvorah says dully. Then, in a harsh whisper, "What have you done with it?"

"I don't have a uniform," I say.

Dvorah rises slowly from her chair, crosses to where I am standing, and comes up close, so that her face is no more than a foot away from mine.

"I know who you are," she says blandly. "I know where you came from and what you're hiding."

Looking into her glassy eyes, I am aware of a tingling in my fingertips.

"It's time to take you back to the unit," I say as calmly as I can.

"It's not time," she says, bearing down on my skull with those eyes. "But I'll go. I have no wish to remain here with you."

She turns and walks to the door, then waits patiently for me to open it. She reaches up to the back of her neck and adjusts the wig she wears for religious reasons, in a habitual gesture I always find oddly touching. I turn the handle, and Dvorah steps out into the hallway.

It is Dvorah's fifth week in the hospital. She continues to be erratic. Some days, she is lucid and rational for much of the session, but something psychotic always slips in. The unit staff report the same pattern; Dvorah might be cooperative, even cheerful, for an hour or two, then slip into a snarling surliness in which she makes accusations or withdraws to her room, refusing to participate in unit activities or even go to the cafeteria for meals. At least she has shown no further violence, which I take as a good sign. I'm hoping that as the new medications reach full therapeutic doses in her blood, the paranoia and delusional thinking will disappear.

I look beyond where Dvorah is sitting, out through the window. I can see the new green foliage budding to life on the giant oak.

"My father told me stories about his life from the time I was very young," she says. "Too young, really, to grasp what he was saying."

Dvorah is in one of her lucid states; her eyes are luminous and steady.

"He told me too much. Too often. Over and over again. He would get this faraway look, and once he started on a story, he had to see it through to the end. I heard them all so many times . . ."

"Do some stick out more in your mind than others?" I ask.

"Yes, I suppose so."

I pause. What I am about to say is risky. I do a quick check in my mind of the pros and cons. Then, I dive in.

"Was there one about a uniform?"

A flicker in Dvorah's eyes—something wary and dark.

"Do you know what he told me? My father?" she continues, ignoring my question, at least for now. "He told me that lying was wrong. All parents tell their children this—it is part of raising them, after all. But he also told me that God would overlook lying if you were a Jew and someone wanted to kill you. Then, he said, it was all right to say you were not a Jew, if you were lucky enough not to look like one so you could get away with the lie.

"That's what my father did during the War. He lied and got away with it because he had blue eyes and fair hair.

"I was four years old when my father told me that, about the lying. I was very confused. I just wanted to know—is it okay to lie or not? A four-year-old mind does not grasp exceptions. I remember going to the bathroom and looking in the mirror and seeing how very dark my eyes and hair were. I remember examining the structure and shape of my features. *Could I get away with such a lie?* I wondered. *Did I look Jewish?* What exactly did it mean to *look Jewish?* And if I did, what would I do or say when the people who kill Jews came to get me? Even supposing it was all right from God's point of view to lie, how would I escape if I couldn't get away with the lie?

"I remember thinking about this a lot, as I got older. I would think myself into a confusing spiral. I looked like my mother, not like my father. Surely, then, I would never get away with lying about my Jewishness, even if I had to. That meant that lying under all circumstances—for me—was wrong. A sin. Not something God would ever overlook. Not for me."

She pauses.

"Ever since then, I've worried that I might accidentally

lie. And that because of the way I look, I'd get no special dispensation like my father had, with his blue eyes and fair coloring. God would hold me accountable, and I would receive a terrible punishment."

An unsavory smile creeps across Dvorah's face.

"But I've caught Him at His own game. I'm *not* in fact culpable."

Dvorah lets out a little laugh. Then, she leans forward and narrows her eyes. Though I've had considerable experience with psychotic patients, I find it particularly unnerving, the way Dvorah swerves so suddenly from seeming normalcy and rationality to that otherworldly, charged, and sinister space of delusion.

"*You'd* know what I'm talking about," she says. "*You* of all people. Yes, I've fooled Him at his own game, because *it's all a disguise. I'm not what I seem. I am something else entirely.* Blue eyes? Why of course. And this wig—you think it hides dark hair?" She laughs again. Now, she seems pleased with herself.

"It's all a game, isn't it. Nothing but a great big fat theme park. Ride the ride, toss the hoops. Some win, some lose. *Kill the Jews.*"

It's enough for today, I think. We're not going to get any further. Dvorah seems to have about fifteen minutes of rationality with me before she veers off into psychotic ramblings.

"Come, Dvorah. Let's go back to the unit."

"Why not?" she says, rising cheerfully. "What have *I* got to lose? I'm going to win, not lose. Though you never can tell with a noose."

At first I don't know what she's saying, as she pronounces *noose* to rhyme with *lose*—it comes out sounding like *nuz*. She's enjoying her own wordplay. My stomach curdles with anxiety.

Yes, I think to myself. *Fifteen minutes at most.* I'll keep our sessions to that until the medication takes full effect.

We walk back in silence. The secret little pleased-with-herself smile stays on her lips, and when I pause to usher her through the unit door, she turns and gives me a knowing sneer.

It is late. I am sitting in my office, going over Dvorah's rapidly growing file.

I turn to the section containing the partially completed case conference, which I have spent a full week of late nights so far preparing, and which I will present at the end of the month. I read over the section titled: "Events Leading Up to Hospitalization."

Two weeks prior to entering the hospital, the patient delivered a healthy baby boy, her seventh child. Pregnancy and delivery were normal. Several hours after the delivery, the patient became very tearful. Her mother, who was with her at the time, reports that she was unable to stop crying for three or four hours. Finally, the patient was given a sedative. She then fell asleep and slept for twelve hours. Hospital staff tried to wake her on several occasions to give the baby the breast—they were concerned about the patient's milk coming in, as they knew she wanted to nurse. On each occasion, the patient did awaken but was very angry and screamed at nursing staff to go away and leave her alone. When they brought the baby to her and suggested she give him the breast, the patient continued to scream at them and, at one point, tried to grab the baby and made as if she were going to strike him. Nursing staff were concerned by this behavior and called the in-house psychiatric resident, who examined the patient when she finally awoke of her own accord, later in the day. (See Appendix for full report from maternity ward psychiatric examination.)

When the patient awoke from her long, sedated sleep, she seemed to have returned to normal. She reported no memory of screaming at nursing staff or any attempt to harm the baby. She put the baby to the breast, and he nursed normally.

The patient was released from the hospital two days later and returned home. Her mother moved in with her in order to care for the patient's six other children, thus allowing the patient to devote herself for a few weeks only to the baby. Her mother had moved in for three or four weeks following the birth of each of the patient's children.

According to the patient's mother, everything proceeded normally for the first week or so, as on her previous visits after the births of her older grandchildren. However, a few days later, the mother began to hear the infant screaming desperately for long periods. The mother went frequently to see what was happening, and each time, she found the patient calm and unperturbed, saying the baby had a touch of colic and that her mother should not concern herself. The mother reports that she noticed an odd look in her daughter's eyes and began to think she was acting in a strange and secretive way.

After about a day and a half, the baby's desperate screaming stopped. But one time the patient's mother went to check on her daughter and grandchild, she realized that the baby was not asleep, as her daughter claimed, but rather listless and limp in its crib. The patient was standing staring out of the window. She was wearing the same nightdress she had worn for two or three days, and the mother realized that *the patient had not washed or brushed her hair for some time and in fact looked quite unkempt.*

The mother became alarmed. She told her daughter she was going to call the doctor to come and see the baby. When her daughter heard this, she turned around and very angrily—in a voice that was not her own—told her mother to stay out of it. "That baby is getting what it deserves," the patient said. The mother reports being terrified by her daughter's behavior, saying, "She seemed crazy." The patient's mother took the baby from the room. She phoned her rabbi, who instructed her to call our hospital and arrange for an ambulance to bring the patient directly here.

The pediatrician determined that the baby was severely dehydrated and had probably not been fed for about a day and a half. He was hospitalized and placed on intravenous fluids. He recovered quickly and is currently in the care of the patient's mother.

It is not uncommon, in cases of psychotic postpartum depression, for a mother to want to harm her baby. What I still do not understand, though, is what Dvorah was actually thinking when she withheld nourishment from the baby. What did she mean when she told her mother: *That baby is getting what it deserves?*

It's true, what I told Dvorah in our session—that I believe postpartum depression is a biological event, and that the medication, we hope, will dissolve it away. But I also believe that psychological conflicts can contribute to the onset of the condition. So if I can help Dvorah dismantle her demons, perhaps another terrible descent into madness can be short-circuited.

I pause to examine this last thought. It is true, then, that

I believe that something psychological—set in play by the stories Dvorah's father told her from the time she was a little girl—may have been a precipitant of her psychosis.

Causes and effects, just as Dvorah said. With one significant difference: Dvorah believes there is some greater force—God, perhaps?—that set all this in motion in the first place. Some greater force that contrived to bring us together not so that I might help Dvorah but so that she might confront me.

It is this last thing that stumps me, though I shouldn't be so baffled; this is, after all, the pivot of Dvorah's psychosis, the point at which reason fails. It is also not so unusual for a patient to draw her doctor into her psychosis.

So why, then, this terrible, creeping feeling?

If I am honest with myself, do I not also at times have the disconcerting—but also exhilarating—feeling, while sitting here with Dvorah, that we have, in fact, been brought together by some mystical force with an unknowable but critically important intent?

"Don't you think it a coincidence? That we're both named Deborah?"

Again, the matter of our names. I repeat what I said in our earlier session.

"Your name is Dvorah. Mine is Deborah. Besides, it's a common enough name."

"I was named after my grandmother. My father's mother."

I, too, was named after my paternal grandmother, though I know nothing about her.

My father told me this that day, when I was a sophomore in college, filling out the paperwork for my junior year abroad, and asked him about his birthplace. After he told me he'd not been born in New Jersey, as I'd supposed, but in Poland, shipped to America after the War as an orphan of ten, he added, almost as an aside: "We named you after my mother. My mother's name was Deborah."

I try to shake this coincidence from my mind.

"And you?" Dvorah was asking. "Were you named after anyone?"

"I'm interested that you would ask that," I say in a somewhat rote manner.

"Don't pull that psychobabble garbage with me," Dvorah says. "You know I see right through it."

"Dvorah, we're here to talk about you, not me. You know that."

"Is that so?"

"To try to—to get you through this."

"A person doesn't *get through* what I've been through. Some things don't get better. Did you ever think of that, *Doctor?*"

She is angry again. She is revving up.

"It's only been three weeks on the new regimen," I say as calmly as I can. "We need to give it a little more time."

"Murder is murder," she says.

I eye the open door.

"Looking for the mental health worker, aren't you. Well, he can't save you from the truth."

"What truth?"

"The truth of who I am. The truth of who you are. Of what *we've both done.*"

I can feel my heart pounding. Dvorah looks like a cornered animal, dangerous and ready to pounce. Under normal circumstances, I could overcome her physically if I needed to. But psychosis is not normal circumstances; I have seen psychotic patients do serious injury to even the most burly mental health worker.

But this is also an opportunity. An opportunity to penetrate Dvorah's delusion. Or at least to get closer to some understanding of it.

"What is it we've done?" I ask quietly.

"You hate the Jews as much as I do," she hisses. "Filthy, disgusting race." Now she leans forward. Her eyes look very black, and also inflamed, which gives them a reddish glow.

"I can't do anything in here—look at me. I'm locked up. You're going to have to do it for me."

Dvorah reaches up with one hand to the nape of her neck and unthinkingly adjusts her wig.

"What, Dvorah? What must I do?"

"The baby—" she hisses. Her hands are in her lap. I see she is clenching them—open, shut. Her knuckles are white.

I've pushed her too far, and now I regret it. Slowly, I rise.

"That's enough for today," I say. "Come, let's go back to the unit."

Dvorah flinches, fear, now, in her eyes. When she speaks, the sound is a rumble coming from her chest—more animal grunt than human speech, though I manage to discern her meaning.

"I'm warning you," she grumbles.

"Come, Dvorah. Now," I say. She remains immobile in the chair, clutching the wooden arms and almost baring her teeth.

"I will expose you," she says. "I swear I will."

Dvorah's attitude toward me alters strikingly from session to session, and sometimes even within the same meeting. She seems to be trying to determine whether I am a trustworthy person, in whom she can confide and take comfort, or a vicious enemy, intent on doing her harm. I do my best to remain steady.

She begins the next session by talking about a dream.

"I have dreamt about that little boy, my father's brother, from as far back as I can remember. My father told me about him—about his brother—when I was five years old."

Dvorah is more lucid today than I've yet seen her. I can almost hear myself holding my breath—hoping against hope that perhaps, finally, the delusions have been kicked out and she is on her way to recovery.

"My father is very involved in the study of Kabbalah. He places great store in numbers. That's why I think he told me this story when I was five years old. Exactly the age his little brother was when he last saw him. When he told him to go and hide in the outhouse in the field."

Dvorah is silent for a moment.

"I was too young to be told such stories. Though I suppose there is no age that would be right. Those dreams terrified me. I would lie awake in my bed, afraid to close my eyes. Many nights, I vowed I would stay awake all night. But sleep always came. The dream was so real. I would hear that urgent whisper—'Go down into the toilet. Stay there. *Do not move.*' And me, I am the little boy, my father's brother.

"It is pitch-black outside. I hear all kinds of sounds—angry voices, orders, pleas, cries. I cannot make sense of any of it. I know only that I must do what my older brother has told me to do. I adore him—he is clever and patient and kind. I always do what he tells me. He is ten years older than I am. I am the youngest of five brothers, and he practically raised me. 'Do not move until I come for you,' he said. His words repeat over and over in my head as I race through the darkness, away from our village. It has always been peaceful and quiet at night, but not this night, no. The men in uniform have filled the streets and are taking everyone from their homes.

"I move quickly across the fields. I know those fields so well, I feel as if I know every blade of grass. Past the linden tree, where the shepherd sits to eat his lunch while he keeps an eye on his flock. Last night, we had rain. The smell of the wet earth rises up and fills my nostrils. Tomorrow morning would be a good time to collect worms, I think. I picture myself digging a hole and carefully pulling away the moist clods. I picture myself coming upon a nice bunch of thick and healthy worms.

"The outhouse is in among some bushes and trees. It is used by the shepherds and by anyone from our village who is out here. You'd miss it, if you didn't know it was there. I creep through the bushes—I do everything by feel; it is so dark, I can see only black outlines.

"Inside the outhouse, there is no stench; I am in luck. It appears it has not been used for a while. The door creaks as I open it. I climb down into the hole. I land on dried dung and bits of old used paper.

"He told me to wait, and this is what I do.

"I do not wait very long before I hear voices. I feel thumpings at the same time. The thumping of many feet, hundreds of people, maybe more. It is like a shudder coming up through the earth.

"I also hear silence. The voices are the soldiers' voices, barking instructions. The silence is that of the villagers: marching feet and closed throats.

" 'Do not move until I come for you.' Isn't that what my brother said?

"Well, perhaps he has come for me, then? I chance it. I hoist myself up, out of the pit, press my face against the rough wooden slats that make the walls of the outhouse.

"I see bands of light spreading across the sky: orange and pink. Dawn. I was right, there are hundreds of people—more, possibly the whole village. Minus one, minus me, little Yanek. It's not my given name, but that's what they call me.

"They are digging, these people I have known the whole of my life. There is a truck, and soldiers in the back are handing out shovels. Dozens and dozens of shovels; the truck is full of them. All the men are digging, the older boys, too. I squint my eyes as tightly as I can and peer through the tiny slit between my eyelids—that's the way I make a kind of magnifying glass with my eyes. I think I see one of my brothers, then a second, but not Robert, not my beloved eldest brother, who told me not to move.

"But wait. That boy over there, to the right. I see him only from behind. The way he raises his shoulders and arms as he digs, that movement is Robert's, I'm sure of it. He's a strong boy—almost a man, sixteen next month. I found a beautiful smooth stone, so round, it's almost the shape of a ball. I have been saving this stone for a while, to give to Robert on his birthday. I am the best of everyone at gathering worms, and I was going to surprise him with some fat worms, and also the stone.

"Yes, I am sure of it. It must be Robert. When he is finished digging, he will come for me. I keep my eyes on his back—I do not want to lose sight of him. There are so many people, such chaos—orders being shouted, an endless echo of clacking and thudding as hundreds of shovels dig into the soil. I wonder what it is they are digging.

"My mother! I see my mother! She is wearing her floral

dress—I love that dress! Spring flowers on a pale blue background, flowers in the sky, I always think. I almost cry out with relief and joy and jump to the door. I will run out! I will run into my mother's arms! I will smell her warmth, she will tell me that everything is all right, I will nestle into the flowers in the sky.

"But no, Robert's voice, it was so urgent, so commanding—*Do not move.*

"I will not move. My eyes sweep back to him—I think it is him—but wait, this boy is wearing a red shirt. I do not remember Robert having a red shirt. I know each of Robert's shirts—one white, for *Shabbos,* the other two blue. He does not own a red shirt, I am sure of it. But those are his arms and shoulders, I am also sure of this!

"I am confused. Confused about the shirt. While I am confused, I see that Robert—is it Robert?—has put down the shovel. More orders from the soldiers. Mama's floral dress—she is moving, with Robert, my other brothers, too—and there is Papa! And Uncle Yosse and Aunt Sarah! My mother tries to take my brother's hand; a soldier whacks her with a stick, and her arm falls to her side.

"Crack, crack. More cracks. They fall forward—into the pit, the freshly dug pit—my eyes shear backward, there, a line of soldiers, holding rifles. Crack. Again crack.

"I dive back into the toilet hole. I remain still, very still. Only now do I register the smell—it is not very bad, as the dung is dry, but it is foul. I think only of the shirt. Robert does not own a red shirt. I am sure of it. But I am also certain it was him.

"This is always when I wake up. Always with the realization that the *me* in the dream—I am my father's little brother—is mistaken. That the *me* in the dream had been right about the red shirt, that Robert, my father, had not owned a red shirt. It had been another boy. Another boy who had stood by my father's parents and three other brothers as they were all shot into the pit.

"You see, Robert survived, of course. He, too, had hidden. Both boys survived, the eldest and the youngest, though they never saw each other again."

"What happened to him?" I ask. "To your father's little brother? The brother you become in the dream?"

Now Dvorah's eyes cloud. "You know very well what happened to him. Same thing as happened to me."

My heart sinks. There it is—the delusion, fearsome and dark. I don't know what Dvorah is thinking, but I take a wild stab.

"The uniform."

Dvorah nods, and gives a faint, unseemly smile.

"Exactly," she says with a note of triumph. "The uniform."

It is Friday at last. I glance down at the calendar on my desk pad and see how long it has been since Dvorah's admission. Only six weeks. It feels like months. I lock my office door with relief. It has been a long few days. I am happy that I am not on call this weekend; I'm aware of how much I need a break from the hospital.

Last night I packed my overnight bag, so I could drive straight from the hospital to my parents' home in New Jersey, the house in which I grew up. When I step out into the new May evening, the cool air leaps up at my face just as I feel the clap of freedom. A whole weekend to myself! No patients, no Ron, only the long drive to New Jersey, the two books in my bag I've been looking forward to reading for weeks, and the inviting, unobtrusive company of my parents. My mother will surely have prepared my favorite meal—roast chicken with potatoes and pumpkin in the pan—followed by her fluffy, delicious dark chocolate mousse.

I take the Whitestone Bridge to avoid the Friday night traffic heading toward Manhattan. I will miss the dual views from the George Washington Bridge, which are among my all-time favorites—Manhattan to the left, and to the right, the opening out of the Hudson River into the sea.

I find myself thinking about my last session with Dvorah, though I'd told myself firmly that I needed a break. *I'll put it all from my mind when I get home,* I say to myself. *Promise.*

I am thinking about the fact that Dvorah's father is from Poland. And though I try to tell myself I'm being silly—superstitious, overly drawn into my patient's psychotic universe—I list out the several coincidences which have arisen. Nothing but the co-occurrence of common facts, I'd said to myself. In addition to our names, the closeness of our ages. And now two more, though Dvorah has no awareness of these; that we were both named for our paternal grandmothers, and that our fathers are both from Poland.

I hear Dr. Finkelstein's voice. "Dr. Erick, think this through rationally." *Okay,* I say back in my head, *I'll do my best.* We are in the New York area, to which hundreds of thousands of European Jews fled before, during, and after World War II. How many thousands came from Poland? Deborah is, in fact, a very common name, especially for women of my generation. Surely, then, there are a large number of Deborahs born to Jewish immigrants from this period. My being Dvorah's doctor is therefore no more coincidental than Kevin O'Malley, our mental health worker, caring for a patient, also of Irish heritage, named Keith, or even also named Kevin. And being close in age—well, that means absolutely nothing. Why should a thirty-two-year-old doctor not be caring for a thirty-two-year-old patient?

How'd I do? I say in my head to Dr. Finkelstein. I see her wise smile. *Fine, Dr. Erick. Just fine.* I breathe out a long sigh. I really am very tired. I look forward to getting some sleep.

I am sailing over the Whitestone Bridge. I was right, I think, to take this route; it was worth sacrificing my beloved views. I don't think I could bear to be sitting in traffic right now.

I don't remember how old I was when I learned that my father was adopted. I knew only that he had loved his adoptive parents. They were much older than birth parents would have been—well into their fifties when he came into their home. They'd both died when my father was in graduate school, before I was born. He kept a framed picture of them on the shelf in his study, though he seldom talked of them. I liked to look at that photograph; a man and woman both with gray hair and warm eyes, and the kinds of smiles that suggest they know the way the world is yet have embraced it anyway.

My mother's parents died when I was three; I have only vague and fleeting memories of them. They were killed in a car accident while on vacation in France, when their car was hit by an English tourist driving on the wrong side of the road. As both of my parents were only children, that left just the three of us.

We floated in a little island of the present: no others to bring memories of their own lives or knowledge of extended family into our world.

This was not so unusual in our close-knit Jewish community, which was largely made up of refugees from Europe. Most of my friends' parents had lost their families in the Holocaust; many were the sole survivors. Perhaps this is why the bonds we formed at the Youth Center were as strong as they were. In our different ways, we were all trying to re-create a lost world.

Being an only child myself, and without uncles and aunts and cousins to fill the house, I spent a good deal of time in the houses of my friends. I don't remember when I was struck by the shroud of silence that seemed to hang in the air at virtually all of these homes; I think, though, that I must have been very young. I recognized it from my own home, though at our house, it seemed less dramatic, if silence can be dramatic. In the homes of my friends, it was as if we were surrounded by two kinds of ghosts, which could never be mentioned. The ghosts of too many relatives, murdered long before their time. And the ghostly pasts of my friends' parents: these, too, were cloaked in silence. We didn't talk about any of this among ourselves. The importance of honoring the code was simply understood.

When I was in eleventh grade, we had a class in philosophy, given by someone on the faculty at Rutgers who was a classmate's father. A scholar of Wittgenstein, he devoted several classes to trying to sketch the outlines of Wittgenstein's later thought. In his final class, he conveyed one of Wittgenstein's aphoristic dictums: "Whereof one cannot speak, thereof one should remain silent." The words struck a chord.

I accepted our tiny little dominion and just threw myself into living. If the present was all we had, I would fill it to the brim.

Every summer, we took a long road trip to see some part of America. One year, we drove through the South, visiting places associated with the history of jazz and the blues. Another year, we traveled through the Northwest, and I fell in love with the gruff vastness of the landscape, which exuded a different kind of silence than the one I knew: a silence that hid nothing. We toured the coast of California, where I stood on bluffs that hung out over an immense and choppy sea, and walked in endless forest, breathing in the gusty, free scent of eucalyptus mixed with pine.

We never, though, traveled abroad. So it was not until I was making plans to go abroad for my junior year of college that I had any need for a passport.

As I was filling in the paperwork, I realized I did not know where my father was born. My father's adoptive family had lived in New Jersey, not far from where I was raised. I'd assumed he'd been born somewhere nearby—perhaps to a teenage girl or single mother. Accustomed to the practice of never asking my father about his past, I was about to write "Rutherford"—the town in which he was raised—in the blank for "Father's birthplace." *What difference does it make,* I thought, *exactly which town he was born in?* This didn't go on my passport; it was just needed on the form.

I paused, pen in hand. I could not bring myself to write in the word. I wanted to put in the right town; I wanted to have the correct information.

Thanksgiving was coming up. I was going home to spend it with my parents, so I decided to ask my father then.

We always had Thanksgiving with two other families, which gave the celebration a festive feel. I was happy to be home. I spent most of the first day helping my mother with the preparations for the feast. That evening we sat around the table drinking hot chocolate. I decided it was a good time to ask my father about where he was born.

"I have to fill in a form for my passport," I began. "For junior year abroad."

"Do you need our help?" my mother asked.

"Actually, I need to put in your place of birth," I said, looking at my father.

"My place of birth," he said woodenly, placing his cup down on his saucer.

"Was it Rutherford? Or someplace else?" I asked.

My mother looked at my father, then back at me. I saw something in her face, but I didn't know quite what it was. An odd mixture of fear, anguish, and blame.

"Actually, no," my father said. "It wasn't Rutherford."

I could feel my mother holding her breath.

My father seemed to be struggling with something. He seemed not to know what to say. When he finally spoke, his voice had an odd, strangled sound to it. Like someone was choking him, but he was managing, against all odds, to say what he intended to say.

"Poland," he said. "I was born in Poland. In Lvov."

Poland. This country had never been mentioned before in our house. And now my father was telling me he was born there.

"Poland," I said. "You were born in Poland."

"Yes," he answered, looking not at me but at my mother.

"When did you come to America?"

Another long pause. Now my mother was regarding me with raw anger. She'd never looked at me this way before, and it made me feel I was a loathsome person who had done something very wrong.

"After the War. I came here after the War."

I knew my mother was willing me to be quiet, but I had to go on.

"How old were you?"

"I was ten. In fact, I turned ten on the passage over."

My mother rose and took my empty cup and her own over to the sink.

"We should all be getting to bed," she said. "We have a big day tomorrow!" She was trying to sound cheerful and nonchalant, but she only sounded angry and closed.

"Yes, you're right, my dear," my father said, also rising. And to me, "Good night, sweetheart. See you in the morning."

I heard their footsteps on the stairs. They went up in silence.

I sat at the table looking out at the front lawn and, beyond that, to the street. It was already very cold; I fancied I could see the coldness in the night sky—the blackness seemed icy and thick. Sitting there, in the kitchen I had known all my life, I felt a terrible aloneness that was as black as the indifferent night sky.

By the time I pull into the driveway of my parents' house, I have left work behind. I turn off the engine and sit, for a moment, in the car, leaving the windows down so I can breathe in the night air and listen to the quiet. No traffic sounds, no voices, only the occasional bark of a dog: and moonlight, bathing the houses and cars and trees in a benevolent glow.

We eat a late dinner—exactly the delicious menu I anticipated; my parents usually wait so we can eat together, though it is often after nine by the time I get there. We talk about the university where my father has been teaching and doing research for almost thirty years and where, some years ago, my mother took an administrative job she has grown to love.

By the time we get to the chocolate mousse, I feel very tired.

"Leave the dishes," my mother says as I scoop the last of the dessert from the crystal bowl. "Why don't you go on up to bed."

I kiss them both and climb the stairs, change into my nightdress, brush my teeth, and fall into bed.

I tumble into a half sleep, glimpsing snatches of disturbing scenes, aware that I am half awake and yet also vividly dreaming. I try to move but cannot. I am tied with four-point restraints to the bed. I wonder, distractedly, how they secured me; the bed I am on, from my childhood, is of the platform kind—it has no posts.

I try to call out to my parents, to tell them that there has been a careless error, that someone has mistaken me for a patient and that they should call Dr. Finkelstein, who will send an order down for my release. But no sound issues from my throat. I have been silenced. I am unable to speak.

I have somehow, though, been released, as now I am crouched down in a small confined space. I am very cold, my stomach contracts with hunger. I am terrified—they are going to find me and kill me, I am certain. They are going to thrust a shovel in my hand, make me dig and dig, and then stand me by the pit and shoot a bullet into the back of my head. I am trembling with hunger, cold, and terror. I want my mother—I want her kind, sweet face, all misty with concern. *Leave the dishes,* she will say. *Why don't you go on up to bed?* I want to throw myself into her arms, I want to cry: *I can eat? Your chicken? Your chocolate mousse? They're not going to make me dig and shoot me in the back of the head?* And she will answer, *No, my sweet love. Nothing of the kind. Just go up to bed, I'll take care of everything.*

But I am alone. I am cold and alone and trembling with terror. I am small, very small. I hear the sound of heavy boots.

I see the beam of a flashlight shining through the gaps in the old wooden boards that make up the sides of the hut. I open my mouth to scream and raise my arm to cover my face. As I do so, I catch sight of what it is I am wearing. It is a uniform, a brown uniform, clean and freshly ironed. I move my glance slowly up and down the sleeve and see that there is a black armband sewn onto the left upper arm, in the middle of which is a bright red swastika that suddenly begins to spurt blood. They have shot me, I think; they missed my head and got me in the arm, smack in the middle of the swastika.

Now I do scream. My voice comes out thinly but with great strength.

I am sitting up in bed. I hear myself screaming and immediately stop. I hope I have not woken my parents.

I hear soft footfalls, and then my mother appears in the room.

"Deborah, what's wrong?"

She sits on the bed, then takes my hand as she did when I was a child, only now her hand is not smooth and beautiful as I remember it from the past but prematurely aged, her knuckles thickened and distorted by the arthritis that hit her early, when she was in her middle forties. It is still a great comfort, and it makes me want to cry.

"Bad dream, Mom, that's all." I am surprised by how shaky my voice sounds.

"Why don't you tell me about it?" she says. Throughout my childhood, I was plagued by nightmares. Many nights, my mother would sit on my bed as she's sitting here now. It has been a very long time since I've told anyone my dreams, although now, as I look into my mother's concerned and loving face, it seems as if all of my life since those long-ago days of my childhood and youth has been itself a dream, or something I've only imagined; as if, in fact, I have been here all along, protected and safe, still living out the ongoing days of a perpetual childhood in my parents' home.

I am about to tell my mother about my dream, but a sob rises in my chest, and instead I find myself saying, "Mama, I'm in trouble. At work. I'm having a serious problem with a patient."

"Oh?" she says mildly.

"A young woman—exactly my age, as it happens. She's Hasidic. Mama, she tried to kill her baby."

Now the sob I'd been suppressing bursts out and I cannot control the tears.

"Postpartum depression, I suppose," my mother says sadly. I nod, reach for a tissue, and blow my nose. I take a few deep breaths and try to regain my composure.

"I don't have the usual distance with this patient. I keep trying to get things back in place, but it's as if—" I hesitate, not sure what it is I am trying to say.

"As if—?" my mother prompts.

"I don't know. It's as if she knows me. This is going to sound a little crazy, but it's as if we know each other from another life, or something. She has an uncanny way of knowing what I'm thinking and feeling. She seems to know things about me she couldn't possibly know by any ordinary means."

"Is she psychotic?" my mother asks.

I start a little at this clinical term. Of course Dvorah is psychotic, it says so in her chart—I've written the word in those pages myself, many times. But here, now, the term seems wrong. It seems like a slap in the face, to me as much as to her.

"Yes, I suppose she is," I say, hesitating again.

"You sound uncertain," my mother says.

"It's just that when you get to know patients, they seem,

well, who they are. I stop thinking about them in purely clinical terms. Words like *psychotic* or *delusional* start to feel
wrong. These patients just inhabit a different world."

"I remember you saying, in the past, that it's not unusual
for psychotic patients to intuit things about the doctors who
treat them."

I nod. "Yes, that's true. But this seems different."

"How?" she asks.

My head is cloudy, I feel confused.

"Dvorah seems to see things about me I don't even know
myself," I say. "Secrets. Hidden secrets I've only ever
glimpsed."

We both fall silent.

For so long, Dvorah has been troubled by the stories her
father told her when she was a child. Stories no child should
have to hear, let alone live through. I wonder if the stories
themselves drove her mad, drove her to try to starve her own
baby to death. I catch myself—I know better than this, me,
the great believer in the biological basis of mental illness,
particularly clean-cut in cases of postpartum depression.

And now, the dreadful stories she was told have found
their way into my dreams.

I myself was told no dreadful stories. I was told nothing
at all.

"Mama?" I say at last.

"Yes, my love?"

"What happened to Papa? During the war?" Never once,
until now, have I ever asked her or my father this question.

"He was orphaned," she says quietly.

"Yes, I know that," I say, impatient. I have waited such a
long time—the whole of my life—to ask this question, and
now, I'm anxious for an answer. "But what exactly happened?"

It is my mother's turn to hesitate. She sits there for what seems like a rather long time, thinking, I suppose, about how to answer the question I have taken decades to ask.

"I've known your father a very long time," she says finally. "We were teenagers when we met."

I know the story, my mother knows I know it: how they were high school sweethearts, how my father proposed to her the night of the senior prom, how they then waited until they had both graduated from college before marrying.

"One of the things I loved about him from the beginning," she continues, "was the respect he accorded to everyone he met. I knew I could trust him with anything; I knew that he would never trespass in any way. I didn't fully understand how important this really is until I was much older, though I did have an intuition about it. I have come to believe that this kind of No Trespassing principle is the secret to a long and happy marriage.

"When your father proposed to me that night—what a serious, mature young man he was; his soul was far older than his eighteen years—I saw something in his eyes. A kind of flash. Like something within him had been to a far-off planet and only barely managed to return. He looked at me for a long time. Well, I was seventeen years old and in love, but I fancied I was seeing the flash of a distant star: pure light, the planet itself long gone, disintegrated to nothing. Before he asked me the question—I knew he was about to propose—it was as if the deepest part of him first needed to communicate something, and not in words, to the deepest part of me. I heard it as this: *Mariana, do not ask. Please. Not ever.* I answered him with my own inner flash: *Not ever.* And again. *Not ever.*

"This has been a long answer to your question. The fact is

I know no more than you do. Which is to say—nothing at all."

I see, through the blinds, which I always leave open, the first shy light of morning.

There is no more to say. My mother rises, pats my hand one last time, and leans to kiss my cheek.

"Why don't you try to sleep a bit more," she says. "You work so hard. You need your rest."

I watch as she leaves the room.

I think about the quiet restraint that has existed these many years between my father and my mother, about the fact that she does not know what my father lived through when he was a small child. That in almost forty years, they have shared so much, and all with an impenetrable fence around my father's early life. *No Trespassing.*

I think about how my entire career is founded on the antithesis of this principle: on the belief in the importance of methodically dismantling such barriers.

For one terrible moment, I am confused.

Is what I am doing all wrong? Am I not shedding healing light but rather causing walls to come crashing in, with potentially disastrous consequences?

I do not, in fact, go back to sleep. I stay sitting up in bed thinking. One thought presses down on me; it is unbearable in its intensity, I cannot push it from my mind. I am awash in a strange kind of anger—toward my father, my gentle, devoted, always beloved father—an anger I have never before felt.

I want to know.

II.

"I think you should consider taking a sleeping pill," Ron says. "You're beginning to look haggard."

"Perhaps you're right," I say, throwing my set of Ron's house keys onto the counter. "I can't face cooking. Let's order in."

I look at Ron, who is sitting at the kitchen table over a hefty-looking legal brief. He seems far away. I am aware of a great sense of effort, as if I'm trying to keep my balance on a tightrope, while pretending to Ron that I'm walking on ordinary, solid ground.

"Middle Eastern?"

I nod.

Ron picks up the phone and places our usual order from the Middle Eastern restaurant. Falafel plate and mixed grill. Then he walks over to where I'm sitting, stands behind me, and begins to massage my neck.

"You're very tight," he mutters, kneading the muscles of my upper back. "Tell Dr. Ron all about it."

I close my eyes, relax into the movements of Ron's hands.

In the four years we've been together, Ron and I have talked openly about whatever might trouble us. Now, though, it feels different. I struggle for words but find myself looking into a dark patch of silence.

He continues to work at my back and neck with his sure hands.

"That feels good," I say.

He says nothing more, but it is as if there is a question lifting from his fingers and hanging in the air.

"I'm just so tired," I say.

Ron's hands stop their kneading; I feel them dropping away. I feel, too, a hardness in the silence.

"Ron?"

A hesitation, and then, "Yes?"

I was right. His voice is hard.

"I feel like there's something you're not saying," I continue.

Another hesitation.

"I'm beginning to get tired, too," he says. I turn to see that Ron is looking out of the kitchen window, out onto the rooftop opposite us, from where, on occasion, we hear a gunshot or two—a gun dealer, we've deduced, allowing potential customers to test the goods.

"I don't know, Deb," he continues. "I don't know what you want from me."

"But Ron—I don't want anything."

"Maybe that's it. Maybe that's exactly the problem."

I am sitting in my office, going over Dvorah's file. I realize it is time to go and get her. I close the file and lock it back into my filing cabinet.

I feel as if I've crossed some kind of line. It's never happened to me before, and I'm not sure how to understand it or what to do about it. I find I look forward to our sessions in a way that doesn't feel quite right—that feels unprofessional. Sometimes, when I ask Dvorah the kinds of clarifying questions that are the stock-in-trade of my profession, I'm just a little too eager to hear the answers. I have a niggling feeling that the treatment is no longer only about Dvorah.

On the unit, I see that today Dvorah is calm.

Back in my office, she sits calmly, expectantly, waiting for me to speak. Finally, I think. The medication is doing what it is supposed to.

"The dream you told me about," I begin.

"Yes, Doctor. I told you about a dream."

There's something a little too pat about her manner—even calculating. As if she decided before the session to be obedient.

"I've been thinking about our last session," I continue. "I have a couple of questions."

"Yes?"

"Well, for one thing, I was wondering how you would know that your father's brother had saved him a stone for his birthday. If it was a surprise and he never got to give it to your father, how, then, did your father know about it, in order to tell the story to you?"

She smiles—pleased with herself, pleased with me. As if she had set a little test for me and I had passed.

"Because he saw it, naturally. He saw it in his brother's treasure box one day, not long before that awful night. And knowing his brother and how he thought—maybe also some little gesture or hint that the boy let slip—he knew he was planning to give it to him."

Dvorah is looking at me so directly, and with such control. I feel unnerved. Is this how patients sometimes feel? Sitting across from a doctor—from me, perhaps—who seems so unflappable and sure of him- or herself, while the patient is awash in uncertainty, and at the mercy of this other person's judgment?

"Dvorah, there's something I want to ask you. Perhaps it won't make sense to you, now that you're so much better."

She smiles gratefully. "The medication really is doing its work now. I'm very thankful for that."

I wait. I'm trying to figure out if Dvorah's polite, good-girl demeanor today is genuine or staged.

"Your question, Doctor," she prompts.

"Yes. Well, when you were—very ill—"

She flinches, and I glimpse, for a split second, that depth of blackness that strips the humanness from her face. Perhaps, after all, Dvorah is only feigning wellness in order to win off-unit privileges and ultimately release from the hospital. I've seen this before—but Dvorah's calm and reasonableness the past day or two have been very convincing.

"The uniform," I say, aware there is something too intense about the tone of my own voice. "Several times, now, you've mentioned a uniform."

"Yes, I did mention a uniform."

"Is it a Nazi uniform? Is that what you're talking about?"

Now, Dvorah looks baffled.

"Why yes, of course. But you've known that all along, surely!"

"Why would I have known? You never came out and said it."

She turns her head to look out the window. She mumbles something to herself, seems, for a moment, to have forgotten that I am here.

"Resemblances, resemblances" is what I think she says. "Is this not the nub of it? *I* see it. But why should *she*? After all—well, it's the law of Mendelian selection. Sometimes the apple falls far from the tree. Or rather, falls far from one tree and close to another."

Her meanings are slipping, again, from my grasp.

"Dvorah," I say. "Help me understand what you're trying to tell me."

When she turns back to face me, she looks miserable.

"I can't," she whispers. "Who could say what I have to say? Who would believe me?"

"Try me," I say. I can feel myself willing her to make the leap back across the divide—back from her delusional world to rationality.

"Don't you see?" she continues. "If we don't work it out together, well, then—"

"Yes?"

"Then we'll both be lost."

"Lost? How?"

"The children shall pay for the sins of their fathers."

I don't know what she's getting at, but behind Dvorah's words I hear a dull gonging: a faint call back to some incomprehensible place where I feel I somehow belong.

"But there's more to it," Dvorah continues. "You see, the children shall also pay for the *sufferings* of their fathers. The two of us, then, taken together—you and I—we are paying a lot."

Dvorah seems to be assuming that I'm following her. I'm accustomed to the way that psychotic patients can turn the usual conventions of conversation on their head—a tangling and distorting of the implicit assumptions that operate between people as they talk. It is harder, though, with Dvorah, to find a foothold in the disorientation. The line between what makes sense and what doesn't has become harder to discern. The craziness seems less crazy; and when she appears to be rational, everything she says is slippery with double meanings and tinged with portent.

"I've often pondered what happens when suffering bleeds into sin," Dvorah is saying, speaking, now, in a calm, pedagogical tone. "It must, you know. It's the natural end point. Just as all rivers must flow into the sea."

Now, I am lost. I sit and listen, hoping that the third ear

that sometimes appears—the ear that filters through the incomprehensible rantings of patients to reveal a pinprick of clarity—will open.

"I realized, when I came here, to the hospital, that it's all of a piece. You. Me. Together. Here. That the fragments are all being brought together, at last.

"Sometimes, it's crystal clear. Like when you take me back to the unit after our sessions. In the moment just before you open the door to let me back in. I watch you—did you know?—as you put the key in the lock. The lock. The key. The way it fits. The way it turns and then opens up the door.

"That's what we are. The lock and key. A perfect fit that will *open the door.*"

Something now seems to occur to her.

"Doctor, do you know anything about string theory?"

I feel like I'm being whiplashed. Just as I begin to get some vague inkling of what Dvorah is talking about, she careens off the road at ninety miles per hour.

"No more than what an article or two in *The New York Times* has taught me," I say.

"Well, it's not just some harmless intellectual endeavor, though maybe that's what the scientists think it is. It's living. It's breathing. It's a monster."

"A monster," I echo. I am looking into Dvorah's eyes. They are not black and red-rimmed now, but open and clear. Gone, the crazed, dark look. I find my own consciousness swimming; I feel the pull of a treacherous undertow that I no longer have the strength to resist.

"It has brought us together," she continues. "This terrible, impossible web of confluences. This is what is really meant by the word *coincidence*. Co-incidents. Random incidents occurring together. And therefore—not random at all. Such co-occurrences—the most improbable things of all; *they happen every day*. Right this minute. *Now*. Impossible. Yes. But *no!* The creationists should take note and abandon their rejection of evolution, of the science that has given voice to the possible impossibilities described by string theory. You see, science does not negate the existence of God, it *proves it*."

Dvorah is excited now; her eyes shine with vitality.

"But here's the catch. It just as surely proves the existence of the Devil."

She raises her hand and sketches something in the air. She makes the same movements, three or four times. At first, I don't know what she's doing, but then I realize she's sketching in the air a large, six-pointed Star of David.

"You. Me," she says. "Past. Present. Suffering. Sin." With each word, she stabs the air at the places where she'd just made the points of her star. "It would be easier to show you if I drew it," she says.

I hand Dvorah a notepad and pen. She sketches a Star of David and labels each point with one of the six words she's just chanted.

"Here, in the middle"—she points to the empty hexagon in the center of the star—"this is the secret at the heart of it all."

"The secret." I seem to have been turned into a voiceless echo.

"Yes. You know what it is."

"I do?"

A ripple of impatience crosses her brow. Then, a faint look of surprise.

"Don't you?" she asks.

"I'm not sure I do," I say.

Dvorah holds up the notepad and taps, with the pen, at the white center of the star, as a teacher might before her class.

"The vacuum of silence," she says. "The inside of a locked-up secret." She is far away, and yet I feel as if I've never been closer to her, never closer than this.

"To which the key—" She continues, speaking slowly, now, oddly drawing out her words. "Has been—" Now, she stops.

"Yes?"

I wait. Nothing. And then.

"—thrown away." She breathes the final word like a sigh.

Dvorah sits back, and weariness seems to pour through her body. She closes her eyes. I have the unsettling feeling that she has gone—that she has somehow climbed out of her own body and wafted away.

"Dvorah?" I say gently, after a time. She opens her eyes. For a moment, they are cloudy and confused; she seems surprised to see me, surprised to find she is still here.

"Doctor?" she says uncertainly.

"Yes, Dvorah?"

"I'd like to go back to the unit, if that's all right with you. Would you take me?"

"Of course."

We walk in silence down the long corridor. I am aware of a terrible feeling that it is not me who is taking Dvorah back to the unit, where I will lock her into a cloistered world of imposed protection and supervision, but she who is accompanying me: that I am the one who will find myself deprived of my freedom and forced to do nothing all day but confront my own demons.

On Friday morning, I arrive early for my supervision session. I sit outside Dr. Finkelstein's office on the antique armchair, studying the tapestry work on the arms. I have sat waiting in this chair now every week for some years—six, to be exact: four as a psychiatric resident, one as chief resident, and now almost a full year since I joined the faculty in my present capacity as attending psychiatrist. All these years, and only now do I notice for the first time that the tapestry on the chair depicts a hunting scene.

I rise so that I might examine the seat. I make out a dozen or more horses, chestnuts, mostly, each mounted by a little rider in maroon hunting gear. Tiny, dime-size hunting dogs in poses of frantic, ground-sniffing motion. A country setting—beautifully rendered trees in different shades of green, stretches of plush grass, and here or there, flowering bushes. I crouch down and search the seat for signs of the fox. Where is the fox? I wonder. With all the meticulous care that has gone into the execution of this scene, surely they could not have forgotten the fox. Perhaps, I think, it is on the panel stretched across the underside of the chair. Carefully, I turn the chair upside down and thrust my head through the four chair legs now sticking upward.

The door to Dr. Finkelstein's office opens. Dr. Finkelstein is understandably surprised to see me crouched over the upturned chair.

"I was just looking for the fox," I say, flustered.

"Yes, of course, Dr. Erick," she replies. She maintains her usual bland, unreadable facial expression, but I fancy I see a trace of humor in her eyes.

"Why don't you come in?" she says.

I put the chair right side up and enter her office.

I've always loved the feel of this space. I came of age here, in this imposing room, gradually metamorphosing from an excited, green student to a trained and self-assured professional. All under the careful guidance of Dr. Finkelstein, who has been mentor, role model, supervisor, and more recently, colleague. I trust her and feel a wash of relief as I settle in my usual place on the right side of the comfortable green couch. Dr. Finkelstein sits, as always, across from me, in the brown armchair.

"So," she begins. "You were looking for a fox."

"I'd never noticed that the chair out there, the tapestry cover—it's a hunting scene. It's beautifully done. Have you ever looked at it? Closely, I mean. I was admiring the handiwork when I realized that it had everything a hunting scene needs—the dogs are even wearing tiny little collars! Except for one thing. No fox."

I can feel myself beginning to flush, the heat rising from the base of my neck in that embarrassing way over which I have no control. Listening to myself speak, I realize how ridiculous I must sound.

"I'm sorry," I continue. "I feel ridiculous."

Dr. Finkelstein looks thoughtful. "What were you planning to talk about today?" she asks.

I hesitate. Of course, I'd been planning to talk about Dvorah, but suddenly, I find I do not want to. I cannot. For a moment, I say nothing. Frantically, in my head, I run through the other patients I am currently treating. I settle quickly on Bernardo, who is suffering with schizophrenia.

"I wanted to talk about Bernardo," I say.

"Go ahead," Dr. Finkelstein says.

I launch into a wooden presentation of how his treatment is going. I dwell on a little glitch that arose some weeks back, which I already discussed briefly with Dr. Finkelstein during a previous supervision session.

Through all this, Dr. Finkelstein sits across from me, nodding in the attentive way she has, making a steeple of her fingers, and every now and then resting her chin on the steeple's tip.

She is thinking about something outside of what I am saying, I know her well enough to know this. But she says little, only listens and nods and occasionally offers one of those supervisor-therapist utterances that help keep the air in a session encouraging and open: "Aaah," or "Yes, I see," or "Go on."

From time to time, I glance at the small gold clock on the antique wooden side table beside Dr. Finkelstein's chair.

Five minutes before the end of the hour, I fall silent.

"I get the feeling," Dr. Finkelstein says, her eyes offering solace, but also a slightly challenging gleam, "that you had something else on your mind when you came in today. Something you didn't get around to addressing."

"Oh?" I say. I feel caught. For the first time in almost six years, sitting in this room, with its huge bay window looking out onto the hospital's impressive and well-maintained formal gardens, I feel wary.

"Hmmm," I add unconvincingly. "Nothing I'm aware of."

"Well," she says, standing now, the sign that the session is over, "if anything comes to mind that you want to discuss, you know where to find me."

I stand, too.

"You needn't wait until next week," she says, accompanying me to the door. On many occasions over the past six years I have grabbed Dr. Finkelstein in the hallway or nurses' station and asked if I could have a few minutes to talk over some concern. But the suggestion of an extra meeting has never come directly from her. She is looking at me now in a concerned, even perturbed way; I cringe at the recognition of the expression. It is one I feel in my own face on a daily basis, sitting with patients. The face of a kindly doctor who knows too much about this person's worrisome affliction, about its signs and symptoms, and of course, sometimes, about the reality of its incurability.

I feel a flash of anger. Who is she to think she knows more about what I am going through than I know myself? How dare she think of me as a patient! *I know what I'm doing,* I think to myself. So what—I turned over her chair and spent a few moments looking for the fox. Does that make me psychologically disturbed? I don't need her to come prying into the depths of my soul, thank you very much.

At the door, Dr. Finkelstein puts her hand on my upper arm for a moment—as a friend might, or a parent—and repeats, in a voice rich with concern, "Really, Dr. Erick. Any time—feel free to call or drop by. I'd be happy to talk, whenever you're ready. Off the record."

Off the record? Is there some kind of record? What is this? Have I been arraigned for a crime—with Dr. Finkelstein a lawyer, appointed by the court? And then, as suddenly as the anger appeared, it dissolves. I am flooded with confusion, and I can feel—how awful!—I can feel my lower lip begin to tremble.

"Thank you," I say. "Absolutely. Yes. I'll do that."

I am flustered all over again and feel desperate to escape Dr. Finkelstein's concerned gaze, with its implicit demand that I address what is unbalancing me, that I acknowledge, head-on, that I am in some kind of trouble.

III.

I'm off to see my parents, again. For some years, I rarely made the trip out to New Jersey, though it's not so very far away from where I live, in Manhattan. I was caught up in my studies and, later, wholly absorbed by the endless days and nights of being a psychiatric resident. It's only in the past year, since being on staff at the hospital, that I've begun seeing my parents again on a more regular basis. And lately, I've found myself craving the quiet and calm of the suburbs. I've found myself wanting to get away—from the city, from my hectic life, even, if I'm fully honest with myself, from Ron.

Of course, Ron knows that something is wrong between us. It's clear he's beginning to feel fed up. But I don't know what to do about it; I don't know, exactly, what is wrong. A shadow has descended over everything, including—especially—over the tentative life we have made together. But I don't want to be worried about or scrutinized. I don't want to have to explain myself to Ron.

I manage to leave my office fairly early, for once; the car clock says 6:26 as I pull out of my parking space. Early enough so that the traffic will not yet be backed up on my favorite route. I shed the burdens of the hospital as I speed along the Saw Mill River Parkway. The effusion of green foliage hanging over the highway seems to absorb my worries the way it inhales the carbon dioxide I breathe out. I turn on the radio, and Fauré's Fantaisie ripples through the air.

By the time I reach the George Washington Bridge, I begin to feel like my old self. I tell myself to trust in my training and what talent I have for the work. I remind myself that confusion and complicated feelings are all part of the work—grist for the mill, as supervisors are fond of saying. I will work it through and all will be well.

As I cross the bridge, I feel more like I'm flying than driving: hanging in the air, midway between river and sky, a good half of the entire island of Manhattan visible to the left, and to the right, the wide water opening out, wedged between sturdy banks.

My mood, though, dampens as I pass through the toll booth of the New Jersey Turnpike.

Cruising along the highway, the vast industrial landscape, which I usually find atmospheric, seems sordid and inhuman. As I speed by Elizabeth, Linden, and Rahway, the working-class houses and apartment blocks, which typically conjure for me images of admirable, hardworking lives, now seem only staunch purveyors of curtailed imagination and stunted dreams.

I realize, just as I'm swerving off the exit ramp, that I've come off the highway too late, at Exit 9, New Brunswick, rather than Exit 10 for Route 287, which would take me directly to Highland Park. No matter, I say to myself. I'll take Route 18, and cross the bridge into Highland Park, then drive the local streets home. It will add no more than ten minutes to the trip. Fifteen, at most.

Only when I am crossing the bridge onto Raritan Avenue does it occur to me that I've not come this way in years, per-haps not since leaving for college, when I was eighteen. I've strolled many times down Raritan Avenue with one or both of my parents—to get bagels, go for ice cream or out for a meal—but I've had no reason to come down this far.

On a whim, at First Avenue, I turn right. Slowly, I cruise down the street and come to a halt before the squat concrete building that was once the Jewish Youth Center. It was sold some years ago and is now a Kaplan Institute for high school tutoring. I pull up in front of the building.

A group of teenagers mills about, some standing, some sitting propped on their backpacks, talking and laughing. One girl puffs nervously on a cigarette, trying to look at ease.

It strikes me as odd that, in all these years, I've not thought to swing by and take a glance at the place where so much of my own youth unfolded. But then that seems to be the way life is: one moves on.

Watching the youngsters with their precarious bravura, I think about my own youth, and am aware of how my treatment of Dvorah has plunged me back into that all-encompassing world of *Jewishness*, with its unshaking horizon and orienting perspective: a world I left behind long ago.

There was another time in my life that I encountered the awful black pit of my childhood, besides my first day as a psychiatric intern, when I looked into the eyes of Mr. Husani, the manic patient. I was a teenager—and it was for me the worst incarnation of blackness I have known. I never, though, made the connection between these two experiences until now. It was here, at what was once the Jewish Youth Center, that for many years I enjoyed happy weekends with a bunch of rowdy, eager comrades and a series of enthusiastic leaders, our *Madrichim*. We learned Hebrew folk dancing and planned events around Jewish holidays which marked off the year in rituals that ranged from festive and ebullient to somber. It was in the cheerful rooms of the Jewish Youth Center that I first learned my Hebrew letters, baked *hammantashen*, fried latkes, and made up comic songs about bad-guy figures from Jewish lore, such as the evil Haman or slave-driving Pharaoh. And here that I developed my first crush; I was always besotted with one of the *Madrichim* and later attached my affections to one or another of the boys in my group. These rooms were a part of my beautiful world, and I loved them as I loved everything in my life, except for the intermittent black nights.

Just after my fourteenth birthday, the Youth Movement

arranged for a two-week retreat at a barracks-style encampment in the nearby Catskills. I was elected a team leader, which involved reporting to the *Madrichim* and sharing some leadership duties. It was to be the longest time I'd ever spent away from my parents' home but this did not concern me. I was ready for it, and besides, I would be with my second family.

We sang Hebrew songs in the bus on the way up, the atmosphere tingling with the charged, erotic energy of a crowd of kids hurtling into adolescence. I don't remember ever having been so happy, so excited, so possessed by a feeling of both deep belonging and endless future possibilities. We sailed out into the wide blue sky; the horizon, which took the impressive silhouette of the mountains, was all my own.

The first week whirled by. In the evenings, I practiced with the choir for a gala performance we were preparing for the last night of the camp.

Mealtimes were especially fun. After our robust fare—salads and hearty stew, soups, and an array of desserts, which included a dark nut and chocolate cake I particularly liked—we would clear the trestle tables and then push them to the sides of the dining hall. Our resident choirmaster, an accomplished Israeli accordionist, would spread the fan of his instrument and the folk dancing would begin. We'd speed around the room, red-faced, smiling, and alive with motion, spinning round and round, buoyed by the music and the spirit, and by a togetherness as ancient and natural and powerful as the force of gravity keeping our feet in contact with the ground.

Then, when our choirmaster put down his accordion, we would collapse onto the floor, sated and laughing and waiting to regain our breath. We would make our way to the trestle table on one wall, where the kitchen crew had set up urns of hot water. We'd put a spoonful of instant coffee and two of sugar into our cups, add a little water, and rapidly froth up the mixture with a spoon, then add more water to fill the cups. This would result in a frothy, whitish head, which gave the impression of café au lait; having just eaten meat, we were required by the dietary laws of Kashrut to wait four hours before we could have dairy.

At the end of the first Sabbath, we gathered in the dining hall to watch a documentary movie. We set out rows of chairs, and one of the *Madrichim* finally managed to erect the screen, which was supposed to pull up easily from a long black metal tube but kept collapsing on itself. Another *Madrich* fiddled with the projector. After an hour or so of these preparations, we all took our seats and someone turned out the lights. The projector flickered to life. I settled into the front row, legs draped over the arm of the wooden chair, and watched as the title burned its letters into the screen: *Night and Fog*.

I was not prepared for what came next, though perhaps there is no preparing for such things.

At first, I puzzled over the image—as I might have puzzled had a sudden twister lifted the room and hurtled it through the air—before grasping the terrible reality of what I was seeing.

A bulldozer, working over piles of dirt. The lighting of the movie was poor; the projector flickered mistily, pouring its black-and-white images through the air, where they smacked up against the screen, then slammed onto the retinas of my eyes to ricochet around my head. Back and forth, the bulldozer lunged and withdrew, turning over its huge piles, which rolled slowly, luxuriantly, against the blades of the plough. Naked bodies, skeletally thin, bony limbs intertwining, coupling, uncoupling, the thin skin of malnourished faces stretched across bony skulls, open eyes, grimacing mouths, this one gaping, that one pressed tightly closed, rolling, rolling, a morbid dance of corpses as they turn and turn and sweep toward the pit. The machine is powerful, it pushes and pulls, finally pushes its load into the pit, then returns, pulling back, to work over a fresh crop of corpses and deliver them to the grave.

My mind seized on a thought—any thought, to rescue me, too, from being plunged down into the ground. *Who was operating the bulldozer?* This thought appeared in my mind as a thin red line of words piercing the suffocating black plunge. *Who was it sitting there, pulling the lever, turning the wheel? Who was he, and what was he thinking?*

Here was the black pit I had trembled before the whole of my life, from the time of my very first memories: here it was, in eerily translucent form, flickering upon the screen. When the film ended, and the screen showed nothing but a large, unsteady patch of illumination, and the lights were turned on, there was an unearthly silence. More than a hundred of us crowded into the room and not one sound. I knew then that the walls of my cheerful world had crashed in, that my childhood was over: that I would never again feel pure happiness. That for me, though the sky might be bright for eight or ten or twelve hours of each twenty-four, my soul would never again, not truly, not fully, know the sun's light.

I sleepwalked through the rest of the retreat.

At night I would lie awake, but the blackness, which I still feared as much as ever, was no longer a mystery.

After returning from the retreat, I felt an intense pull toward the ritual and practice of Orthodox Judaism. My home was decidedly secular, though infused with an inchoate spirit of the religion which had affected my parents' own lives but from which they had, each for different reasons, turned away.

It worked for them, being cut off from Judaism. It must have been disconcerting to have me return from the retreat insisting on maintaining the Jewish dietary laws and wearing the uniform of modesty that Orthodox girls my age wore— ankle-length skirts, sensible shoes, and long-sleeved blouses; a far cry from the miniskirts, platform shoes, and skimpy halter tops I'd favored before.

They took it all with their usual quiet good humor. They stayed out of the way as I threw myself into the rigors that went along with my new identity.

I had studied Hebrew for years. Now I went at it with new determination, adding classes in Torah and Talmud into my already busy schedule. I became a *Madrich* in the Youth Movement and spent every weekend at the Jewish Youth Center. Homework I crammed into the wee hours of the morning, fueled by a kind of urgency I'd never before known.

I was on fire with it all—with the feeling that everything contained some mystical meaning that gave full coherence to the world around me.

One afternoon, I was working with my friend Diane on a school project at her home. The subject was totalitarianism, and we were struggling through a chapter in Hannah Arendt's masterwork on the subject.

I hadn't noticed that Diane's father had come into the dining room, where we had our papers and books spread across the table. We were in heated discussion—the kind adolescents thrive on—about the implications of historical events like Stalin's reign of terror or the Holocaust on the nature and intentions of God. I forget which one of us was arguing which of the obvious sides of this debate; I remember only that we were both flushed with the pleasure of young minds beginning to grasp the intricacies and larger meanings of thought.

Diane's father walked over to the table, displaying the oddest expression I had ever seen—his features suddenly slack and motionless, as if his face had turned into a rubber replica of itself. Diane was in midsentence when her father spoke: I remember the peculiar image I had of her half-spoken sentence extinguishing itself into the air as a small puff of smoke.

"This is the answer you're dancing around," he said in his thick Polish accent. He yanked up the sleeve of his shirt. He'd not thought to undo the cuff of his shirtsleeve, and now a small white button popped from his wrist and sprang to the floor.

We both looked at the skin on the inside of Diane's father's forearm to see the series of murky dark green numbers tattooed into his flesh, the ink fuzzy at the edges, having spread with age.

I had long known that Diane's father had spent two years in Auschwitz, where his parents, his first wife, and their two young children had been gassed. He alone had survived and found his way, after the War, to America. Miraculously, he had made a new life for himself.

"I can tell you what this says about the nature of God. About the 'interplay of man's free will and the poles of evil and good.' "

These had been my words, a few minutes back, and now I cringed at the sound of them.

"This says one of two things. Either that there is no God, or that the Devil and God are one. There's nothing more to be said on the subject."

He yanked down his sleeve and then turned and walked from the room. I heard him add, under his breath: "At least not in my house."

Remembering this now, I start. *The Devil and God are one.* Didn't Dvorah say something very close to this, only today?

After her father's statement, Diane and I said nothing further. Quietly, I began gathering my papers and books and packed them away in my satchel. At the door, I leaned forward to give Diane the usual parting hug. She felt stiff and unyielding; it was like hugging a tree.

We never talked about that moment. Nor did we ever again engage in discussions about God.

That was the first crack in my love affair with religion. The second came not long after—five or six months later.

It was an ordinary Saturday night at the Youth Center. We leadership members were sitting over coffee, discussing the upcoming month's program. I was aware of the deep pleasures of shared background and beliefs and commitment to a singular direction and way of life.

Slowly, strangely, I felt myself being removed from the situation: everyone and everything was suddenly fuzzy and indistinct, as if my ears were stuffed with cotton and my eyes coated with oil. I felt dizzy and faint, and as if I were floating above everyone, peering down through a thick bank of clouds.

Suddenly, all of them—including my dearest, closest friend, Diane—seemed like ridiculous, deluded puppets. *Who is thinking for himself?* I heard a voice say inside my head. The room had become suffocating, and I found myself gasping for breath. Next, I was slumped in my chair. I blinked up to see a group of concerned faces hovering around me— puppet faces, not the people I knew. I heard someone screeching—"Go away! You sicken me!"—and then realized with confusion that the voice was coming from me. In the hazy distance, I heard someone cry out that they should call an ambulance, and sometime later I found myself being hauled away by medical workers and attached to an oxygen mask, and there I was, looking around the tubing at Diane's concerned face, aware of the sensation of speeding through the night.

Later, at the hospital, I listened as the doctor explained to my parents—ignoring me, speaking as if I were not there—that I had had a severe and protracted anxiety attack. They'd administered a sedative, which explained why I was now feeling so pleasantly floaty and calm, though unable to speak, my tongue a dry slug stuck to the bottom of my mouth.

"From what the friend told us," the doctor was saying, "Your daughter has been under a good deal of pressure."

My parents were nodding. "Yes," I heard them say, "she does push herself."

"I suggest she take a rest. A few days off from school. No extracurricular activities for a while."

How odd, to hear my Jewish involvements described as "extracurricular activities"—but in the same moment, I felt a flood of relief.

We went home. I slept on and off for two days, during which I vaguely remember being fed bowls of chicken soup in my room by my mother—the first *traif* food that had passed my lips in almost three years. This did not disturb me. Rather, the taste of the soup carried with it the same relief I'd felt in the discharge room at the hospital, listening to the doctor talk about me as though I were not there.

Whatever happened to me that day—the words *anxiety attack* didn't capture it; it felt larger, more spiritual, less explicable than that—did not happen again, though the gulf between me and my world of Jewish involvement remained. When my friends asked how soon I would be returning to the Youth Center, I mouthed the words the doctor had used: *I need a break, I need to cut back on my extracurricular activities.*

My modest skirts and long-sleeved shirts remained hanging in my closet above my now-unused sensible shoes. I made a trip to Macy's with my mother, where several hours in the juniors' section yielded a new wardrobe of jeans and T-shirts and chunky-heeled shoes, along with a slinky, sleeveless dress nipped in at the waist that was for us a bit of an extravagance.

Soon, my old circle stopped asking when I would return. I threw myself into my schoolwork, which helped me land a scholarship to Columbia University. The next fall, I moved to the student dorms and began my major in premed, with a few philosophy courses thrown in.

Oddly enough, I didn't give much thought to what had happened—to the rupture in my world that changed everything—in the way that young people can blithely alter the course of their lives. My mind was now on other things. I met a new group of friends, and my life became a busy round of hours spent in labs, dissecting small animals or juggling test tubes, or in the library, memorizing chemical equations and cracking my head on the endless impossible physics problems that did not come easily to me. I explored the city, spent long, heady evenings in cafés, and succumbed happily to my first serious experiences of eroticism and love.

On occasion, riding the subway downtown, I would see a Hasidic woman or man, head pressed over a prayer book or other Hebrew text, lips moving noiselessly or forehead furrowed in concentration. I would feel a deep tug somewhere far away—deep inside my being—and I would stifle the feeling and turn away.

Of course, Dvorah knows none of this. Though I confess that, every now and again, when she falls silent in that way she has—not a comfortable moment of reflection but an accusatory refusal, her mouth clamped tight—I feel as if Dvorah knows everything about me, all the details of my past, and is damning me for betrayal.

The little crowd in front of the Kaplan Institute has dwindled, and now the last of them—two girls who look like sisters—climb into a car that has pulled up behind my own. I glance at the clock on the dashboard. Heavens, 9:15. I've been sitting here for more than half an hour. I start up the car and pull away from the curb.

Ten minutes later, I turn in to my parents' driveway. I grab my overnight bag from the trunk and go inside.

My parents are in the kitchen, sitting over cups of herbal tea.

"Darling, you're here," my mother says. "Hope you don't mind—we were famished, so we ate. Yours is in the warming drawer. We held off on dessert, though, so we can eat that together."

I retrieve my plate and join them at the table. My chronic tiredness of late hangs over me. I pick at my food, aware of an intense agitation that makes me feel as if my entire body is prickling with poison ivy.

From the corner of my eye, I see my mother cast a worried glance toward my father that is meant to be surreptitious. I make no attempt at conversation; I sit in a strange frozen gloom, push the food around on my plate, and every now and then place a forkful in my mouth.

"Papa," I finally say. "I wonder if we might talk—" Now I flash a glance my mother's way. "Alone, if that's all right."

"Of course, Deb," he says.

"Go ahead," my mother says, rising to take the plates to the sink. I follow my father to his study. We enter, and he closes the door. I sit in the blue chair by his desk; my father sits opposite me in his leather reading chair.

"Well," he begins. "What's on your mind?"

"I have a patient, in the hospital. I shouldn't really talk to you about her—confidentiality and whatnot. Sitting with her in sessions, I find myself wondering all kinds of things that really concern her less than they concern me."

"Oh?"

I'm not sure how to proceed. I just plunge in.

"She's suffering from a severe postpartum depression," I continue. "She's on medication, and I meet her four times a week for psychotherapy. I'm trying to help her unravel the content of her delusions: she has all kinds of preoccupations that torture her. So that when the medication takes full effect"—I am waiting myself to hear what I have to say—"so that when the medication takes full effect, perhaps she'll be less haunted.

"I suppose I believe this haunting has played some role in setting the biological events on their collision course in the first place. Helped along by the hormones of pregnancy and childbirth. She'll likely keep having children—she already has seven, and she's only thirty-two. If I can help her face her demons, then perhaps, when she's pregnant again, and the hormones go haywire, perhaps there'll be no demons to send her over the edge."

I have been in such a whirlwind of confusion that nothing has been making sense. And yet these thoughts, as they tumble from my mouth, actually sound quite coherent. It's a relief to be talking this way to my father. I take comfort in his kindly, interested face.

"She talks mostly about her father. I think he's a loving

man, but he told her many things when she was a very little girl that have plagued her all her life. I imagine he had good intentions, but the result has been devastating."

A shadow crosses my father's face. I wonder what he is thinking.

"On the one hand, I find myself thinking, How could her father have told her such things? Such terrible stories—true stories—from his own past. Did he not have any concept of the need to let children believe in a safe and just world, at least until they have the cognitive capacity to make some sense of it all? Until they feel secure enough to believe in the possibility of a good world, despite the awful realities?"

Papa's eyes seem to have darkened. It is as if he is burrowing away from me, into a secret and solitary place. I'm afraid to stop. I'm afraid that I'll never again have the courage to ask my father what I want to ask him.

"Papa, I've had such confusing feelings sitting there with my patient, about the way I, myself, was raised."

My father is clenching his jaw. I can see the muscles working along the length of both sides of his face. I can feel that he wants me to stop what I'm saying, but I can't. I must see this through to the end.

"At first, hearing how much she has suffered, I felt grateful that you never told me anything about your past. I know nothing—nothing at all. For heaven's sake, I only discovered you came from Poland when I was nineteen years old.

"But, Papa, sometimes when I'm with my patient, I find myself thinking—Well, as awful as it is, *at least you know*. At least you know who your father is. Where he's been, what happened to him and to his family."

My father is looking at me with pleading eyes. But I can't stop. I won't.

"I sit there, listening to my poor, psychotic patient, and thinking—*at least you know who you are.*"

Now, though, I do stop. I wait to hear what my father will say. He has sunk down in his chair and is looking up at me from eyes that are like deep wells, as if he is peering up from the darkness and out over the edge into the light, where I, his daughter, am sitting.

I wait some time. Then, I see the pain slide out of my father's face. I see the kindliness return to his eyes, as if he has traveled up from the well into which he had fallen and is now, again, aboveground, in the light, with me.

"When I came to this country, I was only a child, as you know," he begins. "But I was a clever boy, if you don't mind my saying so. I had always given everything a lot of thought. I realized that if I was going to grow up to make a good life for myself, the first thing I needed to do was learn English. Really learn it, so that I'd speak like a native."

My father has always been articulate—and has never spoken with a trace of an accent.

"I was lucky enough to be given a wonderful home." His eyes stray to the picture of his adoptive parents on the shelf opposite and rest there for a moment. "I was very grateful for that. It allowed me to just—well, get on with things. I studied harder than anyone I knew, but I also played hard. Every kind of sport that American boys play. Baseball, of course, but also basketball and football and later wrestling and rowing. I was going to become an American, in the fullest possible way."

He goes to the window.

"I very quickly realized something else," he says, gazing out of the window, his back toward me. "That I couldn't be an American—not really, not deep down in my soul—as long as

I was also—" My father's voice breaks off. I give him a moment, but he does not continue.

"Also what, Papa? As long as you were also what?"

"As long as I was also what I was before. As long as I kept the past alive."

He turns to face me.

"I had no choice. I had to bury it all, if I was to go on and become what I wanted to become."

"I see," I say quietly. I am wondering what to do with the angry feeling rising in my chest. I feel like saying something unkind to my father, but I don't. I clamp my lips closed as I've learned to do with my patients and wait to see if he is going to say anything further.

"I never spoke of it because—well, because I was trying to get on with my life. Trying to stay in the new life I'd built. Which of course—wonderfully—had you in it!"

Now he smiles the warm, fatherly smile that has always made me happy. But I can still feel the anger. I am waiting for him to break the cold, lonely silence that I find I'm thoroughly sick of.

"Not long after the Nazis occupied the area—I was five years old—my mother took me on a long journey. We traveled by horse and carriage to a small town some miles away. My father had done business for many years with a Ukrainian. Being a Jew, though, he was no longer allowed to sell to this man—his name was Olansky—and they had gone their separate ways. It was to Olansky's house that my mother took me. I was tired and hungry after our long ride, and happy when the driver of the carriage pulled up in front of a modest, well-kept house on the main street of the town. We were greeted by Olansky and his wife and ushered into their house. My mother talked with them quietly for some time, while I sat by the hearth with their two children—one was younger than I was, and the other a little older, both of them boys. We drank strong, sweet tea and ate thick slices of heavy bread with fresh butter."

"Finally, my mother came to say good-bye. 'We'll come for you, when it's over,' she said.

"I did not understand what she was saying. When I kissed my mother good-bye, I felt a great heaviness in my chest, as if someone were sitting down on me and would not get up.

"I've always had fair coloring—you take after me, of course. I was able to pass as Olansky's nephew. I spent the War years with them.

"When the War was over, an American came to the town and went from house to house, asking if there were any Jewish children who had been sheltered. He was a representative of the Jewish Agency and was offering passage to adoptive Jewish homes in the United States. Several families came forward, including my own. Having spent five years with them, and from such an early age, I had come to think of them as my family. I think they had grown to love me, in their way, but the time had come for them to move forward as best they could. They probably thought it best, in any case, for me to return to my own people. The agency representative thanked them for the risks they had taken on my behalf. I packed a suitcase, said my good-byes, and left with the American, who spoke some German—we'd all been forced to learn German, during the occupation—which allowed us to communicate.

"I came across on the boat with a dozen or more other children like me. We slept together, ate together, and when we landed in America, we all went off to our new homes."

I am looking at my father standing by the window. I am

wondering how it feels for him, after all these years, to be telling me what he's telling me.

"Thank you, Papa," I say.

He walks back around his desk and sinks down into his reading chair. He looks weary, and suddenly much older.

I rise and walk over to where he is sitting, then lean down and kiss his cheek. He takes hold of my hand and gives it a squeeze.

"I guess I'll be getting along to bed," I say.

"Good night, darling. Get some rest. You need it."

At the door, I turn around to give one last good-night smile to my father. He doesn't see me; his elbow is propped up on the armrest, and he is resting his head in his hand. His eyes are closed, but I can see that the flesh of his face is hanging slackly. His mouth is partly open and pulled down in an expression of grief. I quickly turn and leave the room, pulling the door quietly shut behind me.

I spend the weekend reading, sleeping, and taking walks. On Sunday, I arrive back at my apartment in the late afternoon. When I enter the hallway, I hear the telephone ringing. *Ron*, I think. I let it ring, then hear the hollow sound of my own voice as the answering machine picks up. I stand still and listen.

"Deb. It's Ron." A long pause. I hear something in the silence. It's as if I can hear him drifting off far away, out of reach.

"Deb." Again, my name. How can one syllable hold such a clear, sad sense of defeat? I walk over to where the phone sits on the side table and reach down to the receiver. I just rest my hand there, though; I don't pick it up.

"Call me when you can," Ron says, and then I hear the click as he hangs up.

I walk into my bedroom and fall onto the bed. I don't brush my teeth, I don't take off my clothes. I just fall onto the bed and drift unhappily into a blank and dreamless sleep.

I awaken to a pale dawn. I've been asleep for twelve hours. I feel crumpled and crusty. I take a long shower, though this does little to clean away the seedy feel. I dress, skip my usual coffee and cereal, and head out. I may as well get to the hospital early, I think. I have a fair amount of paperwork to attend to, and anyway, I am eager to be in my office.

I feel better once I am back on the hospital grounds. I go straight to my office. The giant oak tree, stationed not far from my window, leans over the grass, shaking its leaves gently in the morning breeze.

I plug in the small electric jug I keep in my office. When it boils, I make a cup of tea and busy myself with paperwork. The morning passes quickly in a round of meetings. Then, I eat lunch at my desk and whittle away at a report until it is time to go for Dvorah.

She is ready, as always, sitting in the blue chair by the nurses' station. She rises when she sees me, and we walk back together to my office in silence.

She begins speaking as soon as she is seated.

"Doctor, I don't know what you know about the Messiah," she begins. "I've been thinking about him all weekend. I wanted to discuss this with you."

"What, specifically, were you thinking about?"

"Well, you must know that the Messiah will come and free all of us—including the dead—when evil and good coex-

ist in the right combination and strength. It is up to the righteous to be as righteous as they can be. This really motivates
people to live good and moral lives. A lot of people I know
take it upon themselves to work as hard as they can in order
to help bring the Messiah about."

She is talking rapidly and is clearly excited. It is the first
time I have seen anything like manic thinking or speech with
Dvorah. I jot down a note about this on my pad; later, I must
give the appearance of this symptom some thought. Now, I
focus on what she is saying.

Dvorah leans forward in her chair. Her eyes are shining.

"One thing that's always intrigued me about the great
Kabbalists is their ability to see a transcendent purpose in
even the grimmest circumstances. You see, for the Kabbalists, the more dire the historical situation for the Jews,
the deeper the symbolic meaning—the closer, paradoxically,
it brings the Jews to the coming of the Messiah. It stands to
reason, if you think about it. When would the Messiah be
more needed, more joyously received, than in the darkest of
times?"

Now, Dvorah sits back. She seems to be waiting for me to
say something. I don't know what to say, so I remain quiet.

"Don't you see, Doctor? We *all* have our role to play. Even
the *unrighteous* among us. I realized, over the weekend, that
the quotient of *evil* is just as important a part of the mix as the
quotient of *good*."

I try to sort out what Dvorah is saying but come up
blank.

She continues: "All this time, I thought I was at odds with
my people. That I was therefore cast out, a fallen angel if you
like. But there's another way to look at it. *God needs the evil as
well as the good.* It's part of His plan for us. How can evil be

routed out of the human soul if it is never given expression?

"Just as Jesus died for the sins of the Christians, so we bearers of evil live out the evil in all human souls on behalf of humanity, so that the coming of the Messiah might be hastened!"

Now she looks at me triumphantly. I had really believed that Dvorah was on her way to recovery—that it would be just a matter of weeks until she would be completely well and could rejoin her family.

"What's the matter, Doctor? Aren't you thrilled? This bears on you as much as it bears on me."

I try to stifle the feeling of disappointment that has risen within me, but I don't have the strength. I flounder to find the right thing to say.

"Doctor, what's the matter?" Dvorah sounds alarmed. "Tell me! I insist you tell me what you're thinking!"

"Dvorah," I say wearily. "You can't just demand that a person tell you what they're thinking."

"Why not? You do it all the time! Do you think it's fair to operate with dual principles? One set of rules for you, another set for me?"

"I'm your doctor, Dvorah. You're my patient. I'm here to help you."

Now she leaps up from her chair.

"*Liar!* Don't you think I'm just as sick of having to put up with your lies? This *treatment,* or whatever you want to call it, is just as much about *you* as it is about *me!* You know this as well as I do."

She looks wildly around the room, as if expecting to find all of a sudden that we are not alone, that our meeting is being witnessed by someone else.

"Don't you see?" she says. *"I've found us a way out!"*

She gulps a little sob, then sits down. She looks down at her lap, where her hands lie like two small limp creatures. Tears stream from her face.

"I thought you'd be happy," she whispers. "I really did. I thought that despite everything—all the role-playing and nonsense that goes on here, 'Yes, Doctor,' 'No, Doctor,' all your comforting little insights—that underneath it all, you recognize as much as I do what is really going on."

I feel blindsided. I feel invaded. I feel like this patient—and after all, *she's only a patient, isn't she?*—I feel she's climbed right into my skin and is ferreting into a place I didn't even know existed within me.

I feel like crying myself.

I don't know what to do.

I do nothing. I only sit here, looking across at this tiny, slight woman who eight weeks ago I'd never met, and who now seems to be destroying my world.

"Well? Aren't you going to *say anything?*" she says.

"I'm not sure I know what to say," I reply.

Now, she looks bewildered. *"You're my doctor . . . ,"* she whispers.

I take off my glasses and rub my temples. *I'll take her back to the unit,* I think. Then I'll go straight to Dr. Finkelstein's office and make an appointment to see her. Today, if possible. This cannot wait until Friday.

"Come, Dvorah, let's go back to the unit," I say.

"But, Doctor," she protests. "I only just got here!"

"I need to think some things over," I say. "We'll meet again tomorrow at our usual time."

I walk her back to the unit. She turns to look at me as I close the unit door. In her eyes, I see something even darker and stranger than I've seen before.

*   *   *

I don't go to see Dr. Finkelstein, however. I return to my own office and sit in my chair for a very long time, looking at the oak tree. In the distance, down by the driveway, a gardener drags a rake over the grass, collecting fallen blossoms into a soft and delicately colored pile.

The next day, Dvorah refuses to see me.

"She's in her room," the nurse explains. "Says she has a stomachache. If it persists, I'll have her looked at later today."

The following day, there's another excuse.

On Thursday, I tell the nurse to bring Dvorah to the dayroom.

I expect her to look defiant, but when the nurse brings her in, I see that Dvorah looks pale and demure.

"Hello, Dr. Erick," she says quietly.

"Hello, Dvorah," I reply.

I am seated at one of the cheerful tables in the dayroom; it is made of light wood with a bright insert of orange Formica. She sits opposite me in a matching chair.

"Look, Doctor," she begins. Her voice sounds controlled. "I really appreciate everything you've tried to do for me, but I think that perhaps I'm just not up to it."

"Not up to what, Dvorah?"

"All your prying and poking about. Sometimes, I feel as if you're a mechanic. Like you're going at me with pliers and wrenches, and will take me all apart until there is nothing left."

I struggle to absorb what Dvorah is saying.

"I'm sorry it's been so difficult for you," I say. What I am thinking at the same time is *I'm also sorry it's been so difficult for me.*

"Perhaps we might approach things in a different way," I continue. I am casting about—uselessly—for something to mask my own sense of desperation and defeat regarding Dvorah's situation.

She raises her eyes and looks directly into mine. I see only a great and all-encompassing sadness.

"I don't really think there'd be any point to that," she says.

"Why is that?"

"We'd only end up going around in the same circles."

"I'd like to try," I say quietly.

Dvorah whispers something so softly I don't hear what it is she's said.

"I'm sorry," I say. "I didn't hear what you said."

"There's a problem," she says a little louder, though her voice is still a whisper.

"What's that?" I ask, keeping my voice low, to match hers.

"There are certain things I can't tell you."

"Why is that?"

Now, her voice drops again. I have to lean forward to catch what she is saying.

"You'd think me even crazier than you already think I am." Dvorah's eyes are glistening with tears.

"You could try me," I say. "Sometimes these things require—"

"Yes?"

"—a leap of faith."

Her voice is still the lowest of whispers. "What would you know about faith?"

"Actually, I know a fair amount about faith," I reply.

Dvorah shakes her head. "It's too late," she breathes. "It's all too late."

"What's too late?"

"You. Me. There, in your office. There really isn't any point. There's nothing either of us can do to change what has happened."

There is a clue embedded in all of this; I can feel it, pulsing somewhere within her words. I just can't bring it to light.

"Remember what we talked about, the first time we met?" Dvorah says, looking at me with such pleading it makes me want to take her in my arms and soothe her, tell her everything is going to be all right.

"You thought I was just plain psychotic—well, maybe I was. But I also knew what I was talking about. It's funny, the whole question of craziness. Being crazy is not what people think."

"I know," I say quietly. "It must be very confusing."

"I told you that nothing changes, not really. That Nietzsche was right—*the eternal return of the same.* And that everything happens for a reason. You told me you didn't believe that. You told me that, in the end, it's just hormones and brain chemistry."

I remain silent so that Dvorah might complete what it is she has to say.

"I realize I can't go on talking with you, knowing you feel that way. We're on different planets. It's like I'm shouting into the vacuum of the space between us. It's not going to get us—to get me—anywhere."

"I appreciate that you've told me all this," I say. "Perhaps we might think of it as a new beginning. Perhaps it's been helpful for you to air your views."

Dvorah bows her head for a moment. I think I see a look of defeat flash across her face.

"Yes, Doctor," she says. And then, nothing more.

We sit that way for a time in silence. For almost ten minutes—an awkward, impossible eternity.

Finally, she speaks.

"May I go now?" she whispers.

"Yes, of course," I say, as kindly as I can. "Tomorrow is the staff retreat. I'll have the doctor on call visit you over the weekend, and then I'll be in again to see you on Monday," I say.

"Very well," she says. She rises and leaves the dayroom, without any further parting glance or words.

It is Sunday morning; I awaken early. Ron is lying asleep beside me. I think about our lovely evening last night. It has been a long time since we have felt so relaxed with each other; in our first few years together, we had many evenings like the one we had last night. Talking over dinner, holding hands while strolling to the movies, and later talking about the film as we sat drinking coffee in our favorite café. I look at him lying there and feel a welling up of fondness.

Last night Ron broached the subject of marriage again for the first time in months. Immediately, I felt the relaxed, happy mood slipping away.

"Maybe now's not the best time. I feel so stressed with work. I'm not sure I can handle planning a wedding. Maybe we could think about it over the summer? I'll take a couple of weeks off. July, perhaps?"

Ron wiped his mouth with the napkin, then looked at me steadily and long. When he spoke, his voice was measured.

"What is it? Why are you so resistant? Maybe we just need to, well, do it."

I looked across at him and realized tears were springing to my eyes.

"Deb," he said quietly. "What is it?"

"I don't know. I just feel sort of—"

"Yes?"

"Lost. I don't know, I feel like I'm slipping into a terrible place."

Ron—he seemed to be drifting away, right before my eyes. I had the feeling that if I were to reach out and take his hand, I would find he was no longer there.

"I can help you," he said quietly. "If only you'll let me."

"That's just it," I say, the tears now sliding down my cheeks. "I feel as if you can't. I feel as if I'm looking at you— and that you're on the other side. Like there's some raging river between us and no way for either of us to cross it."

Ron was silent. Too silent.

Now it was as if my own self was drifting away. As if I were reaching out not for him but for the calm, professional *Dr. Erick self* I have come to rely on, who saved me long ago from a different, frightened self.

Then, I saw the strain in Ron's face. How long had he shown signs of strain? I looked closely at him and realized that something was different about the way his face looked. When did this happen?

"What are you thinking?" I asked.

He looked at me with such sadness and pain. "I'm thinking that perhaps you're right. Perhaps things are different. Perhaps things have changed."

"Work, the hospital—" I faltered.

"Maybe it's more than your job. Deb, I'm at my wit's end. I don't know what to do anymore."

After we came home, we made love slowly, lovingly. It was

as if all the good feeling and affection and warmth of the years we've been together flooded into our lovemaking. When it was over, I lay in his arms, crying softly.

"Sssh, it's okay," he whispered, stroking my hair. But I knew it was not okay. I felt as if all of it—my calm, my control, Ron, my world—were slowly washing out to sea.

Now, I get up and go into the bathroom to wash. Ron rolls over, lets out a sigh, but doesn't awaken. I open my closet and choose a long skirt I bought last summer, a crisp cotton work blouse, and a linen jacket I've not worn for years. I take the large square silk scarf my mother gave me years ago when she was cleaning out her wardrobe and stuff it into the pocket of my jacket. In the foyer, I take my pocketbook and lock the front door quietly behind me.

On the subway, I reach into my pocket and withdraw the scarf. I fold it into a triangle and place it over my hair, tying it in a knot at the back of my neck.

At Seventy-second Street, I change to the 3. We trundle into Brooklyn, and I sit for an age: station after station of unfamiliar names. Finally, I get off at the Crown Heights–Utica Avenue stop.

It is only nine o'clock on a Sunday morning, but the streets are alive with shoppers. After their Sabbath day of rest, people have a lot to do to prepare for the week.

I join the flow of walkers. I see other women of about my age, though none without children. With my long skirt and jacket and hair scarf, I fit right in.

I find myself outside a bakery; the enticing aroma of fresh breads and pastries reminds me that I've not eaten breakfast.

I follow a middle-aged woman inside and join the long line snaking around the small space.

This is Dvorah's world, I think. I look around the shop,

wondering if any of the women here actually know her. Besides her husband and mother, she's not had visitors to the hospital; she's not wanted to see anyone else. Many of the women are chatting in Yiddish. Up at the counter, they are ordering in Yiddish. I find myself looking into the eyes of a woman ahead of me, much younger than I am—she looks like a teenager—who is resting her hands on her very pregnant belly. She smiles a half smile, as if she thinks she knows me but isn't certain, and I smile back. She is radiant, this girl, as she waits in line for her pastries.

The line is moving quickly. The young woman I smiled at is gone. Women leave with large boxes or bulging plastic bags. Others come in and stand behind me.

It is my turn. I survey the glass cases in front of me and the bread bins behind the counter. I feel flustered. My eyes settle on an apple pastry in the case directly in front of me.

"One of these, please," I say.

The lady serving behind the counter seems surprised to hear a customer order in English.

She points to the apple pastry. "A box of these?" she queries. "Yes," I say, growing more flustered by the minute. I suppose that a woman my age does not come into a shop like this and order a single pastry. Especially not on a Sunday morning, when she'd be shopping for her family—at least for today, if not for a day or two in advance as well. A woman my age would be likely to have upward of five children, possibly eight or nine. A husband, of course. And endless relatives dropping by. The woman places a dozen or so of the apple pastries carefully and quickly into a large box, separating them into two layers with a piece of wax paper.

I feel a little hand take hold of mine. I look down to see a girl of three or four gazing longingly into the lower shelves of the glass cabinet before us. She is eyeing a rack of donuts dusted in powdered sugar. She says something in Yiddish which I do not, of course, understand, and then turns her sweet face up to mine. When she sees that I am not her mother, she pulls her hand away and her eyes fill with tears. Before I can look around to find her mother, I hear a voice behind me, calling out "Ruthele," and the little girl runs to her mother.

"Nothing else?" the woman behind the counter is asking.

I spin back to face her. "Aah, perhaps these." I point to a braided roll.

"One dozen? Two?" she asks briskly. The store is filled with customers who seem to know what they want in advance of their turns. I am holding up the line.

"One," I say.

The woman heaps rolls into a bag. I hand her a twenty-dollar bill, and she hands me my box and bag and then, a moment later, my change.

"*Shavua tov,*" she says.

I walk out of the pastry shop, trying to balance the bag of rolls on top of the large box of pastries. I have no idea what I am going to do with all this. Perhaps, I think, I'll give them to a panhandler on the train home. As I walk back to the subway station, I feel the imprint of the little girl's hand in my own.

On Monday, when I arrive on the unit at our usual meeting time, Dvorah rises enthusiastically when she sees me.

"Good morning, Doctor. I'm glad you've come," she says. "I'm ready for my session today."

"Glad to hear it, Dvorah. Come, let's go."

The minute she is seated on the chaise longue in my office, she begins speaking.

"I've given it all a lot of thought, this weekend. I was very busy." She smiles one of her rare smiles. She is in good spirits—none of the weary defeat that was so evident when I last saw her on Thursday. I marvel, as I often do, at how changeable people are—and how especially changeable psychiatric patients can be.

"All this time, you've been worrying so hard about how to help me. We've been going about this all wrong."

"Oh?"

She seems a little impatient. "You know how teachers are always saying, 'I learn so much from my students.' That's a perfectly accepted point of view. That students teach their teachers, even though the teachers are there, in the first place, to teach them."

"Yes," I say.

"Well, why not here? Do you not learn from your patients?"

"Yes, Dvorah. Of course I do."

"Are you not sometimes also helped by them?"

I'm not sure how to answer this question. Of course, she is right. But I don't feel as if this is something I should actually say.

"Dvorah, I'm not sure what you're getting at."

"What I'm *getting at* is that *things are not always what they seem.*" She lowers her voice and leans forward, with a conspiratorial look on her face. "We needn't tell anyone. It could be our secret. Why shouldn't I help you? Why shouldn't I *show you the way*?"

"Show me the way—where?" I ask.

"To your *real life.*"

"My real life."

"Yes."

"What is my real life?"

Now, Dvorah looks genuinely puzzled.

"But, Doctor, you know that perfectly well. Here"—and she reaches up with some suddenness and slides off her wig, exposing her closely cropped head to the bright sunlight pouring in through the window of my office. Tiny dust beads, which must have been settled in the long strands of her wig, dance around in the bright halo of light, jumping about her wispy, dull hair and then falling invisibly in among the strands.

"Here, I know you want this," she says, holding the wig out to me. I have the off-putting thought that she is offering me a small, dead animal.

"Go on," she says, shaking it a little, so that the dead-animal-wig shimmies slightly, sending up a new froth of dust beads that commence their frenzied motion in the sun rays. "Take it. Put it on. It's the only thing stopping you."

"Stopping me from what?" I whisper. My voice has all but disappeared. It comes out thin as the hum of a mosquito.

Dvorah thins out her own voice, as if trying to match the suddenly odd quality of my own.

"From taking your rightful place," she breathes. She says something else, but now her voice is so low, I do not hear it.

"I beg your pardon?" I say. "What did you say?"

"You heard me," she says, a decibel or two louder, just enough for me to make out the words.

"No, I didn't. Not the last thing you said."

"So we can finish this business. Finish what I came here to achieve."

"What you came here to achieve." I falter.

"The switch."

"The switch?"

"Yes, so we can make the switch."

Dvorah rises and approaches me, holding the limp wig before her as if she is bringing me some sort of sacrificial object. I am paralyzed. I want to reach for the buzzer under my desk, but I find that not only am I stuck to my chair as if bolted there but I also seem unable to move my arms. Only my eyes move, following Dvorah's slow, almost ceremonial movement before me. She seems to be in some kind of trance. She is gliding toward me—and now, I realize, she is humming something. Her lips are tightly closed, the wordless humming seems to be getting louder. I recognize the melody, though I cannot place it. A joyous melody that sings out to me from a long-distant past. What on earth is she humming?

Dvorah is upon me. She is raising her hand, the wig is dangling there, the hair hanging downward. I think of a scene from an old movie I saw once as a child, in which an American Indian from the days of the Wild West, outfitted in Hollywood Indian style, whoops into his tepee village carrying a fresh scalp. I want to jump back; I fancy I see droplets of blood flying out from the swinging, hanging hair. I want to shriek—*Stop! No! Not another step!* I want to call for Kevin. I want to leap from this doctor's chair of mine—*Dr. Erick, yes, I'm here for another session*—where I have sat now for some years and listened to all kinds of dreadful suffering and grief. I want to leap from the chair, bound down the two flights of stairs and out through the grand lobby, run onto the driveway, and tear all the way down to the bottom of the hill, leaving my car behind, leaving this office behind, leaving all of it for someone else to worry about.

But I cannot do any of this. I must only sit and watch Dvorah advance. Now, she is swaying her hips, she has closed her eyes. The melody rises and I realize it is a song sung at Hasidic weddings. The song that women sing as they encircle the bride.

She is beside my chair. She opens her eyes and I see that her face is lit with an otherworldly joy. She opens her mouth, and the song bursts loudly and fully from her throat. She has a rich voice that is powerful and extremely loud, especially in this room so full of silence. Just as she is leaning down toward me, just when I realize that what Dvorah intends to do, now, is fit her wig onto my head, Kevin bursts into the room.

"Is everything all right?" he says, then stops short. "Dr. Erick, what's going on?"

My own trance is broken. I rise suddenly, stiffly, awkwardly from my chair. My voice comes out gravelly and low.

"Please, Kevin. Take Mrs. Kuttner back to the unit."

Dvorah looks confused. She is standing now with her arms hanging at her sides. I see that her wig has slithered to the floor. I walk around the desk and bend to retrieve it.

"Here," I say, offering the wig to Dvorah. She looks at me blankly, looks for a second at the wig, then back up to my face, but she makes no move to take the wig from my hand, so I pass it to Kevin.

"The nurse can help her with this when you get back to the unit," I say.

After they have left, I close the door and lock it from the inside. I stand for a long time with my back up against the locked door. I am trembling and feel an unpleasant constriction in my chest. I stand there, up against the reassuringly hard wooden door, looking across the room and out through the window at the lawns and sky, which from this distance, across the length of the room, appear to be both real and unreal, like a beautifully rendered painting.

＊   ＊   ＊

Wednesday. The days are sliding by. I slide along with them. Tonight I cannot bear the look in Ron's eyes; they no longer show concern, only a hardened glaze of forbearance. I look at him and feel lost and alone, as if I have landed on the wrong planet, far from home.

"I think I'll go out for a walk," I say.

"Of course," Ron replies. He is clearing the table—we've just eaten mushroom soup from a can with toasted bagels and butter.

"Anything we need?" I say, feeling very sad.

"Milk, I think," he says.

"I'll probably be about an hour," I say.

I grab a light sweater and step out into the hall, where I wait a long time for the elevator. The hallway is stuffy and close; the elevator has probably broken down again. I take the stairs down the nine flights; my shoes echo hollowly in the bare concrete space, around and down, the murky brown walls closing in on me, the clank and ring of my leather soles unpleasantly filling my ears. It is a relief when finally I reach the metal door at the bottom. It is heavy; I use both hands to push it open. I have the feeling I am bursting up from a turbid lake in which I'd been submerged for too long.

Outside, it is pleasantly cool. I head over to West End Avenue and turn south. The early evening light is pearly, softening everything. For a moment, nothing seems lasting or solid—these buildings I am passing, some eighty years old, others a hundred or more, seem to have sprung up only now and to be fading with the fading light. Around me, people hurry or stroll or stand about hailing a cab or chatting together. Cars honk, a baby wails. At the fringes of everything, coming from different directions, I hear the distant barking of several dogs.

I seem to be part of a little crowd walking down West End Avenue towards some destination—not hurrying, but not ambling, either: just moving with a calm sense of purpose— a young couple, two women pushing strollers, a family with three older children. All nicely and modestly dressed. I am moving among people heading to a synagogue, I realize; it is Wednesday night, so it must be the evening of a Jewish festival. I do a quick calculation, lining up the months with the holidays. It must be either *Lag B'Omer* or *Shavuot*, depending on how the festivals fall this year.

I am still in my work clothes—a navy suit with a mid-calf skirt and white silk blouse; I fit in just fine. We're approaching the Anshei Chesed synagogue, which I must have passed hundreds of times in the years I've lived on the Upper West Side and never once entered.

I turn with the others and climb the stairs to the grand front doors, then move through the lobby and into the sanctuary.

The service is already in progress; I stand at the back of the room and take it all in. Rich royal blues and golds, beautifully oiled reddish wood, glittering lights, and a throng of well-dressed worshipers, the men and women all together, as is the practice in the modern Conservative synagogue. The cantor's voice rises above the Holy Ark; the Rabbi is preparing to remove the Torah scrolls, which he will then parade through the congregation, the cantor behind him singing the praises of God.

The Hebrew words and melody fly from the cantor's throat and are taken up by the congregation, whose voices, too, flutter through the space like a flock of spirited birds. The sounds slam against my ears and knock the breath from me. I feel dragged back to some place that is both troubling and sweet; I want to run toward it and away from it at the same time.

I close my eyes to try to regain my equilibrium.

A cascade of fractured images hurl through my mind in the way of dreams, though I am fully lucid and awake. Desert sands, an enormous temple the size, it seems, of a pyramid. Ecstatic worshipers in flowing robes. Now, a cramped alleyway lined with hovels, hurrying male figures, their long black coats faded and worn and flapping at their legs like troublesome crows, wide fur hats, also black, encircling their heads; hurrying toward a damp storefront up ahead, its windows lit with candles, from which this same haunting melody I am now hearing seeps into the dusk-shadowed air. I am dreaming, I am awake, I am traveling through the time that is clogging my veins. Hurrying, now, a family in frantic flight: after them the clattering of jackbooted feet. Mounds of books going up in flames, sinewy black letters turned to ashes and smoke. *Where they burn books, they will also burn people.* A crematorium of pages, and now, skin and muscle twisting in flames, then evaporating upward, a hellish flesh-smoke, toward a sky believed to be heaven. Ships and boats carrying orphans, and Diane's father, sunken in bereavement and alone. The building of synagogues on foreign soil. Shanghai. Sydney. Buenos Aires. Babies swelling in wombs that had held only grief, pushed out into the world, their thin age-old wails turning, with time, to the song flying now from the cantor's throat.

I open my eyes, clutch on to the polished pillar beside me, emotion punching up at me from within. Tears are dripping down my cheeks. I have no handkerchief or tissue and feel a sudden panic: here I am, in public, at the mercy of a flood of unexpected tears and without a tissue to mop them up. I turn and make my way back out through the lobby and onto the street. Now my nose is dripping, too. I hurry to Broadway and run into the first bodega I see, grab a purse pack of tissues, and throw a dollar on the counter.

I am thinking of my father. Of how he excised religion from his life. Both of them did—my mother and father, both—and yet they also shoved me, quite deliberately, in that very direction. Why else send me, at the age of eight, to a religious, Jewish youth group? They winced when I came back from the Youth Movement retreat all fired up about Orthodox Judaism, but what did they expect? Did they expect simply to offer me the induction into their heritage so that I, too, might walk away?

Well I did, in the end. Walk away. I did what they had done, as a good daughter often does.

I mop up my eyes and blow my nose and head back out into the spring evening.

My father's silence. I am wondering, as I used to, about what it was that made him slam the door on his Jewish roots. I'd glimpsed the outrage and despair of Diane's father that day as he yanked up the sleeve of his shirt, but what about my own father? And what dark urgings of the blood had made him and my mother plant me back in the very soil from which they had uprooted themselves?

I walk up Broadway, though slowly now, with no sense of purpose other than returning to Ron's apartment. Four years together and we still keep our separate places. As I think about Ron, my heart aches with loneliness and longing. Ron, who in a way understands so little about me, who has no inkling of such dark urgings of the blood.

I pass by restaurants that are filling up; they exhale their celebratory moods through open windows. In a bar, a TV screen mounted high on the wall sends down flickering blue-

and-green images. A stationery store is preparing to close. The bagel place, with bins of bagels that are no longer fresh, is empty of customers. The voices of the congregation in the synagogue have fluttered away, but still I hear the resonant, pure voice of the cantor; I complete, in my mind's ear, the melodious prayer he had begun when I fled. The words come back to me, accurate and crisp. They are telling me something, calling me back.

Again today, Dvorah is quiet and withdrawn.

"How was the meeting last night with your husband?" I inquire.

"Oh. Just fine," Dvorah says in a small voice. And then: "Doctor, I've been thinking. Perhaps I shouldn't return there."

"Return where, Dvorah?"

"Home. To their home."

"*Their* home?"

"It's not mine, not anymore."

A husband of fourteen years. Seven children, one of them an infant. No longer her home.

"And why is that?"

Dvorah lets out an impatient sigh. She is stirring to life.

"There's a reason I've had so many children," she says. She points to her wig. "Beyond the obvious. I conceived the first child on my honeymoon. Three months after my eighteenth birthday. I've proven to be quite fertile since then, as you know."

Dvorah pulls a tissue from the box I keep on the side table and holds it in her lap.

"I was planning to keep going as long as I could." She twists the tissue, adding in a whisper, *"Baruch Hashem."* She looks a little embarrassed—as if she no longer really believes the expression summoned to ward off the evil eye—but can't help herself from uttering it, just in case.

"I made my own calculations. I figured if I was lucky, I could bear fourteen children. By age forty-six, I'd be pretty much spent."

Dvorah looks down at her lap and realizes she has shredded the tissue she was twisting. She leans over and throws the scraps in the wastepaper basket beside her chair.

"What happened?" I ask.

"I'm sorry?" My question seems to have startled her.

"Your plan—"

"Yes, of course. Well, the problem was my dreams began to change. They began to go in a very bad direction. Far worse than ever before."

I wait to see if she's going to tell me about how her dreams changed.

"You see, the point of having all those children was to make up for the terrible losses. A lot of women in our community have feelings like mine. From our own wombs, we are going to replace all those murdered Jewish babies.

"It was after my fourth child—I remember this well; I was still in the hospital—that I lay awake one night trying to imagine the faces of one-point-two million children. That's the figure, more or less, that's generally accepted as the number of Jewish children murdered by the Nazis. I lay awake conjuring images of unknown faces until I thought my head was going to burst. This went on night after night. Even after I returned home. I began to despair. I realized that even if I had twenty children, it was such a tiny drop in the ocean that it was hardly worthwhile.

"That was when I started having the dream. I am lying in

a delivery room. My body is being torn apart with labor pains. I am giving birth to one baby after another. I barely catch my breath and the intense contractions begin afresh. Out comes another baby. I am completely exhausted.

"This goes on for what seems like hours. I am on the verge of fainting when suddenly I realize there is an odd, repetitive noise in the background. Something that's been going on for a long time but that, in my state of perpetual labor and childbirth, I've entirely tuned out. It sounds like the cracking of a whip. What are horse riders doing here? I wonder.

"I raise myself up on my elbows, just as another baby pushes out between my legs. I scan the room. It seems suddenly to have expanded. I am no longer in a sterile, enclosed room but on a hospital bed out in the middle of a large field. The doctor is still there, tending to the births, and the nurse is saying encouraging things to help me push out the next baby. I strain up to a sitting position and see that some distance away is a large pit. As quickly as I am delivering babies, they are being taken by a guard and perched at the edge of the pit. Then—again, I hear that sound. My eyes move slowly in the direction of the noise and land on its source: a soldier in a brown uniform has his rifle raised and is firing shot after shot. Each one hits its mark; following each, one of my new babies falls dead into the pit.

"I told my husband about the dream. He told me I must put it out of my mind.

"That's what I did. I endured the dream when it came. I would awaken in a sweat. Then, I would force it from my mind.

"I realized, though, that I could not go on having children forever. I was very tired. So I settled on the number seven."

Now she looks at me as if only just remembering that I'm here.

"The number seven is very significant from the point of view of the Kabbalah," she continues. "In fact, you might say that in this number, the entire world is contained. Even the act of the creation is contained within it.

"There are seven *sefirot* that govern the seven cycles or aeons. Each of these is linked to one of the books in the complete Torah. There were originally seven books, not five. Together, these books contain the entire world."

She looks at me and seems to judge that some of this is going over my head.

"The details don't matter," she says. "The fact is I realized that it made perfect sense to stop at seven. After I'd made that decision—I was pregnant with my fifth by that time—I felt some relief. And the dream no longer came to haunt me. I was able to get on with my life.

"It was after the birth of this last baby that everything went wrong. There was nothing I could do about it. My plan had failed."

Dvorah bows her head a little, and I see that tears are dripping down her face. She does not reach for a tissue. She just lets the tears fall onto her lap.

"That was when my father's brother came to me. In the hospital, maybe an hour after I'd given birth. I saw immediately that he was wearing the uniform. He was very angry. 'What, no more children?' he said. 'But we need them! You have to give us more! We need fresh supplies for our soldiers to shoot. How else are we going to fill up our pits?' "

I have not spoken in a long time. Dvorah is now sitting silently crying.

"Dvorah," I say quietly.

She raises her head and looks at me with the most naked misery I have ever seen.

"Please, help me to understand. Why would your father's brother— He was a little boy who was hiding from the Nazis, a little Jewish boy. Why would he be wearing a Nazi uniform?"

"Because he went over to the other side."

I press on. "Why would he do this?"

Now she looks bewildered. "I don't know. I have no idea. I just know that he did."

"How do you know that he did?"

"Why, because my father told me!"

"He told you?"

"Yes, he had—"

"What did he have?"

"He had evidence. After the War, he did some research. He knew all his family were dead, but he wanted to know how, exactly, they had died. That's when he turned up the— the evidence."

Now she clamps her lips shut.

"The evidence," I repeat.

"Yes," she says tightly.

"Not something you want to share," I venture.

"Precisely."

"Because—"

"Because it's none of your business."

I'm feeling exhausted. I glance over at the clock and see that we have five minutes left.

I wait for the clock to tick away our final seconds.

I realize that I've run out of ideas. That I no longer know what to do with Dvorah. Each week, I intend to talk with Dr. Finkelstein about her in our Friday supervision session, and each week I fail to do so. It's all gone too far. I wouldn't know where to begin. I also fear Dr. Finkelstein would judge me harshly—and rightly so—for having failed for such a long time to address what is clearly a very problematic situation.

Now, when I'm with Dr. Finkelstein, I find myself feeling extremely anxious. She knows I'm in trouble, but she's keeping a respectful distance, waiting for me to speak when I'm ready.

I'm surrounded by people who are keeping a respectful distance. For some reason, this makes me angry.

As I look at Dvorah, sitting there—she, too, seems to be waiting out these last few minutes—I realize that I'm tired of the fact that her psychosis seems not to be lifting. This is not like any postpartum depression I've ever seen.

And then, something snaps clear in my mind. *Oh, my God,* I think. Perhaps this is not in fact a psychotic postpartum depression—or at least, not anymore. Perhaps it is not going to lift, the way such depressions do, with the right medications, and once the hormones and body chemistry have gone back to their normal, prepregnancy condition.

I remember how manic she was a week or so ago and stop, for a moment, to think about the impenetrability of her paranoid delusions. Perhaps Dvorah is suffering from some more enduring form of psychosis.

I see that her face has now taken on that dark, snarling, animal-like hostility that marked our early sessions. Just as I'm preparing to say that we're out of time for today, she angrily speaks.

"When will you have the guts to own *your* piece of it? To admit that you've committed the very same crimes you accuse me of?"

Again, that prickly crawling feel at the back of my neck.

"I'm not aware of having accused you of anything," I say as unthreateningly as I can.

"Don't play the innocent, caring doctor with me," Dvorah

hisses. "Haven't you ever heard of the expression 'it takes one to know one?' Won't you ever *get it?*"

She rises and slowly approaches my desk, behind which I am sitting. She moves in the prowling, coiled way of a wildcat, preparing to pounce.

"Dvorah," I say firmly. "Sit down."

But she doesn't sit down, she takes two more velvety, stalking steps toward me, her face contorted, her eyes sunken and far away.

"I won't," she says. "I won't sit down. I won't do what you say."

"One more step, Dvorah, and I'll call the orderly."

"Call him. Go ahead. Have him strap me to a bed. What difference does it make? I'll expose you, I will. I'm not going to let you get away with it."

I reach under my desk and press the red buzzer. I know I have a minute or two before Kevin will materialize.

"What," I whisper, a little alarmed to hear there is urgency in my voice. "What will you expose?"

"Everything," she whispers back.

She has stopped moving forward. She is standing across from me, gripping the desk with her small, nicely shaped hands, staring with eyes that are looking at me from some other world. They are like a magnetic field; I feel myself being drawn into them.

"You see," she says, and now she leans across the desk, so that her face is only about a foot from mine. "You're just as guilty as I am. You wore the uniform once yourself. I don't know what you've done with it. Maybe you locked it in a trunk and put it up in the attic. But you have it, I know you do. Everything you are—what you wear, what you do. It's false, all of it. Nothing but a disguise."

Where on earth is Kevin? I think. I feel a rise of panic; my breath turns shallow. I concentrate on surreptitiously trying to inhale deeply a few times to get my breathing back to normal.

"Almost as convincing as my own disguise," Dvorah continues. "But not quite."

A mad smile appears on her face. "All of it—my piousness, *oh, what a perfect Hasidic mother and wife! She's so caring and devout! Look how she inspects the broccoli for insects, picks each of the tiny* trait *creatures out with her fingers and squeezes the life from them. How uncomplainingly she bears all those children. Pregnancy after pregnancy and never a complaint. The years of suckling and rocking and soothing to sleep. Truly, she's a marvel!"*

I am sinking down a little in my chair. I hear heavy treads at the end of the hallway, rapidly approaching. Kevin, at long last.

"I'm a master of disguise," Dvorah is saying. "Surely you admire me for this. Being a master of disguise yourself."

Kevin strides into the room.

"Come along, Mrs. Kuttner," he says in his usual forceful, unruffled way. To me, under his breath, he says, "Sorry. Incident on the unit." He takes Dvorah firmly by the shoulders.

"Don't you touch me!" she shrieks, struggling away from Kevin's grasp.

"I'll carry you if I have to," he says calmly, and Dvorah relaxes, allowing herself to be led from the room.

After Kevin leaves, I rise, plug in the electric jug, and wait for the water to come to a boil. I put a tea bag into the mug and then pour in boiling water. I return to my desk and sip my tea, staring out the attic window onto the wide slope of the hospital grounds. The panic I felt when Dvorah was in my office subsides. I think back over the session, pull out my notebook, and jot down some notes.

It is beginning to come clear. I see how she has drawn me in, how Dvorah needs to feel she has an ally if she is fully to confront her demons. I need to start thinking in terms of a new, differential diagnosis. This may be a paranoid psychosis, or else a true case of schizoaffective disorder. Either way, I need to make some changes in the medications and dosages. I consult my weight chart, make some calculations, and then pull out my prescription pad and write an order which I will take down to the unit on my way to lunch. If I don't see a marked improvement in two weeks, I will switch her to another antipsychotic and consider using a stronger sedative.

I tear off the order form and grab my jacket from the hook on the back of the door, glancing unthinkingly at the closet as I leave.

I shudder at the thought of Dvorah's accusation. That I have worn a Nazi uniform and must therefore be guilty of crimes against the Jews. I recall, too, how she jabbed at her temple to indicate that her father's brother, himself in Nazi uniform, came to her in her mind—in a dream, or perhaps in a psychotic vision of some kind. I puzzle, again, at her delusional formulation. Why would her father's brother—a little boy who hid in an outhouse to avoid being shot by the Nazis, who very likely was found by them and killed—have anything to do with wearing a Nazi uniform himself?

Perhaps I am wrong to try to make any sense of it. Perhaps psychotic patients are, after all, "beyond comprehension," as many psychiatrists would believe. Perhaps we can do no more than look over their shoulders into the abyss, providing reassuring words as we wait for the medication to wipe it all out, or at least to make it all a little less terrifying.

But perhaps there are also doctors who themselves get drawn into the abyss: who find themselves being—willingly—pulled over?

IV.

Dvorah has been in the hospital for eleven weeks. It is only two weeks since my last visit to my parents, but it feels like an age.

I look at the small gold clock on the table by the chaise longue and see that it is already 8:30. Damn. I had not wanted to keep my parents waiting again. I close the file I am working on, take off my glasses, and sit, for a moment, rubbing my temples. There it is—that worm of concern, unsettling my equanimity. I close my eyes and focus on what I am feeling. An image of Dvorah floats into my mind's eye—not the angry Dvorah of late, who can be so disarmingly lucid and then floridly delusional, but a different Dvorah, a Dvorah I have never known. A much younger Dvorah. I am picturing her as a teenager, seventeen or eighteen. Her face is fresh and young and very sad.

I'll stop off at the unit on my way to the car, I think.

I unlock the door to the unit and pop my head into the nurses' station.

"Signing off for the weekend," I say to Nurse Harmon. "Just checking in to see that everything's okay."

"All's quiet on the Seven South front," she says wryly.

"I can't say that's the most encouraging news," I reply. "You do remember what happens in the film?"

"Sorry," she says with a sheepish smile. "You worry too much, Dr. Erick, really you do."

"Part of the job description," I say. "Seriously, though, keep an eye on Dvorah."

"Anything we should know?"

I shake my head. "Nothing new, really. You've probably already read my weekly note."

"Yes. I read it over at change of shift. She seems to be doing quite well, from what you say, and from what I've seen of her so far this evening. I saw the adjustments you made to the meds. That makes a lot of sense. Poor dear, she's been through the wringer."

"Yeah," I say. "Mental illness is no bowl of cherries."

"Why are you worried?"

"Just a niggling feeling. I think she's feeling the full force of her sadness at the moment. In some ways, that might be harder than being caught up in the drama of her delusions."

"I'll spend some time with her tonight," Nurse Harmon says. "Let's see—" She reaches for the mental health worker rotation schedule. "Marjorie's on the night shift. Dvorah likes Marjorie. I'll assign her for a one-on-one. She can also chat with her while she's getting ready for bed."

"Good plan," I say. I look at Nurse Harmon and think, for the hundredth time, how lucky we are to have her.

"May I make a suggestion, Doctor?" she says.

"Go ahead."

"Just forget about all of us. For one weekend, lock the hospital out of your thoughts. We'll get along just fine without you worrying."

"Righto," I say.

Nurse Harmon is right. I worry too much. The minute I drive off the grounds, I'll put the hospital clear out of my mind.

I drive with the windows open. Spring is now in full tilt;

in among the evergreens along the Saw Mill, the apple and cherry trees are in bloom. I drive into the sunset, which tints the blossomy crowns of the trees subtle shades of violet and peach. I inhale the sweet, warm air and try to clear my mind.

As I turn in to my parents' driveway, I see that the house is in darkness. I glance at the car clock—10:30 p.m.—and turn off the engine.

I enter the house quietly, flick on the hall light, and go to fix myself a snack.

I'm sitting at the table, eating my bowl of cereal and fruit and leafing through last week's *New York Times Magazine*, when my mother appears in the doorway in her bathrobe.

"Darling, you're here," she says. She takes an apple from the fruit bowl on the counter and joins me at the table.

"Sorry to be so late," I say. "I had a really busy day. Long week, actually."

"Not to worry. You said you might be late," my mother says. "I'm glad you're here. Your father went to bed. He has a bit of a headache."

"Oh?"

"He's been under the weather lately. I told him I want him to see Dr. Patel, but you know your father. He's holding out. Marching around with his nothing-wrong-with-me banner and shouting, 'No more doctors!' along with all the other protesters his age. Honestly, I don't know what it is with men. Refusing to see doctors. It's like some sort of Masons' vow they all take."

"I'll have a word with him tomorrow," I say. "He's due for his checkup, isn't he?"

"Overdue, in fact."

"Make the appointment. I'll talk him into going."

My mother yawns.

"Why don't you go on up?" I say. "I'm going to finish my cereal, and then I'll be up myself."

My mother kisses me on the cheek and heads back upstairs.

I put my bowl and spoon in the dishwasher, turn off the lights, and make my way up the stairs.

I splash water on my face, brush my teeth, and flop into bed. I fall asleep straightaway.

I find myself tumbling through dreadful nightmare images, which slip from my grasp before I can catch hold of them. I jolt awake: one image stays with me, burns itself into my mind's eye. It is my father, sunken down in his chair, the muscles of his face hanging as he tries to keep his grief from bursting out of him. He is turning his face—slowly—and when his gaze meets mine, I see it is not my father's blue-gray eyes at all, looking out at me, but Dvorah's deep, dark brown eyes, wavering with paranoid accusation and rimmed with red.

I look at the clock beside my bed: 3 a.m. Words are swirling around in my mind: *My father lied to me. What he told me about living with the Ukrainian couple was not the truth.*

Absurdly, at the same time, in the background, is a song— the Birkat Hamazon. The Jewish prayer said after meals, which we used to sing on the Youth Center retreats after every meal. *"Baruch atah Adonai, Elohenu melech ha-olam, hazun et ha-olam kulo b'tuvo, b'chein b'chesed uv-rachamim . . ."*

I always loved the rhythm and melody of this long and festive prayer. I rise, turn on the light, and scan the bookshelves for my siddur. Not surprisingly, none of my Hebrew books are here. I long ago removed them. To the attic, no doubt. I grab the flashlight that is in the drawer of the desk.

The house is quiet and dark, alive with the presence of my sleeping parents, filled with the breath of their dreams. I creep through the hallway. I know this passage in the visceral way one knows one's childhood home; the space seems an extension of my own body. I am not walking so much as pouring through it, and having the hallway pour through me. At the end of the passageway, I pause, my hand on the cut-glass doorknob.

On the stairs leading up to the attic, I turn on the flashlight. The heavy dusty scent assails me and the bare wooden boards creak beneath my feet. I seldom came up here as a child; this space always frightened me. I imagined it haunted by a vengeful ghost, awaiting the opportunity to squeeze the breath from some innocent child such as myself.

I swing the beam of my flashlight around; it reveals several old trunks, countless boxes, odd bits of discarded furniture, everything scattered about in disarray. Pretty much standard-issue attic fare, I say to myself, to calm the child's terror that leaps up from the distant past. Everything is hung with the cobwebbed feeling of time passing fatally and unnoticed. An attic, I tell myself, like every other attic anywhere: unused bits and pieces, not needed in the present, and yet still a ghostly part of their owners' lives.

I move a few boxes around, hoping to gauge, by the heaviness of each, which might contain books. I find my old Siddur in the fourth box I open. I set the flashlight on a stacked box and gaze at the Siddur's faded blue cover. This, too, has the visceral feel of being part of my actual body. My parents gave it to me when I entered the sixth grade; I used it daily for many years. The faded, woven cover, with its elongated Hebrew letters, embossed in a shiny aqua blue, feels soothingly familiar. I flip through its pages; the arched, archaic letters jump up at me.

My eyes drift along the beam made by the flashlight;

beads of dust move frantically within it, as if agitatedly seeking to return to their former resting place. My gaze lands on the corner of a large trunk, pushed all the way up against the far wall of the attic, mostly hidden by stacks of boxes.

I don't recall ever having seen this trunk before. I retrieve the flashlight from where I placed it high up on the stack of boxes and pick my way through the cluttered space.

The trunk is very old and heavy, made of wood, painted black, and edged in metal. The metal has tarnished to a mottled gray; the clasp that closes it is rusted but not locked. I release the clasp from the U-shaped piece through which a padlock would be slipped, and the lid creaks open.

The pungent, off-putting odor of mothballs wafts up; inside are old woolen blankets with grosgrain borders. I remove them, and then two feather pillows, which are large, very heavy, and very old; they have about them the smell of forgotten lives.

I peer into the now almost empty trunk. In the corner, sitting on the bare wooden planks of the trunk's floor, is a small metal box, simple and unadorned. I lean into the trunk and retrieve the box, which is smooth and cold to the touch. I turn it in my hands; it looks old and handmade. It is fitted with a lock, the only feature that shows any intricacy or ornamentation, engraved with curlicues and several letters that are difficult to make out in the narrow and not very powerful light of the flashlight, though it seems clear that they are initials. I focus the light directly onto the lock—yes, three letters— *A, G, L*—engraved in fancy script. Not my mother's initials— her name is Mariana Erick, formerly Mariana Neumann—or my father's initials—his name is Jacob Abraham Erick. I assume it is his box. I have no hard evidence, but I feel it to be and I know I am right.

I place the flashlight on the floor; its beam slithers across the dusty boards, disappearing into the space between two stacks of boxes. I pull at the lid of the lockbox, but it does not budge. I pick up the flashlight, examine every corner of the empty trunk, and then carefully unfold each of the blankets, shake them over the trunk, then refold them and place them back inside. Now, the pillows. I remove the worn cases, which are made of fine cotton, and feel all around each pillow, hoping to find a little hole into which the key may have been slipped. I find nothing, though, so I re-dress the pillows and return these, too, to the trunk.

I perch on the trunk, holding my new find. Gently, I shake it. I hear a rustle and a little thud. I can't imagine what the box contains. I think about this for a while, then replace the lockbox into the trunk.

I flash upon Dvorah's face, her eyes narrowed in hostility. *I don't know what you've done with it,* she hissed. *Maybe you locked it in a trunk and put it up in the attic.*

I know the box is my father's—it looks so Old World, something that might have come from Poland—though the initials engraved on it are not his.

No trespassing. I hear my mother's voice. *The secret to a long and happy marriage.*

But he is my father, not my spouse. I feel a rise of anger. Does a parent have the right to make a complete secret of his past?

Is that history not also mine?

I make my way back to the stairs. On the second floor, I flick off the flashlight and continue in darkness. I move quickly and quietly, down through the kitchen and to the door that leads to the basement.

In the basement, I go to the little toolroom and retrieve

my father's toolbox from the shelf above the workbench. I choose a small pair of strong pliers, a wire cutter, and a wrench, then replace the box and return upstairs.

My eyes have adjusted to the dark; I feel like a sly night creature.

Back in the attic, I go quickly to the trunk, take out the lockbox, and lay the tools beside me on the surface of the wide box, then set about tinkering with the lock.

At first, I take care not to mar its metal surface and to avoid marking the engraving on the lock. But the lock does not yield. I realize that, if I am to break it, I will have to damage it, perhaps ruin it altogether.

I pause to think about what I am doing.

What, in fact, *am* I doing? A psychiatrist, with a responsible position, in the habit of promoting privacy, having practiced a lifetime of honesty—even as a child I found it impossible to lie. What am I doing, going at my father's box in the manner of a common thief?

And why this feeling of urgency? This rage growling in my chest like a caged beast? I have the sudden desire to scream, to lash out, to express the growing and unfamiliar fury within.

Damn the stupid box. Damn it, I think. *Damn my patient Dvorah and her psychotic projections onto me.* I'm sick of the whole thing. Sick of being sucked into other people's crazy universes, sick of the burden of it all. Tomorrow I will drive to the hospital and speak to the unit chief; she is covering this weekend and so will be there first thing in the morning. I will request that Dvorah be transferred to another doctor.

I put my head in my hands and close my eyes. I am tired, very tired. I've been skirting dangerously close to unprofessional doings. I know, in fact—now that I am being honest with myself—that I have actually already crossed the line. That my sessions with Dvorah are no longer only about what is best for her while we try, finally, to come up with the right medications to treat what is probably a schizoaffective psychosis with paranoid features.

That her sessions are, at least some of the time, about me. About hoping to shed a glimmer onto the dusty corners of my own being that have, in their dark secrecy, been causing some havoc of their own.

Dvorah's nightmare—the little boy, her father's youngest brother, trapped in the putrid place surrounded by dried human waste—plunges up from the depths of my own consciousness; his terror plunges up within me as if it is my own. I hear my heart pounding and feel a cold, reptilian creeping on my flesh.

Something's here, I know it. There is something in the locked metal box that I must see. *It is my right,* I think, clenching my teeth. And for one brief, horrible moment I can feel, on my face—in my tightly tensed jaw, in the stretch of my neck and cheeks—an expression I recognize as one Dvorah has worn many times in my office when spewing forth rage. I try to wipe the expression from my face, to dislodge Dvorah's crazed anger from my breast, but it will not be shed, which makes me go at the box with even greater urgency.

To hell with the smooth metal surface, I think as I twist with the pliers at the hinge first on one side of the box, then on the other. *To hell with the engraving*—whose initials are these, anyway? Those of the Ukrainian, who took my father in? No, surely not. He and his wife are nothing but fictions, I am sure of that.

Why did my father lie to me?

I stop what I am doing. I have the pliers in my hand. I

hold them aloft as if I, petty criminal I have now become, were about to strike some victim, strike him in the head and leave him for dead.

How could he leave me alone? I think. With nobody to trust. With nobody to show me *the way out.*

Perhaps there is no way out?

Yes, I think. *He deserves this, me meddling with his box.*

I have given up on the lock; I realize I am more likely to break the thing at the hinge on the back of the lid. I alternate between pliers and wire cutter, working less frantically now, my rage of a few minutes ago tamed to a steely band of concentration. I clench with the cutter, then pry with the pliers, back and forth, staring intently at the hinge, which is finally showing signs of giving way.

There, it has snapped.

I am aware, suddenly, of the deep silence around me.

I have a hankering to see the sky and breathe in the night air.

I remember there is a window somewhere up high, under the eaves. I send the beam of the flashlight roaming upward, scan with it, and come to rest on the window—yes, there it is—under the eaves. It has been covered over with black cloth, which appears to be taped to the frame. I wonder who did this, and when, and for what reason. I can't imagine my mother or father wanting to create such an enclosed state of darkness. It must have been the previous owner and my parents had not thought to remove the cloth, or had intended to but not gotten around to it.

The box is in my hands—and it is open, finally!—but I can't bring myself to look inside, not until I've had the chance to breathe in the night air, to gaze, for a moment, upon the sky.

I put the box down and go in search of the ladder I know we keep somewhere up here. I locate it quickly, and carry it over to the window. I'm up in a moment. The cloth pulls easily away from the window; the duct tape holding it is very old and much of the glue has broken down. The cloth would have fallen off of its own accord soon enough.

I pull on the wooden sash. The window, too, is old, possibly the original one, and very stiff. I tug, tug some more, and it gives, pulling up halfway. Flakes of old paint fly down. I lean forward, a little hazardously, and thrust my head through the window. I drink in some mouthfuls of fresh night sky. I realize I am very thirsty—my throat is parched. I look up and see what I was hoping to see: the sky wide and deep above me, hung with flickering stars and a semicircle of moon, which glows senselessly, anciently, and with perfect evenness.

I go back down the ladder. The even glow of the moon, now free to enter this space, has turned what were eerily obscured objects into well-defined angles and curves, giving them a kind of indoor forest feel. For a moment, the child in me half expects a wood sprite to come hopping out from behind a stack of boxes.

I turn back to the lockbox. I draw from it what looks like an official document, made of heavy paper and folded over like a greeting card. I flip it open and shine the flashlight onto it. On the left side is an old, faded black-and-white photograph of a child—a boy; I'd guess his age to be ten or eleven. He is very serious: eyes staring out that are pale in color and yet give the impression of burning blackly. He has fair hair and even features. A handsome boy, though troubled. Something very familiar about the face, though I am certain I have never seen this child before.

On the right side of the card are lines of typescript. Information typed on an old-fashioned typewriter. I can make out that it is German. It seems to be identifying data: height, weight, birth date. Below, at the bottom, is the boy's name. *Jacob Abraham Erlich.*

There's some mistake, I think. That's not my father's name. My father's last name is Erick. My name. Our name. My eyes must be deceiving me.

Dvorah, her psychotic transmissions—all those murky, unconscious goings-on that I must put an end to; they're making my eyes play tricks on me. I know Dvorah as Dvorah Kuttner, her married name. But I also know from the one meeting I had with her parents that her maiden name is Erlich.

I shine the light directly onto the letters. I read the name again.

No, my eyes are not playing tricks on me, that is what is written. *Jacob Abraham Erlich.*

I know, of course, that refugees anglicized their names upon arriving in America; they do it still. But then, I hadn't known my father was a refugee until I was almost grown myself. I'd never thought to ask if our name had been changed.

And here—this serious boy with the light-dark far-seeing eyes of a kind that do not belong in the face of a boy—here is my father, long before he became my father. I've never seen any pictures of my father as a child. I am startled to see the resemblance I bear to him. Age has changed him so strikingly that I'd never thought of myself as looking like him.

I close the heavy card, set it down carefully beside me on the wide cardboard box, and reach again into the metal lockbox.

My hand comes into contact with a piece of crinkly paper

that feels fragile and old. Carefully, I pull it out. It is newsprint, yellowed and brittle and folded into a square. Very slowly, hoping that it will not crumble in my fingers, I open the square, smooth it a little, noting that it has cracked along one of the fold lines, then pick up the flashlight again to see what it shows.

It is very faded; the printed photograph is too yellowed with age to reveal its subject immediately.

I peer more closely—it is a boy, the same boy I just saw on the identification card, only younger, perhaps seven or eight years old. Very serious—something oddly blank about his expression. All around the photograph there is German newsprint. I scan it quickly to see if I can make any sense of it, but I do not understand a word of German.

I look back to the picture, and now I see. My father, before he was my father; this distant, unknowable boy with the face that is simultaneously serious and blank. He is wearing a uniform; his arm is raised in a salute. His arm is raised in a *Sieg Heil*—a terse, properly rendered Nazi salute. This boy, my father, is wearing a Nazi uniform; the swastika stands out blackly on his left arm.

I drop the square of old newspaper as if it has suddenly burst into flames and will any moment bite hotly into my fingers. It flutters down to the floorboards, lost in the shadows.

I don't know what to think.

I am losing my mind.

I hear Dvorah's words echoing inside my head: *You wore the uniform once yourself. I don't know what you've done with it. Maybe you locked it in a trunk and put it up in the attic. But you have it, I know you do.*

Have I slipped over—over to the other side?

Who would believe me? How could anyone in their right

mind possibly believe this find? The ominous coincidence at the heart of all this?

Is this how a madman feels? Convinced that the impossible parameters of his vision—everything coming together *just so,* everything filled with threat, and all of it pointed toward *me*—is the absolute and fundamental truth? The madman, up against a mass of disbelievers with their smug and knowing formulas and reassurances, their prescription pads and four-point restraints, their army of orderlies and ward rules and starchy, no-nonsense nurses. All of them intent on proving *me* to be the deluded one? When all along, as improbable as the details of the delusional system might be, it is I who see and know *the truth.*

There is something else in the box, something that has rolled into the corner. I feel for the object, find it, roll it around in my fingers, then draw it out.

I look down at my hand.

What I see is not possible. What I see is as impossible as the photograph in the yellowed, cracked newspaper clipping. Not reality, surely. How could any of this be real?

What I see is a small smooth stone, almost perfectly round and the color of flint. What I see is a smooth rock so round it is almost a perfect ball.

Somehow, I have made my way down to the kitchen, though I do not remember actually walking the hallways and stairs. I am terribly thirsty. I have poured a large glass of orange juice. I am sitting here, at the kitchen table, looking at the tall glass with the sunny bright liquid, but I cannot drink. I cannot get my hand to reach over and raise the glass to my lips.

I sit and listen to the clock ticking behind me on the wall.

I sit and wait, unable to drink the orange juice, though I look at it with a longing that grows more intense as time passes.

The kitchen windows are covered from midway down with a sheer length of chiffon, so as the dawn rises, the room fills slowly with milky, early light. I listen to the ticking and wait, though I don't know what I am waiting for.

When I finally hear the tread on the stairs, I realize I have been waiting for my father.

It is my mother, though, who enters the kitchen.

She begins to greet me, but I must look awful in some way, as she calls out in fright: "Deborah! Whatever is the matter?"

My mother leans over me and puts a protective arm, a mother's arm, around my shoulder. "Darling, what's wrong?" she says again.

I open my mouth to speak, but my throat is so dry, nothing comes out but a little grunt. My mother lifts the glass of juice to my lips, and I take a few slow sips.

I open my mouth again, and this time a few hoarse words make their way through.

"Papa," I say. "I'm waiting for Papa."

"Jake?" she calls out, making no attempt to mask her mounting panic. "Jake, can you come down here?"

Some minutes later, my father appears. His face, too, clouds over at the sight of me. For a moment, I wonder what it is they see.

"Papa, I'd like to talk to you," I say, my voice now almost restored, and calm, though still odd to my ears.

My father's eyes drift down to my hands, which are resting on the table. He sees that I have something beneath them, that I am cradling something in my hands. He sees that I am cradling the ruined metal lockbox, and his face turns a sickly pallor.

"Mariana," he says to my mother. "Will you excuse us?"

He walks over to me—he seems a little wobbly; I wonder if he might faint—helps me up by the arm, and together we walk into his study. Quietly, he closes the door.

Before he can say anything, I speak.

"The initials," I say. "Engraved on the lock. Whose initials are they?"

It is as if he's been waiting for this question these last fifty years. He answers without hesitation.

"The soldier's."

"What soldier?"

"The soldier who took me in."

"The soldier," I repeat.

"Yes, that's right."

"The Nazi soldier."

"Yes," my father says.

"No Ukrainian couple, then."

"No Ukrainian couple," he echoes.

"Lies, all of it. Everything you told me."

"Yes and no," he says quietly. "Truth in such situations becomes elastic. It's not always easy to know what is reality and what isn't."

I think of my psychotic patients. I think about Dvorah and her nightmares, both the ones that visit her when she sleeps and the ones that overtake her when she is awake.

I hand him the yellowed scrap of newspaper. He knows what it is before he looks at it; his face turns whiter still, and his strong jaw quivers a little, something I have never seen before.

I think about my mother's principle: *No Trespassing.* I feel a shock of shame. I want to snatch the picture away, to shout—"*Forget about it, Papa*"—and run from the room. I want to put it all aside, go back to the unruffled existence I led before meeting Dvorah: to allow my father, too, to remain in the careful chamber he has made of his life, the past safely sealed away.

But I can't snatch the clipping away; it is too late.

"It's you, isn't it," I say.

He stares down at the picture of the little boy in his perfect, neat, miniature Nazi uniform, his hand raised in a *Sieg Heil.* My father seems frozen or turned to salt, all but his squarish chin, which continues to tremble delicately.

I am aware of a faint crowing coming from far away. It sounds like a raven or buzzard. What would a bird like that be doing in the New Jersey suburbs?

Papa hands the newspaper back, then looks at me deeply and long. I expect him to be angry, but there is only sadness in his eyes. Sadness, and something else I've never seen and cannot name. He opens his mouth to speak, but nothing comes out, so I speak instead.

"You were taken in by Nazi soldiers," I say again.

"I was their mascot," my father says mechanically. "I was hiding in a small wooden hut. But they found me. They opened the door and told me to come out with my hands raised."

I see him, a little five-year-old boy, crazed with hunger and fear, emerging from a small wooden hut, hands raised in surrender.

"I only wanted some bread," he continues. "They made us dig a pit, me and about a dozen other people they found hiding in the woods. The shovel was very heavy; I hadn't eaten in days, and I remember worrying that I would drop the shovel. Then, they lined us up, face forward, before the pit. All I could think of was the taste, the smell, the feel in my mouth, of bread. More than anything, I wanted to taste bread one last time before I died.

"I turned around. There were three soldiers. Each was holding a rifle and preparing to shoot. 'Could I please just have one piece of bread?' I asked. I was sucking on the sleeve of my jacket—for days I had sucked it, imagining I was sucking a crust, and it was soft and stretched. One of the soldiers lowered his rifle. He said something to the others, though I couldn't hear what it was. They were conferring about something. None of the others standing by the pit turned around. I'd never seen any of them before—there were two other children among them, though older than I was, probably ten or eleven.

" 'Advance,' the one soldier said. I walked forward. He reached for my arm and pulled me to his side. Then, he raised his rifle, the other two raised their rifles, and I watched as they shot the rest of the people in the back. They all fell forward, into the pit.

"The soldier took me to the truck while the others filled in the grave. It was there, as I was seated beside him in the driver's cabin, that he reached into a canvas bag and pulled out a piece of heavy, black bread. I remember the taste of that bread to this day."

My father falls silent. He looks away from me, toward the window, whose shade is raised and shows a perfect oblong of early morning sky. Still that distant sound, the slightly raucous cry of some predatory bird.

I see in my father's face that this unbearable, unfathomable piece of his past is only the beginning, and that there is so much more to say—that what followed, for him, is as infinite and incomprehensible as the huge sky stretching forever outside the window of my father's study, a room I have known all my life and that has always smelled reassuringly of my father's woody aftershave and the musky breath of his pipe.

Something now seems to occur to him, and he continues.

"I lived with those soldiers for five years. One of them set up a little cot for me in the corner of their barracks. I was made to observe everything they did. For a time, they were a firing squad. Then, they started using vans filled with gas . . ."

Now he trails off and falls silent. After some minutes, he speaks.

"I was always afraid of the other soldiers. But Albrecht—the one who took me in—he treated me like a son."

I wait awhile before speaking.

"Why did you keep the newspaper clipping?"

"They didn't know I was a Jew—the reporter, the newspaper that ran the story on the regiment that had the little boy as a mascot. Albrecht's story was that I was the son of an Aryan farmer and had been orphaned. Because of my coloring, the story was convincing enough."

My father had blond hair as a boy, and bright, bluish grey eyes.

"Yes," I persist. "But why did you keep it?"

Now my father rises, reaches for his pipe, and plants it absentmindedly in his mouth, though he does not light it. He goes to the window and peers out at the nothingness of the sky.

"I don't know, Deborah," he says. "I really don't know."

I walk toward him and move into his arms. I breathe in his familiar scent. What would I have given that my beloved father—as a child, a little five-year-old boy cowering in a hut—might have had the arms of his own mother and father to comfort him, that he might have run into those arms and been safe?

I draw back from him. And then, my father's face crumples. I watch as if in a dream: my father, always able and unremittingly stoic, is hunched over, his crumpled face all but unrecognizable, tears streaming from his eyes, lost in a place of grief pried open by me.

What sort of a daughter am I?

What good is there in any of this? Why must I upset the bones of the past?

I think about the black-red pit of Dvorah's eyes—their awful, impenetrable depth.

The demons are not hers alone. I feel I must put them to rest.

I don't know where to begin. It's all so unlikely. As improbable as the reality of a five-year-old boy watching as his family and entire community dig the graves they then thud into with bullets to the back of the head. Improbable to the point of insanity.

"Papa," I say. "I'm sorry."

He remains hunched over. He blinks once, twice, a look of the utmost bewilderment on his face.

"It could not be helped," he says.

What could not be helped? My prying open the lock? The havoc I have wreaked? Dvorah's psychotic illness? The incomprehensible brutality of his past? History itself?

"Papa," I say again. How can I tell him what I want to tell him?

I've never felt this kind of helplessness. I want to run after the little five-year-old boy racing in the dark, clutching the precious round stone he has saved for his brother. I want to take him in my arms and comfort him, tell him he's safe, take him away from all he is about to experience. I want to prevent it from happening. I want to undo it. Undo it all.

But it is too late. It was too late long before I was born. There is no undoing any of it. There is nothing I can do.

All along, listening to my father, I felt a niggling buzzing behind everything—behind the horror, the reality, the truth he is telling me. Now, it bursts through.

Dvorah's dream.

Dvorah's accusation.

I think of Mr. Husani, his tortured, red-rimmed eyes. The way he approaches the window in the door, the way he reaches up to touch my face, through the glass. So much in his eyes, but also this: recognition. What does he see within me?

Dvorah's dream, Dvorah's accusation. Here they are, hanging in the air of this room. I look down at my hand; I am still holding the news clipping. Here it is, all of it; I am holding the core of Dvorah's insanity here, in the very palm of my hand. A child—a boy, a *five-year-old boy*—cornered, hiding, trapped. In a small hut, my father has said. *What kind of hut?* Could it have been an *outhouse*?

"Papa," I say. That awful, distant, faraway sound—it is my own voice. "What kind of hut was it?"

He turns to me now—I see his eyes. They are black, rimmed in red, and bottomless. Suffering and madness of a different kind than Mr. Husani's or Dvorah's—the nightmare no delusion—but madness nevertheless.

"The hut?" he asks. His voice is a whisper; his voice is filled with pleading.

Again, he turns away. Now his legs buckle, he falls to his knees, grasps the windowsill, and looks up, out the window, into the sky. His eyes are streaming, his mouth is stretched around a silent howl. No sounds but a stifled gasping for air. His shoulders heave, he continues to peer into the heavens.

I do not know what to say. I do not know what to do.

Quietly, I approach my father. I place my hand on his shoulder.

"I'm sorry," I say again in that distant voice that is and is not my own. He does not seem to hear me; it occurs to me that he cannot, as he is not here, but back there, in a past in which he was not my father but a child, in a past in which I do not yet exist.

"Your brother," I whisper—surprised, this time, by my words. My voice is operating of its own accord—I do not know where this is taking me. "You had an older brother."

He turns to me.

"My brother was shot. I watched them shoot him."

"What was your brother's name?"

"Robert," he whispers. Then again, "Robert." He is saying this to himself, as though I am not here. I stay for a moment, my hand on my father's shoulder. After a time, I turn and quietly leave the room.

I walk past the kitchen, see that my mother is busy at the sink, and make my way upstairs, where I splash water on my face and brush my teeth. I head back downstairs, drop my bag by the front door, and find my mother in the kitchen.

"Darling, what is it? What's going on?" she says.

"I don't know, Mama," I say in my frightening faraway voice.

"What do you mean? What are you talking about?"

"I'm sorry," I say for the third time in the space of twenty minutes. "I have to get to the hospital."

"Deborah, it's seven o'clock on a Sunday morning. I thought you were planning to spend the weekend."

"I'm on call," I lie. "It must have slipped my mind."

My mother, too, looks as if she's far away, though she's standing right in front of me. I see her, see the concern in her face—I know she is my dear, beloved mama, to whom I can say anything, on whom I depend utterly—but I cannot *feel* any of it. All I feel is that I must get away, that I must leave this very second.

"Really, Mama, I have to go," I say.

I am moving slowly; something has happened to the air. It is impossibly thick. My mother, too, is moving in slow motion. I see she is struggling to say something, trying to figure out if she should be alarmed.

"Papa," I say. "He's in his study. I think you should go to him." Now the look in her face transforms again. She intuits something.

"Is he all right?" she asks anxiously. She does not wait for my answer. She puts down the dishcloth she was holding and hurries from the room.

Moments later, I am in my car, turning out of the driveway, sailing through the tree-lined roads of my childhood. A gentle rain begins to fall; the early sunlight catches the droplets of water and makes the air itself shimmer.

I turn onto Route 27 and watch as the leafy, suburban streets become more urban and industrial. I pass squat little apartment blocks and tiny houses with front yards that seem scrawny and undernourished, though some show the signs of tenderness and care.

When I turn onto the highway, I am aware that I can breathe again and the air no longer seems thick.

I inhale deeply a few times and allow my mind to float free. Enormous trucks speed by; I stay in the far right lane so I won't need to try to keep up with them.

I startle at the sound of my cell phone ringing. Eyes on the road ahead, I fumble in my purse, which is on the passenger seat beside me, and retrieve my phone.

"Dr. Erick," I say curtly.

"Deborah? It's Pete." Dr. Peter Burton, chief psychiatric resident. "Where are you?"

"On my way to the hospital, as it happens," I say, aware that suddenly my voice is no longer far away, that it feels like it is coming from inside me and like it is, again, fully my own.

"Are you driving?" he asks.

"Yes, I'm still in New Jersey. Route 287."

"I think you should pull over," he says.

Only now do I notice that his voice is unusually steady: effortfully calm.

"Okay," I say. "Hold on."

I pull over to the shoulder, put the car in park, and flick on the blinking emergency lights.

"Okay, I've pulled over," I say. "Go on."

"Deborah, the cleaning staff found Dvorah a half hour ago in the bathroom. The bathroom up by your office."

"She has off-unit privileges," I say, annoyed that she'd been let off the unit without any kind of supervision, and so early in the morning. "She shouldn't be in the office area, however, not without supervision."

"She hanged herself, Deborah. With a belt."

What is he saying? What on earth is this idiotic, irresponsible young doctor saying? One doesn't make such jokes, not in a psychiatric hospital. To call a doctor on her cell phone and—

"What are you saying?" I almost shout.

"She's down in one of the empty rooms of medical records," he continues. "The coroner should be here any minute."

This is not a joke. Dr. Peter Burton, the chief resident, is not joking.

"I see," I say. I do not know what to say next.

"Deborah?" Peter says.

"I'm on my way," I say, then ring off.

By the time I reach the George Washington Bridge, the day has fully arrived. To my left, as I cross, I see the widening river opening out, the trees on both banks in full, new leaf. To my right, the great impossible city, in all its hunched and also sky-reaching enormity, built on wild dreams that too often bloom to garish nightmare. I wonder, for a moment—automatically, force of habit—about the varied lives being lived there this very instant: luxury apartments housing luxury lives; treacherous ghetto hallways; smoked salmon being ordered in the Plaza Hotel; and somewhere else, not so very far away, a young girl succumbing to rape.

Dvorah, in my bathroom. Hanging from a belt by the neck.

I am on the Henry Hudson Parkway. I glance at the speedometer and see that I am speeding. Upper Manhattan reels by, a fast-forwarded film, sending up disjointed frames.

I approach the tollbooth and slow down, roll down the window, and sling two quarters into the bucket, then accelerate onto the Saw Mill River Parkway. An abundance of trees lean over the edge of the roadway, sending out a thick green scent.

I take the White Plains exit and speed along empty roads. I turn onto the winding road leading up through the grounds to the hospital and then, on a whim, curve around the main building and take the back road to the storage house. I park in the lot behind it. Outside the entrance, I sort through my key ring to locate the all-purpose key I was issued last year, on becoming a fully fledged staff member. I slip it into the lock on the door. It turns easily and I enter.

Inside, I do not turn on the lights; sufficient natural light enters through the small windows to allow me to make my way.

I've never been in this building, but I know from the map of the hospital which once, a few years ago, I examined with some interest, that the Supply House, as it is called, is, like all the buildings on the grounds, linked by a network of underground passageways constructed more than a hundred years ago when the hospital was built. The tunnels were made so that staff could easily move among the buildings when there was snow, though I suspect a darker, more mystical motive was at play. How apt, I remember thinking upon hearing about the tunnels: that a hospital for the insane should have hidden, underground passages—a kind of unconscious linking together everything going on aboveground. Linking together the buildings, the patients, the staff: defying the more usual boundaries between dwellings, between people, between mental health and the outer reaches of madness.

The tunnels are seldom used these days, except to store old furniture and various other items, and occasionally by the odd staff member, like myself, who feels drawn to their hidden, atmospheric feel.

I cannot face seeing anyone; I will make my way to my office unseen, I think, through the tunnels that pass from the Supply House to the main building.

I wander through the ground floor, looking for a door leading downward to the tunnels. I move among boxes and neat stacks of cleaning supplies, move in the cool white glow of the new day, aware that today Dvorah will not register the way the light changes here in the late morning, when it goes from thin and clean and transparent to a rich buttercup yellow. It is later in the afternoon that the light turns hot; then, it splashes through the trees and slides to the ground in puddles of gold. But Dvorah will not see this either. I wonder if she'd ever taken notice of the special qualities, here, of the light. I wish I'd told her about it, told her to watch for its changing textures.

I pause and listen to the birdsong always audible here from dawn until dusk; a great variety of species make these grounds their home, unperturbed, as they chirpily hop about, by the slow shuffles and limply hanging arms of the residents who drift along the pathways, or by their odd grimaces or occasional wild utterances.

I continue on. I try first one door, then another. This one leads to a stairway going up, the second is a closet. Ah, here it is. I have found the door. I pass through and descend. At the bottom of the stairs, I hesitate. It is quiet, very quiet, and dim. The twittering birdsong has been snuffed to silence. The natural light of the limpid morning is similarly snatched away, replaced by the dull pulsing glow of low-wattage fluorescent strips placed at wide intervals on the ceiling.

The air is heavy and stagnant. It feels as old as the tunnels themselves. I have the eerie feeling I am breathing the exhalations of long-dead doctors and nurses and patients who many decades ago regularly walked these underground passages. I am moving among ghosts; I am breathing them in.

Around me, as I walk, are the hulking shapes of discarded furniture: chests of drawers and bulky bed frames, side tables and desks and stacks of wooden chairs, long ago replaced, above, by furniture that is cheerful and modern. I wonder why all of this was kept; I cannot imagine it will ever again be put to use. I have the feeling that these objects, too, are exhaling the lives of the countless people who once made use of them, sending out invisible little cloud puffs of lived experience—a shriek of despair as a patient pulls out first this drawer, then the next, in a frustrated attempt at dressing herself; the blank anomie of drugged asylum inmates seated on wooden chairs at a patient meeting; the fervor of a psychiatrist, hunched over his notes, wishing to make sense of his patient's psychotic ramblings. A gaggle of voices and dreads and impossible longings, of the human mind gone haywire, of too many doomed attempts to set right what cannot be set right.

I walk. My feet and heart are heavy. Though the furniture I make use of upstairs—my desk, the chairs in my office—is modern, it may as well be consigned here, to these tunnels that contain all that is discarded, ended, failed. Consigned here, among the dead.

The dim fluorescent lighting is beginning to make my head throb. I realize I have no idea how to get to the main building. I have lost all sense of direction. I round another curve: more tables, more stacked chairs. It is endless, this sea of spent and hopeless lives.

I sink to the floor. I breathe in the useless air of a hundred or more years, breathe in and out as Dvorah will never again do, try to imagine what it is to have a nose and lungs and airways that are seized and unmoving. I close my eyes, and the image I have been warding off in the two hours or so since I answered my cell phone as I was driving along Route 287 snakes to life. Dvorah, sneaking off the unit, the belt perhaps hidden around her waist, under her clothes, tight against her bare skin. Taking the back passage to my office, what used to be the servants' corridor in the time when both staff and wealthy patients were tended by servants.

I shake my head, open my eyes. I do not want the scene to play out.

A lump of grief takes hold of my chest, and now I find I cannot breathe. I gasp at the air, try to open my lungs.

The scene rolls on; it will not leave me be. Dvorah, her face calm now, almost peaceful, as she finds a way to secure the belt to the pipe while permitting enough remaining length to encircle her own neck. Ingenious, the method she devises, but then Dvorah had abundant intelligence.

I want to shriek, I want to push it away, I do not want to see what she does. But I cannot shriek; I feel I am staring into the headlights as a huge truck barrels toward me. I am frozen, unable to stop it, unable to move.

She has pulled a chair to the spot—the chair in the hallway, perhaps she used that? Another of the many hard-backed chairs with the tapestry-covered seats that adorn the corridors—did that one, too, contain a scene of a foxhunt?

Stop! Dvorah, don't do it!

But I can't scream out, I can't breathe. I can't stop her. She has already done it. Already tightened the buckle against her throat, kicked away the chair, heard the sickening snap of her own neck, felt the sudden seizing of her lungs, the cessation of the passage of air through larynx and nose that began long ago as she squeezed into the world through the birth canal, as seven babies, a year or two apart, would later squeeze out through her own body.

I might have spoken to Dr. Finkelstein about Dvorah, about the trouble I was having. That day I searched so ridiculously on the upturned chair for the fox; I might have opened my mouth and talked, and Dr. Finkelstein might have helped me find the kernel of the trouble, which in turn might have allowed me to set things right, so that now I would not be conjuring the image of Dvorah's bulging eyes, her stiff, blue, protruding tongue, might not be watching as the cleaning woman opened the door to discover the dreadful sight that will probably haunt her for the rest of her days.

I can breathe again, but I do not shriek. I fall to the dusty floor and cry. Tears spill from me, they pour out like blood from a gash, they are pouring from my eyes, my nose, my mouth.

I have so many people to cry for; I do not think I will ever be able to stop.

All of it feels like my fault. My father, frozen in terror in the wooden hut—was it the outhouse? How could it not have been? Could there have been two different young boys taken over as Nazi mascots? Two boys who watched as their parents, their brothers, their relatives, everyone they knew, dug their own graves and then were shot to fall face-first into the pit? Horrifying. Unlikely. But in that dreadful reality-hell of suffering and trauma, the gruesome repetition of literally millions of stories might have contained such similar, almost identical situations.

But not the stone. Not the smooth, round stone in the shape of a tiny ball that a little boy delightedly anticipated he would give to his brother: surely not two of those.

I am on fire with it all. I do not think I can bear it.

I feel as if I cannot go on.

This must be what Dvorah felt. I am feeling what she felt as she crept off the unit.

No one, surely, is now aware of what I feel. How could I, then, have known how Dvorah was feeling? How could I therefore have prevented it?

How could it, then, be my fault?

I am a psychiatrist. I was her doctor. I hear her voice, a fragment from an early session: *What have I got to lose? I'm going to win, not lose. Though you never can tell with a nuz.* A noose. A clue, right there, in my office.

I should have known.

I drag myself up from the ground. I taste dust in my mouth, dust from the floor that has mixed with the flooding tears and lodged, now, in my throat.

I remember with a sudden prick of alertness that at certain intervals, pinned high up on the wall, just beneath the fluorescent strips, little signs are posted that indicate which buildings are in which directions. How could I have forgotten? Each bears a letter—*A, B, C, D,* and so on—with connecting tunnels labeled according to origin and destination. I walk along the tunnel and, after a dozen or so steps, locate one of the little wooden signs tacked high onto the wall: *C-D.* Below is a piece of heavy card, faded and yellowed, on which is the key. C is Supply House, D is Physical Therapy. A is the Main Building. I remember, too, that at the end of each passageway a small map is posted. I walk on a ways, reach the place where a staircase leads up to building D, and locate the map, tacked to the wall beside the door. It takes me a moment to make sense of how I need to proceed. When I am sure it is clear, I turn right into passageway D-F, which should intersect with D-A, which in turn will take me where I want to go.

I make my way quickly now, and soon I am climbing the stairs and pushing the door open into one of the familiar grand hallways of the main building.

I pass a nurse and several orderlies, all of whom I know only peripherally as they are not staff on my own unit. I nod my morning greeting. Their eyes are wary and uncertain, the eyes of people who know some tragedy attaches to the person they are encountering and who therefore do not know what to say.

I take the stairs to my office two at a time. I pull out my key and open the door.

Damn it. God damn it, I think. Casebook study. Just as the psychosis is beginning to lift—just as the debilitating heft of the depression is beginning to move off her. This is when the patient has the ability to take action. Still sunk in the black pit, still having to deal with the horror of it all, but now with the energy to plot and execute her escape. Exactly when a patient is at the greatest risk. How could I have missed it? Dvorah should have been on around-the-clock suicide watch.

I flick on the overhead light and go directly to my locked filing cabinet. I unlock the drawer and locate Dvorah's file, then pull it out and set it on my desk.

I stare out the window. It is a beautiful, sunny late-spring day. A medley of chirpings reaches my ears. I curse my stupidity. Curse my cursed profession. Curse this century. Curse, most of all, myself. I stare out into the sunny day that is lightly scented with the sparse apple and cherry blossoms remaining on the branches outside my window and at the same time stare into the awful truth.

I have Dvorah's death on my hands.

I get up from my desk and walk over to where my diploma hangs on the wall. I reach up and remove it, then place it facedown on my desk. I flick aside the little catches holding the backing in place and slide out the heavy, velvet-covered cardboard, then lift the parchment from the glass. Carefully, methodically, I tear the diploma into strips, and then tear each strip into a dozen little squares.

I sit back down and open Dvorah's file. I go to the front section, which contains all the intake information, then find the forms I filled out that very first day, the day I met Dvorah.

There it is, written in my own hand. I write so many notes and reports in the course of any given week, and fill in so many endless forms, that I tend not to retain information that is extraneous to the treating of the patient. But there it is, in the heavy, dark ink I like to use. *Name of Father: Robert Solomon Erlich.*

Robert Solomon Erlich. Dvorah's father's name was Robert. Dvorah's father—the older brother in the story he relayed to her when she was a child, of a little boy he promised to come back and find. He did come back, after Nazi soldiers had taken the boy to be shot, though one of them, for some reason I will never know, instead took the boy and put him into a little SS uniform so that he might be their mascot.

There is a knock at the door. I close Dvorah's file, place it back in the drawer, then go to unlock my door.

It is Peter Burton, the chief resident.

"Deb, I'm so sorry," he says.

"Yes. Well—" I don't know what to say.

I see Peter's eyes stray over to my desk, where my diploma is now a little stack of torn parchment pieces lying next to the empty frame.

"Can we talk for a moment?" he asks.

"Why yes, of course. Come in."

He sits on the blue chaise longue. I sit in my leather desk chair. He pretends not to see what is so clearly evident on my desk. He pulls something from the inside pocket of his white doctor's coat.

"The nursing staff found this when they were clearing out Dvorah's things. It was in the drawer of her bedside table."

He hands me a sealed white envelope. I see my name written in Dvorah's neat, schoolgirl script.

I take the envelope. Seeing Dvorah's handwriting shakes me. It is like seeing the handprint of a ghost. I try to hide my reaction, though my attempt is halfhearted. I am tired of trying to hide how I feel. When I look at Peter, I just let myself be, and find that tears are spilling from my eyes.

"I'm so sorry, Deborah," Peter says again. "Is there anything I can do?" he asks. "Really—anything. You only have to ask."

I've always liked Peter Burton. He is a fine chief resident and will go on to have a fine career. I recognize in his face the confidence and sense of mission that must have shown in my own at his age—not so very long ago—and I feel a sliding sadness at the loss of my faith, both in myself and in my profession.

"Thank you. I'll give you a call if I can think of anything."

Peter rises. "The police will, of course, want to see the letter. I just wanted you to have a chance to look at it first. It's addressed to you, after all."

I nod. "Yes. Of course."

"They'll be here soon. Less than an hour. I'll call you when they arrive."

"Thank you. I appreciate that."

After Peter leaves, I sit back in my chair and open the letter.

There she is—alive, again, in the voice of her words.

Dr. Erick. Or should I say, Dr. Erlich?

When I came to you, I was crazy—I know this as well as you.

I'm not crazy now, though. In fact, I've never felt so sane.

I'm sorry, but the thing is, I've seen too much. And I keep seeing it. The medication has taken effect, you can rest assured about that. But none of it goes away. And it's just—well, it's just too hard.

Some things, I never told you. I couldn't bring myself

to. Who would have believed me? I was crazy, anyway, and what I had to say was crazier than any of it.

You see, my father couldn't help himself. He couldn't help keeping it all alive. He thought he was doing the right thing.

I named my third-born son after my father's brother. After the little boy who went missing from the outhouse, who was not there when my father came back to get him. At my son's bris, *when the rabbi announced the baby's name for the first time to the people gathered there, my father became very upset. He tried to hide it, but I know my father well, and I could see that something was troubling him.*

Once everyone left, I asked him what the matter was. He said that I shouldn't have named my son after his brother. Why on earth not? I asked. It is the Jewish tradition to name babies after deceased relatives. "Because he went to the other side," my father said. I didn't know what he meant, but he was too flustered to say any more, and the baby was crying; I had to go and take care of him.

He didn't say any more about it, though he always had a strained relationship with my son.

One day—it was Jacob's fifth birthday, and both my parents came over to wish him happy birthday. You remember, my father placed great store in the magical quality of numbers. Five years old, the same age his brother was when he last saw him. My father acted strangely throughout the party. Then, just as they were getting ready to leave, he took me aside and asked if he could show me something. We went out into the backyard, and he pulled an envelope from his pocket. From the

envelope, he took out an old newspaper clipping. "This is
my brother," he said. "This is what happened to Jacob."
I saw a little boy dressed in a Nazi uniform. "I came
across this when I was doing research in Washington, some
years ago, to try to find out whether anyone else in my
family survived. It was pure chance that I found it. While
the war was still on, a German newspaper ran this story.
I secretly removed it from the archives, though I shouldn't
have. I couldn't bear the idea that anyone else would
see it."

I didn't know what to say.

So you see, he didn't die, my father's brother. Worse
than that—he was turned into a Nazi. My father didn't
speak for a while. Then, he told me to make sure my Jacob
was always diligent in keeping all the laws. "Watch over
him more than over the others," he said. "You will need to
protect him from the evil eye.*"*

I didn't tell you any of this because when I saw you,
that first time, when I was tied up in the Quiet Room, I
recognized your face. You have the same face as that
little boy.

Remember, I don't believe that anything happens for no
reason. I believe that you were sent to me and I was sent to
you, that we were made to encounter each other. How
unlikely is it that we'd have been thrown together this way
by pure chance? Such things happen in life.

How could I have told you any of this? I was
delusional, remember?

And anyway, though I knew what I knew in my heart,
I couldn't be sure it was really the truth.

The truth is a very murky thing.

I'm sorry to be leaving my children, but I believe they

*will be better off without me. I'm sorry to be letting you
down. You tried to help me—I know you tried your best.*

*I used to look at your face, sometimes. Just look at it. I
wanted to know who you were. But mental patients aren't
allowed to know their doctors. Those are the rules.*

But I did know you. I thought I did. Was I wrong?

*Whatever you say, we were there, in the same room,
day after day. We were there, brought together. How can
any of your rational theories explain that?*

I look up from Dvorah's letter and gaze again out of the
window. I see that under pressure from last night's blustery
wind, the apple tree by the Supply House has thrown down
its last fistfuls of blossoms. Now they glisten, a little, from the
light morning rain.

I am not surprised. I am beyond being surprised. Dvorah
is right. Reality is stranger than insanity. It is reality that
defies comprehension. I turn back to the letter.

*I'm not sure I believe in the idea of patients and
doctors. I do believe in the idea of friendship, though,
and I appreciate the friendship you showed me.*

I'm sorry, Doctor. I tried. I really did.

Could I ask you to visit my family?

The letter is signed simply "Dvorah."

I spend the rest of the day dealing with the coroner, the
police, and the hospital administration. We meet with the
patients on the unit. Everyone is stunned. All day long, wherever I am, I say a silent farewell in my head: to each person I

encounter, to every object, to the Persian rugs on the hallway floors, and most of all, to the light. I think all day about the light, wherever I am walking—and I seem to spend hours walking, from meeting to meeting, up and down these corridors I know so well, up and down stairs.

By three o'clock in the morning, I have finished what paperwork I need to do. I have a pile of telephone messages on my desk, taken down by the hospital operator. I return none of them. I do not call Ron. I do not call my parents. Earlier in the evening, I had the unit secretary call both Ron and my parents and tell them that I'd be very busy until tomorrow afternoon and that they were not to worry about me.

I stretch out on the blue chaise longue and close my eyes. Sleep does not come. I lie there in an exhausted daze, my eyes closed, listening to the sound of my breath moving in and out of my chest.

At six-thirty, I rise and retrieve the small toiletry kit from my bottom drawer. I do not go into the locked bathroom next door. Instead, I go down one flight and use the bathroom on the second floor. I wash my hands and face and brush my teeth. The water tastes of metal. I brush my hair, avoiding my own glance in the mirror.

The funeral is scheduled for this afternoon, according to Jewish practice. By rights, Dvorah should be denied burial in the Orthodox Jewish cemetery, given that she took her own life, which is considered a sin. I was told by the coroner, though, that the family was granted special rabbinical exception, because Dvorah was mentally ill.

I move through my morning responsibilities in a trance. Someone else is mouthing the words I speak; someone else is saying reassuring things to the patients, reassuring things to the staff. Someone else is accepting condolences from Dr. Finkelstein and the other doctors on my unit.

At noon, I lock my office and head down to the car. I drive first to Manhattan, to my apartment, where I take a quick shower and change into a dark blue suit with a long skirt. I go directly back to the car and drive to the Brooklyn cemetery.

There are thirty or forty people at the graveside. Dvorah's husband is there, and all seven of her children. I don't know what the children have been told. Everyone is dressed in black. All have prominent rents in their clothing.

I stand a little away from the others.

I feel like a pariah.

I watch as they lower the pine coffin into the grave and then as Dvorah's husband, father, and brothers take turns with the shovel to fill the deep hole.

No one speaks. There is the sound of quiet weeping from several of the women. Some of the men, too, have tears in their eyes.

I say what I have been told to say—*I wish you long life*; I asked the coroner, who has had some experience with such things. I say the ritual words of condolence to each of Dvorah's family members.

I have come to clean out my office. When I gave my notice two weeks ago, Dr. Finkelstein did not seem particularly surprised.

"What are you going to do?" she asked.

"I don't know," I replied. "I really don't."

All the files have been packed up. Medical Records will

come up later today to take them downstairs. Before I close up and tape the final box, I retrieve Dvorah's file, turn again to the intake information section, then pick up the telephone receiver and dial the number of her father. The phone rings emptily into what feels like the silence of an abandoned house. I sit in my office, under the eaves of the magnificent old mansionlike building, aware of the hollow space on the other side of the wall, the bathroom that is now padlocked shut. No one will answer, I think. Not after the twenty or more rings, and yet I clasp the phone to my ear and listen intently to the ringing, as if it is a code I must decipher. In a moment, the line will cut out.

Just as I'm about to restore the handset to its cradle, I hear a click and then a voice.

"Hello?"

"Mr. Erlich?"

"Speaking."

"This is Dr. Erick," I say. "Dvorah's doctor, from the hospital."

"I know who you are," he says. His voice is sad, nothing more. The accusation I hear is an echo, coming from me.

"I know this is going to sound a little odd, but I was wondering if we could meet."

He hesitates.

"Yes, that would be all right," he says.

"Could we meet at my New Jersey office?" I say, scrambling. I have no New Jersey office. "It's actually a little closer for you, coming from Brooklyn, than driving up to the hospital."

"Why yes, if that's what you'd prefer."

"Two o'clock? This afternoon. Would that suit you?"

"Yes, that would be fine."

I give him the address of my parents' house, and then detailed directions for how to get there from Brooklyn.

I drive beyond the house I grew up in to the end of the block and turn around to park so that sitting in the car I'll be able to see the front door. I turn off the engine and wait.

I wonder if they will know each other at once.

I wonder if I have done the right thing.

Perhaps, in such situations (are there others like these?) there is no right thing.

I wonder if, finally, so very long after that birthday—a distance measured not in time but in some other indecipherable dimension: part nightmare, part insanity, part hell—my father will give his brother the smooth round stone, the stone that tickled his fancy, shaped, as it was, so unusually, like a ball.

A car turns onto the block, a neat maroon car, spotlessly clean. It comes to rest in front of my parents' home. The door on the driver's side opens, and Dvorah's father, Mr. Erlich, steps out. Even from this distance I can see the stamp of grief in his face. I imagine it will be there until the end of his days.

I imagine that one does not recover from the death of a child, especially when the death was at her own hand.

Slightly stooped, he walks up the path to the front door. He rings the doorbell and waits.

I wonder which of my parents will open the door.

I will go to see Dvorah's husband and seven children, I think. Not very professional, but then I have torn up my diploma. I am no longer a practicing psychiatrist. Dvorah asked me to visit them, and I will go.

I want to see their faces again—the faces of the children.

The baby, only a few months old, the eldest already bar mitzvahed. I am interested in them all, though I confess I am especially interested in the boy she named Jacob.

Several minutes pass. My parents, of course, are not expecting anyone. Perhaps they are not even home. This possibility had not occurred to me. I feel the rise of anxiety in my chest.

Then, the door opens. I can see, from where I am sitting, that it is my father. My father has opened the door. He is standing there, trying to make sense of what is before his eyes.

Notes

"The Porcelain Monkey"

53 An exhibition entitled "Prussia—Taking Stock" was mounted by the West Berlin Senate in 1978. A member of the advisory board wanted to include one of Mendelssohn's porcelain monkeys, but his request was denied. A pretty porcelain monkey, found in the Hohenzollern Museum, was included instead.

66 Hitler presided over the 1936 Olympics and stood by German medal winners at their awards ceremony. The female athlete in this story is entirely fictional.

67 There were young men and women in Nazi Germany, determined to be of "pure Aryan breed," who were brought together for the purposes of mating.

74 James Simon was a prominent Jewish industrialist of his day. Known as "the cotton king," he was an important donor to Berlin's new art museums in the late 1800s. He owned a mansion on Lake Tegeler, where he displayed the kinds of paintings that appear in this story. The mansion was not to my knowledge ever used as a nursing home.

I am grateful to Amos Elon's brilliant book, *The Pity of It All: A History of the Jews in Germany, 1743–1933* (New York: Metropolitan Books, 2002), for his account of Mendelssohn's life, his passages about James Simon, and his footnote mentioning the 1978 exhibition.

"Dark Urgings of the Blood"

In a newspaper article, I read about a Jewish boy who was taken to live among Nazi soldiers as a kind of mascot; a boy-sized Nazi uniform was made for him. During the war, an article was written about him which appeared in a German newspaper, along with a photograph of the boy in his uniform, arm raised in Nazi salute. Elsewhere, I read about a child who hid in a latrine in a field to escape the Nazis. I have incorporated both of these real occurrences into "Dark Urgings of the Blood"; the charcaters I create, however, and all other aspects of this story are entirely fictional.

Acknowledgments

These stories were inspired by Amos Elon's brilliant book *The Pity of It All: A History of the Jews in Germany, 1743–1933.* I am deeply thankful for the life-altering experience of reading his book.

My utmost appreciation to the Australia Council for the Arts Literature Board for their generous support.

Thanks to Jed Horne and Charles Palliser for their openhearted attention and acute remarks, and to Doreen Nayman and Ilana Nayman for ongoing involvement in and support of this project. Deep gratitude, as well, to C. Michael Curtis of *The Atlantic Monthly.*

My writing bears the indelible stamp of three people— Louis Sass, Andrea Masters, and Michele Nayman—whose remarkable sensibilities and unending generosity are enriching beyond words.

I feel especially fortunate to have the incomparable Aaron Priest as my agent, with the able additional help of Lucy Childs and Lisa Vance, and to have landed, through their efforts, with Scribner. The book could not have had a more expert and dynamic stewardship than that provided by publisher Susan Moldow, editor Alexis Gargagliano, and head of publicity Suzanne Balaban. Sincere thanks to them all, with a special tribute to Alexis for her fine sensibility and talents.

I shall long remember the kindness of the staff at the Gran Hotel and the Villa San Jose; I greatly appreciate the serene and muse-friendly environment they afforded.

About the Author

Shira Nayman grew up in Australia. She has a master's degree in comparative literature and a doctorate in clinical psychology, and has worked as a psychologist and a marketing consultant. Her work has appeared in numerous publications, including *The Atlantic Monthly, The Georgia Review, New England Review,* and *Boulevard.* She is the recipient of two grants from the Australia Council for the Arts Literature Board, and lives in Brooklyn with her husband and two children.